Acting the Nabob

by

Caitlyn Callery

Acting the Nabob

Cover Art by *Teddi Black*

The Wild Rose Press, Inc.
PO Box 708
Adams Basin, NY 14410-0708
Visit us at www.thewildrosepress.com

Publishing History
First Edition, 2025
Trade Paperback ISBN 978-1-5092-6120-8
Digital ISBN 978-1-5092-6121-5

Published in the United States of America

Dedication

To Amanda Giles.
Long may the stories flow.

Chapter One

May 1818

Alice followed the rest of the dancing troupe off stage. At the last second, before she disappeared into the wings, she kicked her leg up and grinned at the audience. The young bucks in the stalls cheered and hollered and whistled. Just as they were meant to do.

Offstage, her grin turned to ballooned cheeks and a heavy sigh. That was her last show of the day. Soon she could change into something more respectable, wipe the greasepaint from her face, and go home. She looked forward to her supper and a decent night's sleep, before she had to come back and do another three shows tomorrow.

There was a thunder of heels on wooden boards as the dancers went down the steps and away from the stage area. Nobody was supposed to speak until they reached the narrow corridor that led to the dressing rooms. If they did, Mr. Tate, the theater owner, worried the audience would hear them and the illusion of magic the show relied upon would be destroyed.

The wings were dimly lit. They had to be, so the audience couldn't see the actors standing here, ready for their entrances. Accordingly, the walls, the ceiling, the wooden floor, all were painted black.

"I'll be glad to get these boots off," Sally said, in the

worst stage whisper Alice had ever heard. If it wasn't for the clowns making the audience laugh out there, they would probably have heard her in the gods.

Sally put her left foot down and winced. She'd been favoring it during the performance, but now she actually limped.

"Is there something in it? A stone, perhaps?" Alice's own whisper was more muted.

"Mayhap. Or the stitching is coming undone. Whatever it is, I can feel a blister forming."

Alice rubbed, sympathetically, at her friend's back. "I have salve."

"Watch your backs, ladies." Peter, the stage runner, whose job was to ensure the show ran on time and all the performers were in place when they should be, pushed past, roughly shoving them aside. With one foot off the floor, Sally stumbled. Alice put out a hand to steady her, at the same moment somebody else did the same.

Their hands met across Sally's back. His were warm and dry, large enough to completely cover hers. A zing of electricity shot through her, startling her, and she glanced up at Benedict Summersby. The theater's lead actor stared back, his dark eyes wide, his thickly painted eyebrows arched, creasing the greasepaint on his brow. His surprise said he'd also felt the shock of their touch.

After the briefest of moments, he turned from Alice and looked instead at Sally, who had managed to right herself. He smiled and gave her a reassuring wink, then walked to the stage.

"He winked at me," said Sally. They watched him square his shoulders, take a deep breath, and step out, to rapturous applause. Sally sighed. "Benedict Summersby winked at me."

Alice shook herself, as if that could somehow rid her of the residue of shock his touch had caused. "Come on," she said. Her voice sounded strange, so she cleared her throat. "Come on," she repeated, more normally, and she tried to lead Sally away. "We'll get…"

Sally wasn't ready to leave. "My shoulder strap's come adrift. Can you fix it?" All the dancers came to Alice when they needed a quick repair. They knew she was good with a needle, better than the women who were paid to see to the costumes, if truth be known.

"I should think so. Come on." Again, she tried to steer Sally away.

"Do it here."

"I can't do it here."

"Please, Al. What if it snaps halfway there? I don't want the crew getting an eyeful."

Alice didn't think it would really bother Sally too much if they did. A gentleman admirer had once told her that her breasts were magnificent. Sally had never forgotten it, and she never wanted others to forget it, either. She relished any chance to prove it to onlookers.

"It's not likely to happen between here and the dressing room," Alice said.

"But it could." Sally peered out at the stage, where Benedict interacted with the clowns.

"My threads are in the dressing room, Sal."

"Just tie it together for now." She fidgeted until she could see past Alice. "Benedict looks good tonight, doesn't he?"

Alice thought of that moment when his hand had touched hers. He'd looked at her, and for a moment she'd been able to look back, to study him without awkwardness, without pretending that wasn't what she was doing. Those big eyes of his, the color of moss mixed with tree bark and acorns, were ringed with long lashes which needed no burnt cork to enhance them. His cheekbones were high and his beard was thick, covering much of his lower face and neck, though his moustache was trimmed neatly. He wore a wig, the same color as his own dark curls, but she knew his real hair was respectably short, while the curls he sported for the show touched his shoulders. With his broad chest, narrow hips and powerful thighs, he looked like the pirate he was currently playing.

Yes, she thought. He looked good tonight. So good that, when he'd touched her hand, Alice hadn't felt the usual panic. Even with the shock that buzzed through her—or perhaps because of it—she hadn't pulled back and run away. Which, in itself, was dangerous, and a reason to panic.

"I mean, he looks good every night," continued Sally, oblivious to Alice's musing. On the stage, Benedict was twitted by the clowns, and the audience roared with laughter. "But there's something about him tonight. A certain Jenny Say Queue."

Alice stopped tying the shoulder strap and stared at Sally, convinced she'd misheard, because she couldn't make any sense of what her friend had just said. "A certain what?" she asked, when she realized she could ponder it all night and not work out the correct words.

"Jenny Say Queue." Sally preened. "That's French, that is. Lord Hudson told me. He said I had it. 'Sally, my girl,' he said, 'you have that certain Jenny Say Queue.' "

Alice nodded, completely lost. She didn't speak a word of French. "So it's a good thing?"

"Yes. It means 'I don't know what.' "

Alice frowned. "How do you know it's good, then?"

Sally giggled, then covered her mouth with her hands to stop the sound, though it could not have been heard above the audience. "You ninny," she said. "I don't mean, I don't know what it means. I mean, 'Jenny Say Queue' means 'I don't know what.' It's French for 'I don't know what.' And, having a certain Jenny Say Queue, like what I've got," she straightened her shoulders proudly, undoing the repair Alice had just made to her costume, "it's what they go mad for. That's what Lord Hudson said."

Alice nodded and felt thankful she hadn't got it, then.

"Benedict Summersby's got it, too," Sally continued. "Enough of it to fill this whole place. And then some." She gave Alice an exaggerated wink.

"If you say so." Alice made the repair again. The last thing she wanted to think about was the man's Jenny Say Queue, thank you very much.

"I do." Sally chuckled. "More good words." She sighed. "I. Do."

Alice rolled her eyes. "They're only good if you say them to the right person."

"I will. You can bet on that."

"Good for you." Alice stepped back, having done all she could for Sally's shoulder strap. "There. That should hold till we get to the dressing room. Come along."

Sally looked out at the stage. For a moment it seemed as though she would argue, but Peter stepped into her line of sight, a scowl on his face. He didn't say a word, simply pointed toward the corridor. Sally pulled a face, but she knew better than to argue, and she led the way out of the wings and into the narrow walkway that

5

took them to the back end of the theater.

"He winked at me, you know," said Sally, once they were clear of the stage area.

"Peter?" Alice couldn't imagine that happening. Peter was more likely to wink at Benedict than at Sally.

"No! Not Peter."

Which left Alice at a loss as to who her friend meant. Somebody in the audience, perhaps? "Lord Hudson?" she guessed.

"Not Lord Hudson." Sally laughed. "He's had to go back to the country for a few weeks. Something about paying his respects to his mother, or something."

Alice suspected his disappearance had more to do with avoiding his creditors than visiting his mother, but she didn't say so.

"I meant Benedict." Sally sighed the actor's name. "It was a proper, definite wink, too. Not one of those, did-he-blink-or-did-he-wink type of winks." She demonstrated the wink Benedict had given her. It was far more salacious than Alice remembered him making.

"Perhaps he had something in his eye," she said, and hoped she looked blandly innocent.

Sally glanced over her shoulder. "You have no romance in your soul, Alice Buck."

I certainly hope not.

"Do you think I should go to his dressing room?"

"What? Now? He's on stage."

"I meant in the interval. No point going when he's not there. And he did wink at me."

Alice suspected Benedict had already forgotten The Wink. She didn't want Sally to get into trouble. A word from his leading man, complaining he was being harassed, and Mr. Tate would fire her. "He'll be busy in the interval, going over his lines for Act Two."

Sally made a sound, halfway between agreement and disappointment. "Should I wait until the show is finished?" She spun around and walked a few steps backwards, so she could face Alice. "I don't know why I am asking you. You'll only say no. You always say no."

Alice interpreted that to mean Sally wanted to hear a yes. Before Alice could respond, though, Sally grinned and went on, "You should say yes now and then, too. It'd do you good."

A cold shiver ran the length of Alice's spine. The very idea made her feel sick.

"Sometimes," Sally continued, "I wonder why you work here. You don't take advantage of any of the benefits."

Alice's smile did not reach her eyes. She wasn't interested in the 'benefits.' She knew what she wanted, and she was working to get it. Her dream would not be helped by the things Sally saw as 'benefits.' In fact, they could destroy everything for her.

She was well aware that she could get more money, more quickly, by following Sally's lead. She knew Sally, and most of the other dancers, earned far more after the show than they were paid for dancing in it, but that method of making money was not for her. It never would be.

Not that she'd condemn the others for it. They had to survive somehow, and Lord knew, things were hard enough at the best of times.

"I don't think he's in Act Three," Sally said. "So perhaps I could go to him then." She frowned. "But should I?"

"If you want to go to his dressing room, go. You

don't need my blessing, or anyone else's."

"I know I don't. But then…he's only an actor. The lead actor, I grant you, but still just an actor. I suppose he could speak to Mr. Tate for me. Get me better roles. But…" She shrugged.

"You have a better offer?"

Sally pulled a face that indicated she did have, but was uncertain about it. "Come to the Green Room tonight, Al." The Green Room, which wasn't green at all but painted in rather muted shades of blue, was where the opera dancers entertained their admirers after the show had finished. Here, gentlemen looking for a new mistress could make themselves known to women in search of a protector.

Alice had never been to the Green Room during the "entertainment" hours. She didn't see the attraction of it. To her, there was nothing enticing about the way a man slobbered all over a woman's face and neck, like an over-eager puppy, before nipping at her, pinching her, bruising her, his fingers digging in, hands pawing, ripping away her bodice, her skirts… Alice shuddered.

"What do you think of Lord Greensborough?" asked Sally. "Only, he's been giving me the eye. And he's wealthy. Wealthier then Lord Hudson, I think. Certainly a lot wealthier than any actor. He's got a nice, thick wad." She gave Alice a saucy wink, to emphasize her *double entendre*. "Then again, Greensborough's old and wrinkly. And with Lord Hudson away, Benedict is… Oh!" She growled in frustration. "It's a Jenny Say Queue all of its own! On top of which, I still have to sort out this wretched boot in time for tomorrow's shows." She turned around again and limped along the corridor toward the dressing room.

Alice shook her head and made to follow, then stopped, alarmed, when a man moved out of a shadowed alcove and into her path. Alice gave an involuntary squeak of alarm and tensed, prepared to bring her knee up sharply into his sensitive parts. A quick scream would bring Fred, the stage doorman running to her aid, but if this man tried to hurt Fred, or demanded he was fired...Alice didn't want that on her conscience.

Then she recognized him and breathed a sigh of relief. "Byron," she acknowledged her older brother. "You scared me."

"Didn't mean to." Byron spoke in the clipped tones of the *ton*, the accent their mother had used. Alice had grown up speaking in the same way, although she'd quickly learned to mute it if she wanted acceptance in the circles they truly inhabited.

Her brother ran his hand over his short, honey-blond hair, making it stand up in spikes, like a hedgehog's spines. His eyes, a darker blue than Alice's own, were unreadable in the dim corridor. Not that she needed to read them to guess why he was here.

"I need to see you," he said.

Alice tensed her jaw. She was so tired of this. "I'm working, Byron. And you're not supposed to be here. Only performers and crew are allowed backstage while the show's running."

"But—"

He was interrupted by Sally's indiscreet stage whisper, her friend's way of trying to help. "You've got to change, Alice. You're running out of time."

Alice hoped Byron didn't know she had no more performances this evening. "I'm coming."

"You have to go," Sally told Byron. "Mr. Tate's on

9

the prowl. If he sees you here, he'll have your guts for garters. And, more importantly, Alice'll be in trouble, too."

"This is a private conversation," Byron retorted, looking down his nose at her.

Sally sniffed. "Nothing is private in the theater, I'm afraid." She turned her back on him and spoke to Alice. "Get rid of him, Al, and come along."

Byron glared at Sally, appalled at her lack of respect. He did not move out of Alice's way. Obviously, he wouldn't leave until he'd said what he needed to say.

On a sigh, Alice said, "I'll just be a moment, Sal."

Sally did not look convinced, but she nodded and walked away.

"Who does she think she is?" muttered Byron. "I could have her fired for talking to me that way. For deigning to talk to me at all."

Alice's hackles rose. "You need to leave, Byron. Now."

"Not until we've spoken. It's urgent, Alice."

I'll bet it is. There was only one reason Byron would seek her out. Only one reason he ever sought her out.

"I've nothing for you," she told him.

He cocked his head to the side and adopted a wide-eyed, pleading-puppy expression. "Don't be like that."

"That look is wasted on me, By. I've seen it all my life. And I'm serious. I have no money." *Not for you, anyway.*

Byron narrowed his eyes. "You only got paid the other night."

He was keeping an eye on when she was paid?

"I settled my bills with it." Which was true, insofar as it went. Byron did not need to know that, after paying her rent, she squirrelled away as much of what was left as she could. It was, after all, her money, meant to finance her plans. Plans that would never come to fruition if she lent it to Byron.

"I'll pay you back."

"That's what you always say." He had never repaid a single penny.

She appeared on this stage thrice nightly, showing off more of herself than she was comfortable with to those leering men, to earn those coins so that, one day, she could open her own dress shop. She had the talent, and she had the desire. All she needed now was the cash.

Her shop would, perforce, be outside of London. She could never save enough to pay Town rents.

Byron still stood, asking her for money. Alice still shook her head in refusal. The conversation was going in circles. So she tried to end it by pushing past him.

He was having none of it. He grabbed her upper arm and held it tightly, keeping her in place. She felt the bruises forming where his fingers pressed into her flesh. Tears stung her eyes. She was damned if she'd let them fall.

"You're hurting me," she said, as evenly as she could.

"I need money," he replied, his teeth gritted.

Alice fought against the pain and raised her chin, defiantly. "Go and earn some, like everybody else has to."

That made him angrier than ever. "Don't be ridiculous. I am not a working man."

"Then do without."

"People like us do not 'do without.' And we don't work. I am not a working man. You are not a working woman." His teeth were clenched, his lips thinned. "Or you shouldn't be."

"Yet here I am." She struggled to free herself. He tightened his hold even more. She bit her bottom lip to stop herself crying out. "Let. Me. Go!"

"I need money. Ten pounds will do for now. Although I'll need more tomorrow."

Alice stared at him, astounded. Ten pounds was her entire wage for a month. "I don't have ten pounds! And if I did, it'd be to pay for things like food. Not for you to throw away at the card tables." She tried to pull away again, but he was too strong.

"I am not throwing it away. It's an investment. I need money to make more money, to take back my rightful place. *Our* rightful places."

Alice shook her head, despairing of him. She'd heard it all before. He was like a parrot, repeating the same few words over and over again. "It's not your rightful place, By. It was Mama's place once. She didn't want it, and they didn't want her. They certainly don't want us. Let me go, and get out."

He leaned closer, his eyes boring into hers, glittering with dark anger. She could smell stale brandy on his breath, the slight hint of sweat underneath his cloying cologne. There were lines around his eyes and bracketing his mouth. Lines he was far too young to have.

"Listen to me, Alice Lucinda Buck," he whispered. "I need money. You will give it to me. Or—"

"Is there a problem here?"

Suddenly, Byron let go of her arm and took several staggering steps back. Reflexively, Alice rubbed her arm, soothing the pain and restarting her circulation. It was a few seconds before she realized she'd been rescued. It was a couple of seconds longer before she figured out her rescuer was Benedict Summersby.

At five foot eleven, Byron was taller than many men. However, he seemed to shrink next to Benedict, who stood a few inches over six feet. Alice looked down and was stunned to see his boots had no heels: the height was all his own. His lean face was a mask of contempt even his beard couldn't hide. He bristled as he pushed Byron back a few more paces.

"Now, see here…" Byron blustered.

Benedict's answer was soft and low. "No. *You* see here. This is a restricted area. You are not permitted to be here."

Byron drew himself up. "Do you know who I am?" he demanded, in the most cut-glass accent he could manage.

Alice rolled her eyes. Byron couldn't claim to be anybody, so the question was ridiculous. But even if it hadn't been, even if he had been a royal duke, she didn't think it would intimidate Benedict Summersby. Rumor had it that the actor had titled relatives of his own. Although, Alice reminded herself with another eye roll, rumor had it that many things were true when they weren't.

Titled relatives or no, Benedict was unimpressed with Byron's grandstanding. "Do I look as if I care who you are?" he asked. "Get out. Before I throw you out."

Alice didn't want that to happen. If the leading man ejected somebody from the theater, it would be noted. Mr. Tate would get to know. And once he knew who Byron was, Alice would lose her job. Her position in the troupe wasn't strong enough for him to be forgiving.

Byron pulled his shirt sleeves down below his coat

cuffs and tried, unsuccessfully, to seem nonchalant. "I was just going." He pointed at Alice. "We're not finished." Then he stormed away toward the stage door.

Alice waited until he was gone before she said, "Thank you."

Benedict gave her an empty stare. She could not have read his thoughts on his face if her life had depended on it. Not that she needed to read them, because he voiced them.

"If I were you, I would sever your connection with that…gentleman." The advice was delivered in a flat tone that conveyed both disgust and disdain. Whether that was for Byron or herself, Alice didn't know.

"Would that I could," she answered, under her breath.

Benedict raised a haughty eyebrow. "Up to you, of course. Remind him of the rules. Gentlemen callers are permitted in the Green Room, when the show is finished." He skirted around her and walked away, leaving Alice wide-eyed with shock.

Gentlemen callers? Who did he think Byron was? She shook her head in disbelief. *More to that, who does he think* he *is?*

She watched him until he disappeared from sight. Sally was right, she realized, begrudgingly. The man was handsome. His legs were long, his thighs well-muscled. In contrast to Byron, who was turning to flab, Benedict's stomach was flat, his chest muscular. His back, under the piratic shirt he wore, was broad, his hips narrow, his buttocks firm and tight.

Not that she should be noticing a man's buttocks. Such things did not interest Alice. Not in the slightest. She was merely being observant.

It was being observant that made her notice his eyes seemed more brown than green in the sparsely lit corridor, and that even his beard could not take away from his beauty. That was a surprise: Alice had never found a man with a beard remotely attractive before. He smelled of greasepaint and citrus, and clean, honest sweat from his performance.

Yes, Alice had to admit it. The man was very handsome.

If you like that kind of thing.

But, Alice thought next, Sally should beware. For handsome was as handsome did and, in this case, handsome was standoffish and unfriendly, superior and contemptuous. It was beyond her comprehension why a woman like Sally, popular and never short of company, would even think of spending time with a man like that.

"You can only look at a handsome face for so long, Sal," she muttered. "If his character doesn't match his looks, you're on a hiding to nothing."

Alice started toward the dancers' dressing room, then changed her mind and headed for the stage door instead. She would ask Fred not to let Byron in again. Not even when the other Green Room Galahads entered the building.

"Right you are, Missy." Fred was a decent sort, with daughters of his own. If any man made a nuisance of himself, Fred always took the dancer's word for it and barred him. It was rumored he'd once barred a marquis, and even Mr. Tate could not get him to admit someone if Fred considered him *persona non grata.*

He now had Byron's name. And that, Alice hoped, was that.

Chapter Two

Ben paused at his dressing room door and peered along the corridor to where he'd left the dancer. Al, the others called her. He'd seen her around the theater over the past few months, ever since he'd returned from his sojourn in the country. He didn't know much about her, except that she turned up, performed well, and had, as far as he knew, never missed a show.

Which didn't mean she wasn't trouble. In fact, he rather thought she would be. Even now, instead of making for the safety of the dancers' dressing room, she walked briskly along the corridor toward the stage door area.

"Never say she's going after that worthless fop?" Ben shook his head, even as he muttered the words. "There's no saving some people."

Briefly, he wondered why women accepted the treatment those so-called gentlemen meted out to them. A woman who looked like she did had no reason to settle for a vicious wastrel like that! And yet, she moved purposefully, clearly trying to catch up to him.

"What a waste," he said. She was one of the prettiest dancers in the troupe, with her honey-blonde hair and her heart-shaped face, those big, blue eyes, and lips he suspected could drive a man to the edge of insanity without any effort at all. "The face of an angel," he mused. And a body made entirely for sin, with a generous bosom, curvy hips, and long, shapely legs.

She wasn't tall, about five foot three, but those legs made her seem taller. The gold thread sewn into her costume caught the meager light as she walked, her hips swaying. The movement was provocative but seemed completely unconscious.

That she captivated men by the dozen was not in doubt. A month ago, when Ben had had no role in the show, he'd sat in the audience. Tate wanted to promote one of the dancers to speaking roles, and he'd sent Ben "Front of House" to watch her and give his opinion.

Hannah, the dancer in Tate's sights, was ordinary, at best. She was late with her steps and relied heavily on the others to cover for her. She'd been totally overshadowed by Al. Al had leading-lady charisma, the kind that could not be taught. The eye was drawn to her, the other dancers all but forgotten. She shone.

Tate disagreed. He wanted Hannah. Ben knew better than to point out Hannah's shortcomings. Tate owned the theater, he paid Ben's wages, and he could easily turn him off. If he wanted Ben to act opposite Hannah Albright, Ben would do so, and he would put all he had into his performance, to cover the woodenness in hers. While Al would dance in the background and probably steal the show.

Ben suspected Al was being punished by being held back. She'd probably rejected Tate's advances, not a clever move for a woman who wanted to rise through the ranks in this theater, although Ben couldn't be sorry, if that was the case. The thought of her warming the theater owner's bed made his chest tighten and his jaw clench, although he couldn't have said why. Opera dancers were a penny a dozen. They came here, slept their way as far up the ladder as they could manage, and left with the best protector they could find. It was the way of things. Al was no different.

A male actor was nowhere near as vulnerable. Although, Ben thought wryly, there'd been a time when he'd found himself trapped, with no way out that didn't lead to the gallows... He pushed the thought aside. He'd survived, and he would never put himself into such a position again.

"You all right there, Ben?" Peter, the show runner, brushed past him on his way to call someone up for their next scene.

"Fine," Ben said, with a smile. "Just thinking about something."

"Dangerous thing to do, that." Peter's smile faded. "You seem preoccupied. You sure everything is all right?"

"Couldn't be better."

Peter nodded, and continued on to find his quarry, leaving Ben with his thoughts. Thoughts that, far too quickly, returned to Al.

Although they had worked in the same theater for months, tonight was the first time he'd actually been within touching distance of her. Twice.

The first time had been accidental, as they both reached out to save Sally from falling. An innocent contact, but it had hit him like a fully laden brewer's dray, almost knocking him off his feet. Electricity shot through him, lifting the hair on his arms, sending his heart into a frenzy, and making his stomach somersault. She'd looked surprised, which made him think she felt it too. Yet Sally had stood, unfazed, as if she noticed nothing untoward.

Scared out of his wits by what had happened, Ben withdrew his hand sharply and turned away before he made an even bigger fool of himself. He even gave Sally a wink, to reassure himself he felt nothing for Al that he didn't feel for her friend.

On stage, he performed mechanically, relying heavily on the clowns, for whom he was supposed to be the straight man. They'd picked up their cues, like the professionals they were, and got him through the show. He didn't remember a moment of it.

Then came the second time he got close to Al. He'd been walking along the corridor, trying to get his mind back onto his performance, when he saw her being manhandled by that idiot. The way the man shook her, leaned over her, threatened her… Ben saw red. It was all he could do not to knock the man down, see how he liked being attacked by somebody bigger and stronger.

Conscious that might make things worse, Ben kept his temper under control and settled for separating the abuser from his victim.

After her attacker had gone, he had looked at Al. Even in the dark corridor, he saw the bruises on her arms. She would need a lot of greasepaint to cover those for a week or two.

"I should have given him a black eye," he told himself now. "If I see him again, I might just do it."

Thank God, the bruises on her arms seemed to be the only damage the man had inflicted upon her. Her face was paler than Ben expected, but that was because she wore only a thin layer of greasepaint, just enough to stop the harsh limelight completely washing out her color. Because it was such a thin layer, he saw that her complexion was clear. There were no lines or pockmarks on her skin, her eyes were bright, and she had a full set of teeth, in good order. Considering her life was made up of late nights, drink, and gentlemen, she was in remarkably good condition.

Ben wondered, briefly, if he'd been fair to her. Many opera dancers were little more than prostitutes, true, but not all of them. Was he unjustly tarring this woman with that brush?

No. He was not. He knew exactly what Al was. Only a few weeks ago he'd turned away in disgust when he saw her in the alley behind the theater. She had been three sheets to the wind and swaying like a boat on choppy waters, while hurling foul-mouthed abuse at the top of her voice and sounding like a veritable Billingsgate fishwife.

But even a drunken fishwife should not be treated the way she'd been treated tonight. That man had hurt her, marked her. That was unacceptable.

She probably wouldn't thank him for it, but when he was dressed, he'd have a word with Fred, and have the "gentleman" barred. Then Ben could say, truthfully, that he'd done his best for her.

Of course, if she continued to meet with the man outside the theater, that was not Ben's affair. If she chose that, on her own head be it. One could only do so much.

He felt in his pocket for the key to his dressing room, then stopped when he realized he didn't have it. He knew it hadn't fallen out on stage; the pocket was too secure for that, and the altercation in the corridor had not been enough to dislodge it, either. Which meant...

Ben turned the handle. The door opened easily, confirming he'd left it unlocked. He groaned, a low, despairing sound, as he remembered.

He'd missed the final call for his scene. Peter had had to fetch him, something that never happened. The runner had ushered Ben out and, in his hurry, he'd forgotten to lock the door.

"Idiot!" he castigated himself. "You don't have the wits you were born with!"

He wasn't worried about robbery. It might happen, but it was unlikely. Not only would the pool of suspects be small and the thief easily caught, but Ben didn't have anything worth stealing.

No. What worried him was that he might find a woman in here. One he hadn't invited and didn't welcome.

Hannah Albright had been making eyes at him for weeks. She made no secret of the fact that she'd like to be more to him than simply his co-star. Which was all he needed. She was Tate's, and Ben was not stupid enough to get involved with her, even if he had been attracted to her, which he was not.

After she'd tried to sneak into his dressing room once before, he'd taken the precaution of keeping the door locked, hoping she would tire of the chase. So far, she showed no sign of it. Although why she would risk losing the goodwill of the theater owner for the charms of a mere actor, Ben couldn't say.

Perhaps she'd heard the same rumors Ben had heard. Rumors that Tate was thinking of selling the theater, lock, stock, and actors to a local gang boss, Milton Percival. Without the theater, and the ability to further her career, Tate had nothing to attract a woman like Hannah. And, if she had any sense, she wouldn't move her attentions to Percival, no matter how many theaters he owned.

21

It had come as a shock to Ben to hear that Tate wanted to sell. But he hadn't had to think about it for long before he realized that, if Percival was involved, saying Tate *wanted* to sell, as if he had any choice in the matter, was akin to saying a fish chose to swim.

It left Ben seriously contemplating his career choices. So much so, he'd missed his curtain call tonight, because he knew, if the rumors were true, he needed to move on before doing so was no longer an option.

If it still was an option, even now. Ben knew, all too well, if a powerful man like Percival wanted him, no other theater in London would employ him. And then where would he be?

"Let tomorrow worry about tomorrow," he reminded himself. "For now…one thing at a time, Summersby."

Carefully, he pushed the door fully open and peered inside. The room looked exactly as it had when he'd left. The blinds were pulled over the long sash window that gave a view of the alley. The lamp still burned on his dressing table, but now the flames sputtered a little behind the safety glass as the wick burned down. Tate would have him hung, drawn and quartered if he knew Ben had left it lit. With the preponderance of wooden furnishings, and flammable substances like paint, greasepaint, costumes, and papier-mâché props, theaters stood no chance in a fire. It was a measure of Ben's preoccupation that he'd been so careless.

Satisfied there was nobody in the room, he stepped inside. The things on his dressing table had been moved. His greasepaints were pushed back to the mirror and his cologne bottle was out of place, the stopper slightly off-center, as if somebody had opened it. His armoire was open, the costumes rifled through, though none had been removed. He kept nothing in there with them, except the obligatory mothballs, and sachets of herbs to make them smell better.

The chaise longue was where it should be, his street coat draped over the raised end. The rest of his everyday clothes hung on the side of his armoire. They had not been touched.

He checked his coat pockets. His watch was still there, and his money pouch. The coins inside jiggled together, so he definitely hadn't been robbed.

Something glinted on the floor. He picked up a large sequin, recognizing it as coming from one of the theater's costumes. He grimaced.

He had a good idea who the intruder had been and, knowing how persistent she was, he checked inside the armoire, making sure it contained nothing it shouldn't. He pushed his costumes into a tidy row, closed the armoire, and locked it.

His shoulders finally dropped, and his breathing steadied. Then everything tensed again when somebody rapped on the door. Warily, he opened it, and was relieved to see Peter, a letter in his hand.

"Sorry to bother you again, Mr. Summersby," he said.

Ben frowned. He didn't think he had any more scenes just yet. "Did I miss another call?"

"No, sir. Fred asked me to deliver this." He handed the letter to Ben, who took it and turned it over, then froze when he saw Lord Liverpool's seal. Why would the Prime Minister write to him? Ben had hoped that part of his life was finished. Obviously, it was not.

Judging by the lack of intrigue and curiosity on his

face, Peter didn't know whose seal it was. Probably best to keep it that way.

"Thank you," said Ben, and he started to close the door.

"By the by, sir," Peter went on, "your door was unlocked while you were on stage. I know you prefer it locked."

"Yes, I do. I'll be more careful in future."

"Thought you should know, I chased out Hannah Albright."

It didn't make Ben feel better to know he'd been right. He really must be more careful.

"She said you were expecting her, to go over lines for next week."

"Did she?"

"She did. But she was, erm, changing her costume."

With a heavy sigh, Ben nodded. "Thank you. I will be sure to lock the door in future." He handed Peter a shilling. Peter gave him a small smile and a slight bow, and walked away.

Ben locked the door. If he must lock it when he was out, he certainly needed to lock it when he was in here. He didn't wish to find himself trapped with any of the actresses or dancers. Especially not that one.

He put his wig onto its stand, and ran his fingers through his short hair, feeling relief at the loss of the warm tightness of the hairpiece. Then he sat, cracked the seal, and unfolded the letter.

It was, indeed, from Lord Liverpool, signed by the man himself. Warily, Ben read the Prime Minister's words.

Summersby,

A small matter has been brought to my attention. It

needs dealing with at the earliest opportunity. You have the necessary skills to undertake the task, and I would prevail upon you to consider helping, as a personal favor to me.

As if Ben was going to turn down a request from Lord Liverpool! He owed the man his life. Ben read on.

Viscount Fremont will meet you in the theater's Green Room at three of the clock tomorrow morn, a time that should ensure you will not be observed or interrupted. Please consider assisting him.

Yours,

Liverpool.

Ben ballooned his cheeks, then blew out a hard breath. He wasn't happy to be dragged back into the world of government intrigue, but really, he had no choice. Last winter, Liverpool could have insisted upon his arrest, and possibly his execution. Instead, he had allowed him to walk free, with no stain on his character. This was Ben's chance to repay him for that. He hoped the job would be simple and quick, and that afterward Liverpool would consider Ben's debt canceled and allow him to go on with his usual life, a free and unfettered man.

He put the letter into his coat pocket and set about removing the greasepaint from his face.

****

It was almost midnight and the final curtain had just dropped. The opera dancers' dressing room was a hive of activity, with women changing their costumes and hanging them up, some parading around in their shifts, while those who had dressed plumped their breasts until they threatened to spill over the top of tight bodices.

A woman pleaded with her friend to lend her a blue

dress because, "He says it sets off my eyes."

"It sets off something," her friend retorted. "He ripped it off you last time. If it hadn't been for Alice and her sewing needle—"

"I won't let him do that again," argued the borrower, but her words did not move her friend.

Others had scrubbed away the greasepaint and replaced it with rouge on their cheeks and lips. Some used burnt cork to paint around their eyes.

Only Alice, it seemed, was dressed in her everyday clothes, hair tucked into her bonnet, face clean. Her coat was buttoned to the neck, even though the dressing room was hot from the number of bodies in it, and she twisted the strings of her reticule in her gloved hands as she waited for permission to leave.

"You can go home anytime," Sally said. She daubed her nose and decolletage with rice powder.

"As soon as Peter says I may," Alice agreed.

"That's not what I meant. Come on, Al. What's at home that's so wonderful?"

Alice sighed, longingly. "Bread, cheese and ham, and a nice, warm bed."

Tonight, that sounded like heaven. Not only was she tired, but her arm throbbed where Byron had grabbed it. She wanted to be gone before he returned to pester her again. She'd asked Fred to keep him out, but the doorman would be busy with the Green Room Galahads, and Alice didn't want to risk Byron sneaking in and cornering her again.

"There's a veritable feast in the Green Room," argued Sally. "Bread and cheese can't compare."

"I have ham, too," Alice said.

"Very funny. You wouldn't believe what Mr. Tate

puts out for the gentlemen. No expense spared by him, which encourages no expense spared by them." She lowered her voice. "Don't tell him, but most gentlemen don't eat it. We dancers, though, we save a fortune on food. Can't remember the last time I had to buy my own meat. Or bread."

"Have a good time," said Alice, and she looked to the door. What was keeping Peter?

"I certainly will." Sally grinned. "Lord Greensborough's coming." She gave one of her saucy winks. "Said he might bring a friend, so you wouldn't be surplus to requirements."

Alice laughed and shook her head.

Finally, Peter came. "Another sterling performance, ladies," he called. "You're free to go."

The noise rose in volume as women surged forward, most eager to get to the Green Room. Although she was keen to leave, Alice stayed back, waiting for the initial crush to die away.

"One of these days," said Sally, wrapping a robe of Chinese silk around herself and pulling the belt tight. "I will get you to that Green Room, one of these days."

Not in a hundred years. Alice watched her friend leave with the others.

When most of them had gone and the room was quiet again, she made to leave herself. Two maids hung up costumes and folded stockings, tidied pots of greasepaint and re-stoppered perfume bottles. They wiped up globules of makeup, straightened feathers in headdresses, and generally cleared away the detritus of ten dancing girls. They took no notice of Alice, until she said a soft goodnight to them, and then they both bobbed curtsies at her.

The corridor was deserted now. She could hear the cheerful voices of the gentlemen at the stage door, pleading with Fred to let them in. Fred's cockney tones cut through, assuring them that Mr. Tate would be out in a minute, and they could come in when he said so and not a second before. Alice knew Tate didn't care when the gentlemen came in. The delay was another of Fred's efforts to look after the dancers—he wanted them to eat before they were eaten, as he'd once said.

With the stage door crowded, it wasn't prudent to leave that way. Alice wasn't permitted to join the patrons filing out of the front doors, so she went to the delivery bay at the very back of the theater, as she did every night. The large space, where the crew stored scenery flats, larger props, and furniture, had a huge door through which big items of stage ware could be delivered. It was dark and deserted now, and nobody ever noticed a lone actress slip through the side door and out into the night.

The alley at the rear of the theater was narrow to Alice's right and left, although straight in front of her it was wide, a short road about fifty yards long leading to the main thoroughfare. This road was used by the delivery wagons that brought supplies to the theater every day, and it was always swept clean. It turned into a second alley, which ran back, along the side of the theater building, past the stage door and out toward the front. That alley was also kept clean, and was wide enough to accommodate the coaches of the more private gentlemen. The care taken of it gave the impression that the back of the theater was as well cared for as the front.

That was, of course, an illusion. Away from there, in the parts the public never saw, the premises were tired and unkempt, the paths uneven and broken, with large holes filled with puddles. The wooden doors and window frames back here were soft from years of exposure to the elements, the paint bubbled and peeling. Torn notices hung off the bricks, the top layer peeling away from old posters beneath. Rats scurried, keeping to the shadows as they searched for last night's food waste.

Alice shivered. It was in just such an alley that Milton Percival had once found her.

She reached into the pocket of her coat and felt for the knife she'd carried since that night. Its heavy handle and sharp blade reassured her now.

Ironically, in view of the way Percival had attacked her that night, these alleys were the safest way for a woman of her class to move about the city. Provided she kept her wits about her, she could travel through them, all the way from the theater to her lodging house, without encountering any trouble at all.

The same could not be said for the front of the house. That side of the building was majestic, its well-lit facade made up of washed sandstone, gleaming windows, and wide doors manned by liveried servants. Its whitewashed steps led to a wide, clean pavement, before a wide, clean road, on which beautiful, well-appointed carriages awaited their beautiful, well-appointed passengers.

But despite its respectable appearance, and the crowds, it was not a safe place for a lone female. There, an unescorted woman was assumed to be of a particular sort. She'd be disdained by the truly respectable, and propositioned by their less well-mannered friends.

Alice was far safer in the back alleys. Even though that was where Percival had…

But then, that had been no random attack. No crime born of opportunity. Percival had not lain in wait in the vague hope that "somebody" would pass by. He'd waited for Alice.

He'd hidden near the supposedly safe stage door and watched her leave, threading her way through the young bucks, ignoring their lewd remarks and good-natured banter. He'd heard her call goodnight to Fred. She'd walked away, and Percival had followed her.

Fred had suggested, many times since that night, that she should wait for other dancers to come out with her. "Safety in numbers," he'd said. "You should all walk home together."

Since several of the dancers lived in the same boardinghouse as Alice, what Fred said made sense. But she didn't want to stay, waiting for them to finish "socializing." Besides, they often went on to other places with their gentlemen, and if that happened, they would completely forget Alice. She would end up walking home alone anyway, so what was the difference?

She turned into another alley, relieved to be almost home.

The boardinghouse was tall and narrow, like all the buildings lining the street. The walls were dark, blackened by soot and grime, the windows thick with city dirt, although Mrs. Brown's doorstep was always clean. It stood out, proudly gleaming in the glow of the nearby streetlamp. The road smelled of sewage and stale sweat, old cabbage, and despair. No stars showed in the sky—few could be seen even in the nicer areas of the city, hidden as they were by tall buildings, smoke from chimneys, fog rolling in off the river, and the lights from houses and businesses, streetlamps, and cabs for hire. Here, the stars had fled completely.

All was quiet in Mrs. Brown's house. Most of her

tenants would not be home for another hour or more. Between one and two in the morning, they would arrive, mildly drunk, laughing, and shushing each other loudly enough to wake everybody in St. Giles'. Most of them would have a few extra shillings in their pockets, enough to buy a new bonnet, or a pair of warm gloves for when winter came. As far as Alice was concerned, they'd earned every penny, for tolerating being leered at and pawed and pestered by men who thought the word "no" meant they were playing hard-to-get to stoke the fire.

Even slapping them away didn't always deter such men, Alice had found. Some thought it was part of the game. They actually relished the idea of being sternly treated. It took a lot to convince them she meant what she said. Indeed, one particular "gentleman" had recently been so persistent that, in desperation, Alice had stood in the alley, playing the drunk, swaying, slurring her speech, and shouting obscenities at him until he was finally embarrassed enough to go away.

Sally had watched that performance, her eyes wide. She'd since told anyone who would listen that Al was, "an actress born, who should be a leading lady."

Alice didn't want to be a leading lady. If she became too well known as an actress, people wouldn't consider her respectable, and they wouldn't come to her shop when it opened. She was happy to be an anonymous dancer, although she would have welcomed the extra pay for speaking roles.

She pushed such thoughts aside as, bone-deep weary, her bruises throbbing, she climbed the stairs to her room. She could almost taste the ripe cheese and salted ham she'd put by for her supper, and her bed called seductively to her. She'd be asleep quickly tonight.

Or perhaps not.

Chapter Three

The minute she opened her door, Alice's eyes were stabbed by the light of not one but all of her precious candles. The smell of tallow filled the air. She knew she hadn't left them alight—she'd gone to the theater in daylight, so there would have been no need to light them. And besides, she only ever lit one candle at a time. She couldn't afford to be extravagant. Which meant someone else had been in here.

Every nerve on edge, ready to run and scream, she looked sharply around the room.

There, on her bed, his boots shedding mud on her blanket while he ate her supper, was Byron. As she came in, he moved, rucking the blanket and depositing more mud. He popped the last piece of bread into his mouth, clapped his hands together to dust off the crumbs, and grinned at her. The grin turned to a wince and he raised one hand to his swelling, shining, black eye.

"I thought you'd be home ages ago," he said. He sounded strange, as if his nose was blocked. Her eyes now fully adjusted to the light, Alice saw it was crooked, and there was a smattering of dried blood above his upper lip.

"What are you doing here, Byron?"

She looked around her room. It was a mess. Her clothes were scattered on the floor, her few pieces of crockery pulled from her cupboard and strewn across the tiny table. She gritted her teeth, knowing he had found the money she'd hidden. Cursing herself for not putting it under the floorboards, she faced him, held out one hand, and said, "Give it back."

"Give what back?" It sounded more like, "gib whap bag?"

"My money. I know you have it."

"No, I don't."

She narrowed her eyes and he stood, pulling the blanket to the floor.

"I only got five pounds. I couldn't find the rest. Where is it?"

"There is no 'rest.' That's everything I have. It took me months to save that much."

Byron sneered at her. "Don't give me that." He came toward her, although his movements were slower than they had been earlier and there was a stiffness about him, as if the effort hurt him. "You must have more. God knows, you aren't spending it." He looked around the room with contempt.

"No, I'm not. I'm saving it. Now, give it back."

"Where's the rest?" The nasal whine took some of the menace from his tone, but she knew he could still hurt her if he had a mind to. "Don't tell me this is all of it. I've seen those bucks at the theater, throwing money at their ladybirds like it burns their fingers to keep it."

Alice bristled. "I am not a ladybird."

Byron gave her a half smile. "That's what I told Percival."

The name stopped her cold. A shiver ran through her, stirring nausea in her belly. She could barely breathe. It took several seconds to tamp down the panic enough to let her speak.

"What has he to do with this?" Her voice was low, not much more than a whisper. She heard the quiver in it, although Byron didn't seem to notice.

"I owe him." He dipped his head, looking like an errant schoolboy who hoped to charm his way out of a caning. But errant schoolboys did not owe money to the likes of Milton Percival.

"Then you're an idiot."

Byron clicked his tongue in irritation. He rolled his eyes, winced, and touched the shiner again.

"Percival is nasty," she said, more to calm her own nerves with the sound of her voice than to tell her brother something he must already know. "And, from what I've heard, he never takes excuses."

"I know all that," answered Byron, testily. "That's why I need the money."

Alice's stomach roiled. Hot bile rose to her throat. She swallowed hard, pushing it down, but she could still taste the burn. "How much?"

"Doesn't matter. What matters is, he wants it. One way or another, I have to find enough to satisfy him. Five pounds won't do that."

She looked at her brother's face, the black eye, the crooked nose, the specks of blood. He'd got off lightly so far. Was this a warning? Or had Byron stopped the beating by making Percival believe he had the funds to pay him?

Oh, God, had he told Percival *she* had the money? Would that monster come here, looking for her to pay her brother's debts?

Her heart did a strange somersault. Her throat dried, and she shivered, uncontrollably, in the warm night air. This could not be happening.

"How much?" she asked, again.

Mayhap she could borrow the money. If it was less than fifty pounds, Sally might help her. Lord Greensborough was generous with Sally, and she knew Alice would pay her back, no matter how long it took. It would set Alice's dream back years, possibly forever, but that was better than being at the mercy of that man. He would kill Byron without blinking. And after he'd killed Alice's last surviving family... She didn't even want to think about what he'd do to her.

"How. Much?" *Please, let it be below fifty pounds.* Knowing Byron as she did, she had no hope of it being much lower, but that was the limit. Lord Greensborough was generous. He wasn't a fool.

Byron winced again. "A monkey."

She gasped and grabbed at the table to stop herself falling. Her breaths came fast and shallow, and her heartbeats ricocheted between her ribs. *Five hundred pounds?*

"Oh, Byron!" That was more than four years' wages to Alice. "I can't possibly help you with that sort of money."

Byron ran his hand through his hair, then limped to the window. He opened it and peered down to the street. Then he turned back to her, his smile regretful. "Actually, you can."

Confused, frightened, she moved to him and looked out herself. On the street were three men. They were stocky and hard-looking, and she knew, instinctively, who had sent them.

Panicked, she pushed at Byron, moving him away from the window. "Mayhap they didn't see you. They don't know you're here. Get out. Go to a coaching inn, any coaching inn. Whichever has a coach leaving soonest."

"Alice," he called at her. It sounded like he had said her name several times already.

"You haven't time," she protested.

At the same moment he said, "They're not here for me."

It took a moment for his words to register. "What?"

"They aren't here for me." A flicker of shame chased across his face, but it was gone in an instant. "What was I supposed to do, sis? He was going to kill me."

Alice was vaguely aware that she backed away from him. She shook her head in denial, her eyes so wide they hurt, her throat trembling. "No," she whispered.

"Percival puts a very high price on you. Something about the fish that jumped off the line." Byron shrugged. He plainly had no idea what that meant.

But she did. Oh, she did.

Suddenly, she was back in the alley behind the theater, pressed against the wall, rough brick snagging her hair and tearing at her clothes. Percival leaned against her, his weight holding her in place. His hands pawed at her, and his mouth was all over her, slobbering and biting at her like a dog. She screamed, but hardly any sound escaped. His hand grabbed her face, and his fingers pushed into her cheeks. He gave her his rictus grin, then tore her bodice, squeezed, pinched, pressed his fingers into her flesh…

There was a shout. More than one. Running feet. Her scream had been heard. Fred rushed to her, several of the young bucks behind him. That night, they'd lived up to the nickname the opera dancers had given them.

Every one of them was a Galahad.

Had it just been Fred, or perhaps two men, they would have paid for their intervention with their lives. But even Milton Percival couldn't stand against half a dozen men. Not on his own. And he knew as well as she did that rape was a hanging offense. If he was taken by these men, gentlemen from families of quality whose word carried weight, it wouldn't matter that he hadn't succeeded in his crime. He would swing. So he'd lobbed foul words at her, promised this was not finished, and then he'd run.

Her rescuers escorted her back to the theater, where they gave her brandy for the shock and a clean, undamaged dress Fred found in the wardrobe stores.

They'd all acted like the gentlemen they were supposed to be that night. One of them had escorted her home in his carriage, seen her safely to her room, asked if she needed a doctor. He'd even offered to pay for it.

It had been months before the nightmares faded, though. Months before she dared go out alone. But there'd been no more sightings of Percival near the theater. Instead, there was talk that he'd taken over another man's area, growing his "manor," and with it his power. There were even rumors of him spreading his influence outside London, muscling in on lucrative ventures in Brighton and other places along the south coast.

All of which led Alice to think he'd forgotten her. She was just one insignificant dancer, after all. Gradually, her fears subsided, and her confidence grew, until she thought she was safe. That Percival had bigger fish to fry.

"I was the fish that jumped off the line." The words

hung in the air, barely audible. In her head, they sounded like screams, as she finally understood. Percival had been thwarted. He was not prepared to let that stand.

"Personally," said Byron, his face scrunched in confusion, "I think the man's mad."

I know *he's mad.*

"I mean, five hundred quid for a tup? No offense, Al, but you're not worth a monkey."

His words brought her crashing back into the here and now. "What did you do?" she demanded.

Byron looked affronted. "What do you mean? I didn't do anything, except play a couple of hands. No, this is on you. You're the one who's been flaunting herself. You're the one who caught his eye."

She shook her head in rapid denial.

"I couldn't pass this chance up, Al. It was the deal of a lifetime. Not only is he not going to kill me, he's forgiven the damn—dashed debt. All for a night with you. Just one night." He chuckled, but it sounded forced. "That's some allure you've got there. You should bottle it. We'd be rich."

Alice gave Byron a look of contempt, then glanced out of the window again. The three men headed toward the corner of the street. Once they rounded that corner, they'd be within three yards of Mrs. Brown's gleaming doorstep. There was no way Alice could get downstairs and out of here before they reached the door.

Up. She could go up. Perhaps she could hide in somebody else's room. Or in a closet. It would give her a few moments to think of something, a longer-lasting escape.

Thankful she hadn't taken her coat off yet, she grabbed her reticule and the miniature of her mother, the only thing in here she valued, then turned to the door. She managed two steps before Byron grabbed her arm, his hand pressing on her bruises, making her cry out.

"No, you don't," he said, and he pulled her round to face him. "It's just one night."

"It is not 'just one night.'" Even if Alice thought she could survive the rough treatment Percival would mete out, and get through the trauma, humiliation, and ruination she faced at his hands, it would never be "just one night." Only a featherbrain would think he'd just release her afterward. Not a man like Percival. Once he'd tired of her himself, he would set her to work and get a profit from her.

That was not going to happen.

"He says he only wants one night with you." Byron sounded as if he actually believed that. Surely, he was not so naive? "One night," he repeated. "Weighed against my life!"

He pulled her back, knocking her off balance. She grabbed at the table to steady herself, and registered the cupboard contents he'd put on it during his search. As well as the plate, the cup, and a few other pieces, he'd pulled out the heavy enamel jug she used to fetch soup from the street vendor on winter evenings.

Alice didn't even think about it. She picked up the jug with her free hand and swung it in a wide arc, all her strength propelling her.

The speed of her action caught him completely by surprise. He didn't even have time to raise his hand in defense.

The jug hit him squarely on the temple. She heard the thunk of metal hitting bone, felt the vibrations jar her hand and wrist. His fingers loosened on her arm, and he corkscrewed to the floor before he could utter so much as a grunt. There, he lay still.

For a second, she thought she'd killed him. Then his chest moved as he took in an unconscious breath, and she sighed her relief before making her way to the door again.

Through the thin walls she heard Mrs. Brown shout, "Oy! Where do you think you're going? I run a respectable house, I do. I pay Mr. Percival to protect me. He'll have you, barging in here like this."

There was no way out through the door. The men would see her. Alice looked around, frantically searching for a hiding place. There was none.

She had one chance. A slim one, but…

Shoving the strings of her reticule up her arm to her elbow, Alice climbed through the window and balanced on the narrow ledge that ran around the building. She'd worried about this ledge when she first moved here. Then, she'd been frightened that one of her less scrupulous neighbors might use it to reach her window and break in. Now, she was grateful it was there.

Carefully, clinging to the wall, her fingers digging into the mortar work between the bricks, she inched along, away from her window and toward the corner. If she could just hide herself in the night shadows…

Once, she looked down at the ground, three stories below, Hard pavement and cobblestone road wavered. Her heart bounced into her throat. She closed her eyes tight and lifted her head, determined not to look down again.

The door to her room banged open and bounced off the wall. Men's voices cursed.

Alice held her breath. Her spine was rigid, her

shoulders stiff. She turned her face away from the light, and hoped her coat was dark enough to blend in with the nighttime.

"Wake him up," commanded one man. He sounded disgusted. "Where is she?"

Byron groaned.

"Where is she?" asked the man again.

"She hit me," whined Byron. "She hit me."

"Not hard enough," said a second man.

"You," said the first man, "check all the other rooms in the house. If she's here, find her."

"Stupid cow can't have gone far," said the second man. "We'd have seen her."

"She bloody well hit me." Byron was no longer groggy, no longer whining. Now, he sounded outraged.

I should have hit you harder.

"She's not out here," said the third man. His voice was close, as if he was out here with her.

"'Course she's not out there. She's not a bleedin' sparrow."

"I was just looking." The third man's voice faded as he withdrew back into the room. Alice breathed out as quietly as she could. A long way off, Mrs. Brown raised her voice, objecting once more. She was joined by a chorus of disgruntled women.

"Sorry to disturb you, ladies," called the first man. "My colleague will give you all a shilling for your trouble."

Somewhat mollified, most of the women stopped protesting. The subsequent quiet told Alice they'd returned to their rooms.

"I'll want a lot more than a shilling," complained Mrs. Brown. "I pay Mr. Percival so this kind of thing don't happen. Wait till I tell him what you three done."

"It will be made up to you, madam," promised the first man.

"She's not here," reported the second man.

"Right," said the first man. "Go back and get help. Check all the coaching inns. Leave someone watching each one. Because even God Almighty won't get you out of this if she slips past you. She escapes, Mr. Percival will wear your eyeballs as cufflinks."

Feet clattered down the stairs. Mrs. Brown yelled, "And don't come back!"

Alice heard flesh hitting flesh, and Byron yelled, "Ow!"

"On your feet. You're coming with me," said the first man.

"It wasn't my fault," cried Byron. "She hit me."

"Mr. Percival will want to see you."

She heard the thud, thud, thud as he was dragged down the stairs, protesting loudly. Tears filled her eyes at the thought of him facing the vicious and vengeful crime boss, but there was nothing she could do.

And then, there was quiet.

Alice stood on the ledge for a long time, frozen in place by terror. How could Byron have done this to her? Her own brother!

One thing was certain. Those men would be back. They knew this was where she lived. At the moment, they thought she was on the streets, hiding, but they'd expect her to return. So it wouldn't be long before they came back, too. She needed to be gone before they did that.

But where could she go? Nowhere in London would be safe. Even the theater could only shelter her for so long, before somebody discovered she was there and betrayed her to Percival. She couldn't ask anybody to help her, either—to do so would be to sign their death warrant.

In the distance, a bell tolled two. It surprised her. It seemed to her that a lifetime had passed since she'd found Byron in her room. In reality, it had been less than an hour. But now, time was running short. The other opera dancers would be home soon. They'd find their rooms disturbed, their possessions rifled. There would be outrage, anger, chaos. Alice ought to be gone before they arrived, before any of them saw her. It would only take one woman, disgruntled over her room being searched and blaming Alice. Or someone attempting to ingratiate herself with Percival. Whatever their reason, there was bound to be somebody who would tell him they'd seen her.

She didn't just need to be out of this boardinghouse, she realized. She should get out of London altogether. Although how she was to do that, she didn't know. Men had been sent to the coaching inns to watch for her. Even if they hadn't been, where was she to find the money for a ticket? Byron had taken hers.

Perhaps, if she could elude Percival for a few days, he would scale down the search. Even he couldn't afford to have men standing idle outside the inns of London for long. If Alice could remain undiscovered for, say, a week, she should be able to make an escape.

Meanwhile, there were plenty of dark corners in the theater. Hiding there long term wasn't feasible, but a few days should work. She could live off the leftovers in the Green Room, and perhaps search the stalls and boxes Front of House for dropped coins. There were bound to be some. She only needed a few, just enough to buy a ticket out of the city.

Slowly, carefully, Alice moved back along the ledge to her window. It seemed to take forever. Her gloves were torn and her fingers raw from gripping the mortar, her boots scuffed beyond repair by the brickwork, the threads on her coat snagged and pulled. But she was alive, and still free.

She took one dress, a shift, and her hair brush. She had to leave everything else. She couldn't carry it, and, really, it wasn't important. As long as she had her life, and her mother's miniature, nothing else mattered.

As quietly as she could, she crept down the stairs to the front door. Just as she reached the bottom, Mrs. Brown stepped out of her room. She stood, hands clasped at her waist, and studied Alice. Alice watched her right back, ready for whatever the woman would do.

Finally, Mrs. Brown nodded. "I never seen you tonight."

Alice breathed out the breath she'd held so tensely. "Thank you."

The woman gestured with her eyes. "Best get out of here before somebody does. Not everyone's lips are as tight as mine."

Alice nodded, and hurried from the building.

Chapter Four

At ten to three, Ben unlocked the stage door of the theater and stepped inside. The corridor was completely dark but he didn't wish to light a lamp. Although there should be nobody around to see the light, Ben didn't want to take the chance, so he made his way carefully along the corridors, hands out in front of him to feel his way. He tripped over something, cursed and righted himself. His shin smarted from the contact and he felt foolish, but needs must.

He reached the Green Room door and realized he could see a light, flickering in the gap between the bottom of the door and the floor. Did that mean somebody was still in there? He hoped not. He didn't want to explain his presence to some drunken lord and his doxy. Fremont certainly wouldn't want to explain his.

Deciding the best form of defense was attack, he flung open the door, intending to scold the errant lovers and send them on their way. Hopefully, they would assume he'd been given responsibility for the theater's security tonight and wouldn't argue.

There was nobody there.

Warily, Ben looked around the room. There were chairs and chaises longues, occasional tables on which were stacked plates, some with crumbs on them, some with half eaten food—bread, meats, cheeses, apples, cake. A garter lay abandoned on the floor next to one of the chaises longues.

Along one wall was a long table covered in a cloth. Big enough to cover the table and its legs right to the floor, the cloth was stained and littered with the evidence that people had served themselves none too carefully. On top of it were plates of bread, slices of chicken, beef, and ham, plus blocks of cheese, platters of cakes and sweetmeats, marchpane shapes, a half-eaten pound cake. There were bunches of ripe green and black grapes, apples, and berries, though the Lord knew where Tate had found those at this time of year. The theater owner must have very good connections if he could procure—and afford—such fruits out of season.

Ben saw bottles of wine, mostly red, some half drunk, and a bowl of punch, its contents a decidedly sickly orange, with a few slices of sorry-looking, over-soaked fruit floating in it. Spots of dried wine and punch dotted the tablecloth.

It was on this table that the lamp glowed, the one that had showed beneath the door, although its light wasn't strong enough to make the room bright. Ben smiled, wryly. The dim lighting was, almost certainly, deliberate. Tate would not want the gentlemen to see the dancers too clearly. The late nights, layers of greasepaint, and the extracurricular activities that made up their everyday lives would not have enhanced their beauty.

Although, he mused, those things did not seem to have ravaged Al's good looks, from what he'd seen in the corridor earlier. Her skin had not been sallow or marked, her eyes had glowed clear, and her honey-colored hair was thick and lush.

But then, the lighting in the corridor had been no

better than the lighting in here. In the harsh light of day, he made no doubt, the woman's allure would be much diminished, and the evidence of her lifestyle all too evident.

Ben pursed his lips, annoyed with himself for bringing her to mind. He did not dally with opera dancers. Never had. Never would. And that being the case, there was no reason for him even to have thought of her. He was, he reminded himself, here for a reason, and that reason was not to dream about come-hither eyes in a doxy's face.

He left the door open so that light spilled from the Green Room into the corridor to ease Fremont's way. This room, with no windows, was perfect for their meeting, but it wouldn't do for the viscount to break his neck on his way in here.

At the long table, Ben helped himself to some of the food. The bread was hardening, but the rest of it was still good, and Ben was hungry. He hadn't been able to eat his supper earlier because he'd been on edge over this meeting. He didn't really feel like eating now, truth to tell, but he knew he must. Hunger dulled the senses, and he had a feeling he'd need every one of his.

Perhaps this cold collation wouldn't turn his stomach the way a hot meal would have. On that thought, he piled the plate with slices of beef, a few grapes, an apple and some marchpane.

As he moved away from the table, he heard a noise. His first thought was that he'd heard the viscount moving along the corridor, but then the noise sounded again. It was a soft rustle, and it was coming not from the corridor but from within this room.

Ben put down his plate and looked around. The

room seemed deserted, although it didn't have the feeling of emptiness one usually got when no living thing was present in a space. All was silent now. But he knew he had heard something.

Thinking to catch the culprit unawares, he jerked up the tablecloth and peered under the long table. He could see nothing in the dark space below.

Next, he crossed to the wall opposite the door. Here, as on all the walls, drapes hung from ceiling to floor, the blue velvet giving the room a plush, expensive look. He lifted a drape and looked behind it. The whitewashed wall was stark.

He stood still and listened. He could hear nothing now. Had it been a mouse? With all this food left overnight, rodents wouldn't be a surprise, although a mouse would still be scurrying, moving along, tapping on the floorboards and rustling over the detritus.

Quickly, he checked the curtains covering the other walls but still found nothing and nobody. He was, as far as he could tell, the only living being in here. Satisfied with his search, he began to relax, then tensed again when he heard a scuffling sound, followed by the distinct ring of boot heels against the corridor floor, alerting him to Fremont's arrival.

"Summersby?" asked the viscount, from the doorway.

The man was younger than Ben had imagined he would be. He'd expected a contemporary of Lord Liverpool, who was in his late forties, but Viscount Fremont looked no more than thirty-five. He was tall, almost as tall as Ben, and trim but well-muscled. He looked very much as if he could take care of himself.

He stepped farther into the room and gave Ben a

perfunctory bow. "I asked Lord Liverpool to set up this meeting," he said. "I believe you can help me with a certain matter."

Ben gave a reluctant nod. He'd hoped his days of "helping" people with "certain matters" were behind him. Although, he acknowledged, if he found himself back in a world of subterfuge and lies, he had nobody but himself to blame. If he hadn't been so eager the last time, mayhap he wouldn't be here now.

Mayhap you would be dead. The voice in his head reminded Ben that the men who recruited him last time had given him the illusion of choice, but if he'd said no, they would not have left him alive to tell the tale.

Which was no excuse. In all honesty, he couldn't blame his poor decision on their ruthlessness. He'd said yes, willingly, long before he'd known their true characters. This time, he was less willing. Although he would still say yes.

Hopefully, this time he would earn his redemption.

"I'll come straight to the point," said Fremont. His voice was deep and reassuring, his accent expensive. "I have a job I wish you to do."

Ben nodded. "When?"

"Tomorrow. Or later today, should I say? First light. I need you to go to Broseley, near the Ironbridge."

"In Shropshire." Western England, almost in Wales. A long way from London, it was not a place Ben could hare off to and be back by tonight's show.

"I know where it is." Fremont sounded the least bit impatient.

"I can't just go to Shropshire on a whim. I have a performance tonight."

"That's been taken care of. Your understudy is

preparing himself."

Ben didn't have an understudy. The company finances didn't allow for it. Apparently, Fremont's pockets were deeper.

"He'll do a fine job in your place."

"Not too fine, I hope. I'd like a job to return to."

Fremont grinned. "He isn't after your position. He'll satisfy the crowd, but they will be glad to have you back."

"Good to know."

Fremont moved around the room. He reminded Ben of a cat, his movements long and seemingly lazy but with an underlying readiness about him, as if he might pounce in an instant. "The theater manager will not penalize you for missing the last two performances of this week's show. On top of which, I've seen the schedule for the next three weeks. You have no roles to play in that time."

"Three weeks?" Ben was shocked. Three weeks was a long time for an actor to be resting. Long enough that Tate might well cast about for another actor to take Ben's place permanently.

"Mr. Tate has been adequately compensated for your absence. He has agreed that, at the end of your time away, you can retake your position here, without fear or favor. You will, of course, also be handsomely rewarded for your services. I'm not a man who calls in a favor and expects that to suffice. I like to think I deal fairly with people."

That was welcome news. Ben might have been willing to do this for nothing, but he could not deny that payment would come in handy. "What do I have to do?" he asked.

"Be Josh Summersby."

"What?" Ben was horrified. "You jest, sir."

"I have been known to," agreed Fremont, his deep voice tinted by his slight smile. "But in this instance, I am in earnest. I need you to play the role of Josh Summersby."

Ben shook his head. "Last time I did that, a number of people, including myself, were very nearly killed. And afterward, I was lucky not to hang for treason."

"I am aware of what happened. This time, your performance will be officially sanctioned. Liverpool himself has given the endeavor his blessing. As has your cousin."

"My cousin agreed to this?" Ben was unsure about that. The real Josh Summersby had been less than happy about Ben impersonating him last time.

"He has. I discussed it with him last week. Just after I attended his wedding in Frantham, actually."

Ben smiled at that news. "My salutations to them both. Miss Bell is a lovely woman." A lovely woman who had eyes for nobody but Josh. Ben was happy for them.

"That she is," agreed Fremont. "Luckily for us, she's also a rare type of young lady. Despite her mother's aspirations, the new Mrs. Summersby did not want a large Society wedding, which, in her words, would involve inviting, 'a lot of people she didn't know, who didn't care for her in the least, and who hadn't deigned to give her the time of day when she was plain Amelia Bell.' "

Ben laughed. "That sounds like Amelia. I am truly pleased for them both."

"As am I. But for our purposes, the upshot of Mrs. Summersby's no-nonsense attitude is that they had a quiet, country wedding, for close friends and family only. A notice will appear in *The Times*, of course, if it hasn't already, but not many people outside the Rotherton area of Sussex have met the bride. And because of Josh's time in India, few people know him, either. Nor is it common knowledge that the happy pair set sail for a honeymoon in Italy immediately after the wedding breakfast. All of which gives you the perfect opportunity to appear, as Josh, in Shropshire."

"Where I'll be on my wedding trip?"

"Precisely."

Ben frowned. "Forgive me, Lord Fremont, but the Ironbridge is not somewhere that springs immediately to mind when one mentions a honeymoon."

"Josh is a consummate businessman. As such, he has, rather practically, combined his honeymoon with a search for investment opportunities."

"Romantic to his core," Ben muttered. Fremont chuckled. "Enlighten me," continued Ben. "What investment opportunities is Josh Summersby seeking?"

Fremont shrugged his shoulders. "Who knows? There are plenty to be had in that region." He counted them off on his fingers. "Canals. Iron. Potteries. Slate. Coal. To name but a few. Your task will be to investigate as many of those opportunities as you can. I'm particularly interested in schemes that are looking for discreet investors. If they don't wish for the details to be spread abroad, then I wish to know about them. It's my belief that if they think they have a juicy fish like Josh Summersby on the line, they'll do all they can to reel him in. Which should allow you to discover a great deal more about them than the average person would ever be permitted to know."

"Then what?"

"You pass the information to my agent, who will pass it to me, and I'll do the rest."

This did not sit well with Ben. Impersonating his cousin, playing a role, that he could do. But collecting information, deciding which of it was useful to this man and which was not…

"You must have someone better qualified for the task," he said. "I'm just a jobbing actor—"

"Don't be so modest, Mr. Summersby." Viscount Fremont smiled at him but it was too predatory to make Ben feel better. "You are actually a very good actor. You're more than capable of pulling this off. On top of which, you bear an uncanny resemblance to one of the richest men in the country. I have nobody with better qualifications for this task."

Ben's uncertainty must have shown on his face, because Fremont let out a frustrated growl. "For crying out loud, Summersby!" he said. "You are exactly the man I need. The people I'm interested in will be interested in doing business with your cousin. Nobody but you could persuade them that is what they are doing."

"We're not identical," Ben tried.

"As near as makes no difference, you are. Good God, man, you fooled Josh's own father."

"An elderly man who hadn't seen his son in more than a decade."

"Very few others have seen him in that time, either." Fremont sighed, heavily. "I grant you, it is possible—not probable, but possible, that you could run into a friend of his from his time before he went to India. If that happens, it would be all to the good, for you're so close to him in looks they would merely confirm your identity."

"And if I should meet someone who knew him after he went to India?"

Fremont grinned. "Your chances of doing that are slightly longer than your chances of swimming to Spain and back in a night."

Ben nodded. "So," he clarified, "I go into Shropshire as Josh Summersby, nabob and heir to a viscountcy, who is using his honeymoon trip to explore investment opportunities?"

"Yes."

"And is there…" Ben's question died as he heard a scrabbling and rustling that was far too loud to be a mouse. The cloth covering the long table moved several times as something, or some*one*, bashed against it. Fremont threw Ben a suspicious glance, then pulled a pistol from his coat and aimed it at the billowing linen. Ben took a step back, allowing the armed government man to deal with whatever this was.

A moment later, Al crawled out. Her coat was streaked with dust and dotted with crumbs, and her bonnet was skewwhiff, disheveling her hair. She coughed once, presumably because of the dust she'd been wallowing in, then gave Ben what she clearly meant to be a winsome smile. An instant later, she saw Fremont's pistol pointing at her, and her smile disappeared.

"Don't shoot," she whispered. "I can help."

Fremont clenched his jaw. "Who are you?" he demanded.

At the very same moment, Ben asked her, "What the hell are you doing here?"

Chapter Five

Alice gulped. She hadn't thought this through, she could see that now. If she had, she'd probably still be crouched under the table, hidden in the dark. She certainly would not be facing a man with a gun in his hand and a dangerous look on his face.

"What the hell are you doing here?" asked Benedict Summersby. His tone was less than friendly, and the glint in his eyes made her wonder if escaping Percival's henchmen had led her into something far more dangerous. The villains in her room had not, to her knowledge, carried pistols.

"I, erm," she began, then realized she needed a plausible reason for being here. It was all well and good having overheard their conversation and seen a way of making their plans work in her favor, but if they weren't satisfied as to why she'd been there in the first place, she had a feeling it would not go well for her.

She could tell them the truth, of course. After her encounter with her brother and the other men, she'd made her way back to the theater, arriving as the last of the dancers left with their gentlemen. Fred had watched them go. She knew he committed to memory every last man, even as he pocketed the tips those same men gave him. He left them in no doubt that if any of the dancers were hurt, or worse, he would recall who had been with them when last seen.

His care for the dancers brought a lump to Alice's throat. He was a good man, and she hoped that what she was about to do would not bring him too much trouble.

Not that it should bring him any trouble at all. Provided she hid herself well and didn't get caught, Fred would not be called to task for admitting her.

While his attention was diverted by the departing dancers and their guests, Alice had managed to sneak in through the stage door. Walking on the balls of her feet so her heels didn't click against the floor, she moved along the corridor to the props bay and hid behind a stack of flats—the large pieces of wood used for scenery. She stayed there, standing still for so long her back ached, and the cold emptiness of the theater seeped into her bones, chilling her through and through.

Fred did his rounds, checking the dressing rooms and the Green Room for stragglers. He didn't come into the props bay. He had no reason to do so.

Alice heard the thud as the stage door closed, the clink of the key turning in the lock. Then nothing but silence.

Carefully, quietly, she came out of the bay and made her way along pitch dark corridors to the Green Room. There, she knew, she would find food for her empty stomach, and a lamp she could light, in a space where no one would see it. The Green Room was surrounded by other rooms and corridors and, as such, it had no windows. Alice thought this was deliberate—if they couldn't see outside, the gentlemen lost track of time, which gave the dancers longer to encourage more money from their pockets. Money, Alice was certain, that Mr. Tate shared in. He wasn't exactly a panderer for the women, but he was little better. For their part, the dancers accepted his demands as the price of allowing them to meet their gentlemen in comfortable, safe surroundings. It worked for them all, and nobody complained.

Alice found the lamp and the tinderbox, and soon the room was bathed in its soft, subdued light. She piled a plate with ham and cheese and a piece of hardening bread, then added the luxuries of a cake and some fruit. Compared to the supper Byron had stolen from her, this was a feast, and she savored every mouthful.

After eating her fill, she sat on one of the chaises longues to contemplate her immediate future. That she must leave London before Milton Percival found her was obvious. But how was she to manage it when the gang boss was actively searching for her?

She could not say. All she could do was stay here for a few days, secreting herself in the dark alcoves that made up this building, eating the leftover food in the Green Room each night, and sleeping where she could. God willing, her game of hide-and-seek would last longer than Percival's willingness to search for her.

A noise in the corridor startled her. She stood and looked around in alarm, realizing she had nowhere to hide.

A man cursed. Had he come looking for her? It was, she saw now, when it was far too late, her most obvious destination.

Her breath caught in her throat. Her heart beat eighteen to the dozen against her ribs. Shivers wracked her body, and fear turned her legs and her brain to jelly. It was more by instinct than design that she ran across the room and scrambled under the long table, curling herself into a ball in the darkest corner, head down to keep her face from showing, should anybody look under here.

Too late, she remembered she hadn't extinguished the lamp. Would its presence draw her pursuers, raise their suspicions, and lead them to her?

The footsteps she heard were those of a man. Heavy, sure and confident. The Green Room door was thrown open, with force. Alice froze. She didn't even dare to breathe more than a sliver of air. Every muscle tensed, every nerve stood on end. She smelled the oil burning in the lamp, the dust under the table, the yeasty stale bread, and the fruitiness of the old wine.

She buried her face deeper into the coarse wool of her coat as he came farther into the room. He moved around, then stood near the table. She heard the rattle of plates, the crunch of an apple being bitten.

A cramp seized her calf. She flexed her leg, hoping against hope that it would help. It didn't. She bit her lip to stop a cry of distress and used her gloved fingers to press against the nastily contracting muscle.

She must have made a noise, for the cloth lifted suddenly, and light spilled into the first few feet under the table. Thankfully, Alice's hiding place was beyond the illuminated area, and she prayed, like she had never prayed before, that he wouldn't see her, wouldn't make out her shape in the darkness.

Her prayers were answered. The cloth dropped, darkening the space. There were more footsteps. Then voices. She recognized one of them as Benedict Summersby. The other voice she didn't know.

The cramp in her calf subsided and she sat, her eyes wide with shock as she listened to their conversation. They mentioned Lord Liverpool. Did that mean Benedict worked for the government? And what did he mean, he was lucky not to have hung for treason?

They spoke of his rich cousin. Alice wondered if Benedict, too, was rich. No, she decided, he couldn't be. A rich man would hardly strut the boards in a second-rate theater, would he?

She listened harder, trying to make sense of it all.

As she pieced the story together, an idea formed. She had, she thought, found a way to leave London. When Benedict said the trip would be, officially, a honeymoon trip, Alice seized her chance. She knew she'd never get a better one.

Although now, faced with not only the thunderous looks on their faces but the gun the stranger held, she wondered if she'd jumped from the pan into the fire.

It was, of course, too late to change her mind. She would just have to brazen it out. In the same moment she realized this, she also decided it might not serve her cause to tell them the truth about why she was here. If they thought she might be pursued by the likes of Milton Percival, they might consider her too much of a risk and refuse to take her. She could not chance that happening.

So, when Benedict asked her what she was doing here, she came up with a Banbury tale that minimized the risk to them, although it was a story a child of five could have seen through. Whatever else she might be, Alice was not a natural liar. She couldn't come up with a convincing story at the drop of a hat, the way some of the other dancers could. Alas, her honesty was a virtue she lamented now.

"I, erm, lost an earbob," she said. She crossed her fingers and hoped Benedict didn't know that she never came into the Green Room. "I dropped it when I was in here earlier. It rolled under the table. I was lucky to find it."

Shut up. Liars often gave themselves away by saying too much. Byron had told her that. Now Alice understood why. Her nerves encouraged her to keep talking, embellishing the tale, layering detail upon detail to make it believable when, in fact, that would have the opposite effect.

The look on Benedict's face told her he already knew she was lying.

Worse, though, was the ice in the other man's expression and tone of voice. The hand pointing the pistol at her was rock steady as he asked, again, "Who are you?"

She had one chance. A moment to sell herself as an accomplice to these men and escape London. So, with a deep breath and her heart in her throat, Alice went for broke. "I'm the one who'll put the finishing touch to Mr. Summersby's disguise, and ensure he is believed."

Both men stared at her, as if waiting for her to elaborate. She spoke quickly, before they could change their minds and demand her silence instead. "You say he's to play a man on his wedding trip? You cannot have a wedding trip without a bride. The people you encounter will soon become wary if there is no Mrs. Summersby to accompany him, will they not? I can play her."

Benedict bristled. He looked insulted. At the thought of her playing his wife? She wasn't that bad! True, she had no beauty to inspire poets and painters, and the nabob he was playing might expect better, but the role needed an actress. She was an actress—sort of—and she did not see anyone else auditioning for the part.

"You most certainly cannot play my bride."

Benedict's words were soft. Which, somehow, made them worse.

The other man glanced at Benedict, though the gun did not waver. She wished he would lower it. She was frightened enough without the threat of being shot.

"Who is she?" he asked.

Alice opened her mouth to answer but Benedict beat her to it. "She's nobody," he said. His hand sliced the air in front of him as if to underline that. "A drunken opera dancer."

"I am not!"

"She probably passed out under the table, and her friends left her there to sleep it off."

"How dare you!" she said, between gritted teeth. "I don't even drink!"

Benedict laughed. "That's a lie. I saw you."

Alice frowned, then recalled that night in the alley, several weeks ago now, when she played the drunkard to get rid of a persistent, unwanted suitor. Had Benedict seen her performance? If he'd believed it, perhaps it had been more convincing than she'd thought.

"What you saw—" she began.

"Doesn't matter," interrupted the man with the gun. He gave her the sternest, most terrifying glare she had ever been subjected to. "What matters, young lady—"

Benedict scoffed. "Lady?"

Both she and the other man scowled at him, though she suspected their reasons were quite different. Her annoyance even overrode her fear of being shot, just for a moment.

"What matters, young lady," repeated the man with the gun, enunciating each word deliberately, "is that I have your word this conversation will go no further than this room. If you breathe a word of it, I can, and will, have you arrested. Do I make myself clear?"

Alice gulped. "Yes," she whispered.

At the same moment, Benedict said, "Best to go ahead and lock her up. She'll surely talk of it when she's in her cups."

How could a man make her so angry that she forgot to be afraid of a powerful government agent who could, quite literally, destroy her? For that was the effect Benedict Summersby and his aspersions had on her.

"For the last time," she told him, "I. Don't. Drink!"

She turned back to the other man to plead her case with him. Government agent or not, she sensed he would be the more reasonable of the two. "Why would I tell anyone?" she asked. "I don't want to tell anyone. I just want to be Mrs. Summersby."

Benedict snorted his derision.

Realizing what she'd just said, Alice added, quickly, "For the duration of this…whatever this is, I mean. Not a permanent arrangement. I don't want to be Mrs. Summersby in reality."

"Thank the Lord for small mercies," muttered Benedict.

She ignored him. "Think on it," she implored the other man. "You cannot have a wedding trip without a bride. Where do you plan to find one? Do you have one in your greatcoat pocket? You do not. But you do have me. I'm an actress, and I'm perfectly capable of playing this part."

"You are not an actress," Benedict said. "You've never had a speaking part in your life."

"Which doesn't mean I'm not capable of taking one, and making a success of it."

"That's enough," said the other man. He spoke quietly but it was as if he had shouted. Both she and Benedict turned to him. He had, thankfully, put away his gun. Alice breathed a little easier.

"This is not some jolly jaunt, my dear," he told her. The endearment set her teeth on edge. Byron used it whenever he wanted to patronize and make her feel smaller than he was. She had a feeling this man intended it to have the same effect.

"Summersby isn't going on a honeymoon trip," he said. His voice was mellifluous, almost hypnotically so. She wondered if he practiced that. "He's undertaking a business trip. And, as I'm sure you're aware, business trips are something a man can generally accomplish on his own. Thank you for your kind offer of assistance, but it is not needed."

From the corner of her eye, Alice saw Benedict's smug smile. It raised her hackles and all she wanted to do was wipe it away. So she smiled her sweetest smile and spoke in her sweetest, most-reasonable-woman-in-England voice.

"That's all well and good," she said. Both men must have picked up the warning in that short sentence, because both their smiles slipped. "It was just a thought on my part. By all means, go without me. Don't take a bride on the trip. But don't blame anyone but yourselves when the entire scheme you've concocted slides into disaster like a cliff edge crumbling into the sea."

"A flair for drama," smiled the stranger. "It must stand you well in your profession."

"A flair for seeing the obvious flaws in something stands me well in all areas of my life," she replied. "This Mr. Josh Summersby. Your cousin?" She glanced at

Benedict. He nodded, curtly. "You mentioned he's just married."

"He has. He's halfway to Italy by now, so there's no chance of somebody bumping into him in a different part of England, if that's what concerns you."

"It isn't. I sincerely hope he and Mrs. Summersby have a wonderful time. I understand the notice of their marriage is in *The Times*. Inevitable, I suppose, when he is—how did you put it? 'One of the richest men in England.' "

She saw the moment the government man understood. His shoulders stiffened almost imperceptibly, and his eyes hardened, although in less than a second he was fully in control of himself again.

"Your point, madam?" asked Benedict, impatiently. His irritation made her looming triumph all the sweeter.

"They take *The Times* in Shropshire, you know. It may be a day or so later than its appearance in London, but it is the same paper, and it carries the same notices. The people you seek, businessmen in search of investors? They'll be sure to take *The Times*. Therefore, they'll know of the recent marriage of Mr. Josh Summersby. Don't you think they'll wonder where he's put his wife? Don't you think they'll ask why she's not with him, so soon after their happy day? Her absence will surely raise their suspicions."

Benedict glanced from her to the government man, then back to Alice. There was a mulish glint in his eye. "Businessmen do not tend to dwell on the Society gossip pages."

"I think some of them do." She smiled. "And even if they don't, their wives will."

He narrowed his eyes at her. His hands on his hips,

he drew himself up to his full height and glared at her down the length of his nose. He probably thought he would intimidate her but, sadly for him, it would not work. Alice had seen the same tactics employed throughout her childhood, by both her parents. If anything, the haughty stance had worked better for her mother, who had been born to it, than for her father, who had merely learned it.

"Amelia Bell is a lady," said Benedict. "What on earth makes you think you could convince anybody that you are?"

"I say, Summersby. Steady on."

Benedict did not so much as flick a glance at the other man. Instead, he stared straight at Alice, reinforcing his words. Words he would pay for. Later. When she was safely out of London.

Now, though, she contented herself with raising her chin and turning her back to him, giving him the Cut Direct as she addressed the other man. She used the cultured tones of her mother's world, the accent she'd long ago abandoned in her efforts to fit into the life that was now hers.

"I can help you with this scheme of yours, sir. I can be the most modest blushing bride, and the veriest lady. I will lend this…gentleman…countenance, and all I require in return is money to the equivalent of the wages I would have earned here in three months. Plus, you may supply the clothes I need for the venture, and I will keep them when the job is done."

The man from the government twitched his lips, amused. She didn't know what expression Benedict adopted. She refused to look his way.

A long minute passed.

Then the man said, "Three months' wages and a wardrobe of clothes sounds reasonable. Congratulations on your accent, madam. It would not be out of place in Mayfair."

"You cannot trust her!" She heard Benedict's boot heels click as he paced the floor behind her. "She likes the sauce too much. She drinks, and when she's drunk, she screeches like a fishwife. I have heard her! What if she should do such a thing in Broseley?"

Alice raised her chin a little higher. "I have already said, I don't drink."

"She. Is. A. Drunk."

The other man bent and sniffed at Alice's breath. She did not back away, though she did raise a haughty eyebrow, the way she'd seen her mother do on many an occasion.

"She isn't drunk now," he said. "Not a whiff on her."

"Fremont—"

"She's stone-cold sober, Summersby. Whatever she was doing under that table, it was not 'sleeping it off.' And she's correct. The world and his wife know Josh Summersby has married. It would cause far less speculation if his bride accompanied him on this trip."

Benedict groaned. Alice's spirit soared and it was an effort to keep the triumphant grin from her face.

"I accept your terms, miss," said the man. "Be at the stage door at seven of the clock. Sharp. If you are late, the coach won't wait for you."

"I'll be there," she promised.

"I will ensure that a small trunk of clothes is packed and loaded for you. It won't be much at such short notice, but it will be adequate for your needs until you reach Abberley, where you'll stay with the baron and baroness for a few days before moving on to Broseley and the Ironbridge. I will arrange for more clothes to be waiting for you at Abberley."

"Thank you, sir."

Fremont nodded. "Your help is appreciated. But know this— You do anything to jeopardize this mission, and you'll find my retribution is swift and thorough, and easily outweighs my largesse."

She bowed her head in understanding. "You have no reason to worry about me."

"Let's hope that's a promise she can keep," murmured Benedict.

Fremont left and Benedict glared at Alice, all his fury showing in his eyes, the thin line of his mouth, the tenseness of his jaw. She decided this was a case of "least said, soonest mended" and stood silent. She had, after all, got what she wanted: safe passage out of London. Now, if he would just go so she could settle down without letting him know she wasn't going to leave the theater…

"You'd better go home and collect whatever you need for this journey into disaster," he said, through gritted teeth. He held his hand out, ready to escort her from the room.

She stepped back and held her head high. "It will not be a disaster," she assured him. "And I don't need to collect anything. I have all I need here with me. So, if it's all the same to you, I will stay here to wait for the carriage to arrive."

His smile was, to say the least, sardonic. "You don't trust me."

"Should I?"

They stared at each other for several long seconds. Then he sighed, defeated.

"As you wish," he said. "For myself, I'm going home. Fair warning. I have to lock the stage door when I leave. Once it is locked, you'll be forced to stay in here until it's unlocked again at first light, whether you wish to do so or not."

"I have already said I don't plan to go elsewhere."

"Your choice." He turned and walked away, his boots sounding loud in the empty corridor.

Once he'd gone, Alice helped herself to a small bunch of grapes and sat down, contemplating the day ahead as she popped them, one by one, into her mouth.

Chapter Six

Ben seethed. He wanted to shake the silly chit until her teeth rattled. How dare she insinuate herself into his mission? This was his chance to prove his loyalty and gratitude to Lord Liverpool and wipe away, once and for all, the taint of treason that he felt had clung to him since his ill-fated trip to the country last winter. He needed this job to restore his good name, to say nothing of his own self-esteem. If the little opera dancer jeopardized that...

What had Fremont been thinking? Ben could see, albeit reluctantly, that a newly married man should have a wife by his side, but really? This woman? She was a drunk, no matter her protestations to the contrary. He had seen her, slurring her speech and swaying, calling out obscenities at one of her gentleman callers.

"She's not even a proper actress," he muttered as he stepped outside, pulled the stage door shut, and locked it securely. The night was warm, the air tinged with the smell of horse droppings, unwashed bodies and grime. This was not the best area of London to be in. Another reason to lock the theater securely.

He walked away, his thoughts on Al. Proper actress or no, he had to admit she was good. He'd been as impressed as Fremont by the authenticity of her upper-class accent, and the ease with which she adopted it. And hadn't he noticed her presence on stage himself? The way she shone and drew the eye?

Other dancers were more conventionally pretty, that he could not deny. And some of them were far more obvious in their come-to-bed allure. Al was…subtle about it, he supposed. Subtle enough that she didn't immediately strike a man as being wanton. Other than when she was drunk, of course.

He would simply have to ensure she stayed sober until this job was done. He could do no more than that.

Ben pushed at the door and tested the handle, then walked away along the alley. He had just enough time to go home, pack his valise, and shave off this infernal beard. It fitted the roles he'd been playing for the last few months. It did not suit Josh Summersby. Truth to tell, he'd be glad to shed it. It was too warm, especially now summer was coming. It was heavy, and all encasing, and it made his face itch.

Engrossed in his thoughts, he didn't see the men at the corner of the alley until he had to sidestep sharply to avoid a collision with them.

"Watch where you're going," snarled a man in the sharp accent of the upper ten thousand.

"Apologies," murmured Ben, then he frowned. The voice was familiar. He looked around and saw the man's face in the scant light of a street lamp. It was the dandy who'd pestered Al. His scowl said the man's humor had not improved since then, and his face was rather more battered, one eye swollen shut and surrounded by a dark bruise. There was lesser bruising under the other eye, and his jaw was misshapen. Perhaps someone had taken an even stronger exception to his mistreatment of women than Ben had. Served him right. No woman, whatever her class or profession, deserved to be manhandled the way this man had manhandled Al.

Then Ben registered the man walking with the dandy and his breath caught in his throat. His heartbeat sped up, and his stomach muscles tightened with dread.

Milton Percival.

The gang boss was not a big man. He stood no more than five feet ten, and though he was stocky, he was not overly big, even when bulked out by the caped coat he wore. There were men in London who were bigger, stronger, and more capable in a fair fight. But then, Milton Percival had never been caught in a fair fight in his life.

Underneath the low-crowned hat, Ben knew, Percival's head was completely free of hair, though whether that was through natural loss or because he shaved his head Ben couldn't say. All he knew was, the bald pate and the ice-blue eyes that could turn a man into a quivering wreck at a glance were more than enough to get him whatever he wanted, the moment he wanted it.

But what was Percival doing with this dandy? Were the cuts and bruises the gentleman sported courtesy of Percival's fists? And why were they skulking in the alleys around the theater?

Ben's first thought was that Al had arranged to meet them here, which would explain her reluctance to go home. He immediately dismissed that idea. For one thing, she hadn't demurred when he'd said he would lock the doors. She couldn't open them without a key, which meant she hadn't planned to admit these men. More, she'd been arguing with the dandy earlier.

Besides which, whatever else she might be, Al did not strike him as stupid. She might keep the dandy hanging on a string. She might give a dozen men the come-hither and use their money to buy gin. But, surely, she knew better than to become embroiled with Milton Percival.

It was none of his business. If the woman had dealt with the devil, it was on her own head. Although, he thought with a groan, it was on his head, now, too. He was about to undertake work for the government and she was coming with him. The last thing he needed was for her to tip the wink to Percival. That truly would turn the trip into a disaster.

On that thought, Ben turned back and peered from the corner of the street into the alley. In the dim light, he saw the taller, thinner man, the dandy, rattle the stage door. It sounded as loud as cannon fire on the night air.

"It's locked," he said, in a whiny, nasal voice.

"You said she'd be here," Percival answered. He gave the door a bad-tempered kick that would have splintered anything less sturdy.

"I thought she would be."

Percival kicked the door again. "Where else?"

"I don't know. Honestly, I don't." The dandy whimpered. The sound of Percival's fist smashing into the side of the man's head reverberated in the narrow alley.

"Where. Else?"

"I thought she'd be here." The dandy cowered, his hands covering his head. For all the good that would do him. If Milton Percival wanted him to hurt, he would hurt.

"Where else?" The gang boss was not even breathing heavily as he hit the dandy again. Ben thought he might have to intervene to save the man's life. He didn't want to. He'd rather they didn't know he'd seen this. For one thing, he needed to leave London without worrying about being followed by an irate villain. For another, when he'd finished in Shropshire, he'd have to return to London. He didn't want to spend his life looking over his shoulder.

At the same time, he couldn't stand idly by and watch a man die.

Thankfully, the dandy's next words stopped the beating. "Even if she's not here now," he sniffled, "she will be later. She's got to come to work. Never misses a show. Wants the money too badly."

"She won't need money where she's going if she keeps leading me a merry chase." Percival's voice was a low growl. It carried on the night air, as clear as a shout, and twice as menacing.

The dandy moved from his cowering crouch to being on his knees, his face turned up to his tormentor.

Don't say another word. Ben willed the advice toward the man.

Percival grabbed the man's cravat and held him up by it. He lowered his own head until their two faces almost touched. The dandy yelped, but he didn't resist.

"You'd better pray she's here tomorrow." He let go of the cravat. The dandy fell in a crumpled heap. Percival aimed a swift, sharp kick at his middle, then sauntered away along the alley, whistling tunelessly, as if he hadn't a care in the world.

His breath coming in loud, gulping sobs, the dandy pulled himself up, using the wall for support. He got to his feet, bent over, and emptied his stomach. Then he staggered along the alley, holding the wall with one hand, clutching his stomach with the other. Twice more, he stopped to be sick. The final time, all he did was dry-heave.

Now, the street lamps picked him up and Ben saw the sweaty sheen on his too-pale face. His nose had bled again and his lip was split. He wiped his nose on the sleeve of his coat, then moved on. Ben stood back, hidden in a narrow alcove, and watched him reel down the street.

If the dandy had any sense, he would keep on going. He wouldn't even stop to pick up his possessions at his home. He'd find a seat on the first coach out of London and put as much distance between himself and Milton Percival as he possibly could.

Then again, if the man had any sense, he wouldn't have been mixed up with the villain in the first place. Although, Ben allowed, keeping away from Percival could be easier said than done. Hadn't he worried for his own livelihood earlier, after hearing rumors of Percival buying the theater? The gang boss's reach was long, his grasp tight.

Ben didn't want to work for him, which meant he might have to consider relocating outside London if the man did buy this place from Tate. Come to that, he might be wise to consider a whole new profession.

That was a decision for the future. For now, thank goodness, Ben was not in Percival's sights. Whereas, it seemed, Al was. Ben had no doubt now—she hadn't been waiting to meet those men. She'd been hiding from them. That was why she'd been inside when everyone else was gone. Why she'd been crouched under the table in the dark. And why she'd been so eager to join him on this trip. What safer way was there to leave London than in a private coach?

Although he had some sympathy for her, in the same way he would have sympathy for anyone Percival set his sights on, Ben was also angry with the little minx. She'd clearly done something to draw his ire, and now she'd embroiled Ben in it. For two pins, he'd try to intercept the coach before it reached here, and leave her and her sack of woes behind. It wasn't as if she'd be much of an asset to him if she did come along.

Although he'd been shocked to hear how well she mimicked the precise tones of the *ton* when she auditioned for the role. Fremont had been right; she would have been at home in every drawing room in Mayfair. More, adopting the accent had seemed to transform her, raising her, giving her a quality he hadn't noticed in her before.

The woman had never been as broadly cockney as some of the dancers, but she'd never struck Ben as anything more than of her class, either. Yet once she adopted the Mayfair voice, she'd lifted her head, straightened her shoulders, and looked every inch a debutante.

Which was not to say she'd be a success masquerading as a member of the Quality. There was far more to being a lady than putting on an accent and looking the part. Al was an opera dancer, as common as they came. She wouldn't know the first thing about acting as a lady. She'd know nothing of table etiquette, for instance, which cutlery to use for which course. She'd be confused about the right way to curtsy, and how to change it subtly, depending on the rank of the person she curtsied to. There were a whole host of other things she wouldn't know as well, things that would be as natural as breathing to a real lady. Ben would have to teach her everything and hope she was a fast learner.

He probably couldn't even write down the lessons

for her to learn and revise. Chances were, like most opera dancers, Al was unable to read or write. At best, she might have been taught the basic letters that children of the slums learned from well-meaning ladies looking for something to occupy their time, while their husbands were...

He stopped dead as that brought another potential problem to mind. A problem far worse than being unable to read, or than picking up the fish knife to use on a steak. It was a problem he couldn't prepare for in advance, nor could he overcome it if it happened. It could destroy everything and ensure their mission ended in abject failure.

Because, what if, when they reached Broseley, one of the gentlemen looking for investors had spent time in London, had visited the theater, and had encountered Al in the Green Room after the show?

Ben hung his head in despair. This job was shaping up to become his worst ever nightmare.

****

Alice settled onto a chaise longue and tried to sleep. A couple of hours wasn't long, but it was better than nothing and would take the edge off the weariness creeping over her. Tonight had been more than busy, and she could feel the tension of it fizzing through her. It prevented her muscles from relaxing and made her thoughts tumble one over another in her mind, until her head ached. A doze would be the best thing for her.

Unfortunately, it wasn't going to happen. The building was old and, as it settled, it creaked and groaned, snapped and rattled. Each new noise startled her, making her listen more intently. Were those footsteps she heard in the rooms overhead? Or simply elderly floorboards settling one against the other? It was lonely, empty, and dark, and she easily imagined long dead actors stalking the place, practicing their lines and reliving their finest hours.

How long had it been since Benedict Summersby had left? Alice had no timepiece of her own, so she couldn't know. There was a clock, but it was in the foyer at Front of House, and to consult it she'd have to leave the Green Room. Ridiculous as it sounded, even to herself, she was unwilling to do that now, when she was the only *living* being in the place.

She'd listened to Benedict leaving. He shut the door firmly and turned the key in the lock, decisively. Then, a few minutes later, he came back and checked the door again. The handle's rattle was followed by what sounded like two hefty kicks against the wood.

That had annoyed her. He must have very little faith in the theater's security if he thought the lock would succumb to her attempts to pick it. And, if she could have escaped from here, what did he think she would do? He was clearly worried she planned something nefarious, though what he suspected that might be was beyond her.

Stealing, perhaps? She doubted there was anything of value in here for her to steal. Any precious metals would be firmly attached to the walls, part of the fixtures and the fittings at Front of House. Alice was hardly likely to prize it off and carry it out in her reticule, was she?

Perhaps he thought she'd take the props to the nearest pawn shop, or make off with the best of the costumes. There was nothing else of value.

"Idiot man!" she whispered. "He makes a fool of himself, all because he's determined to see only the worst in me." Which didn't bode well for several days together in the close confines of a private traveling coach. "He doesn't want to work with me," she allowed. "But then, I'd rather not work with him! If I didn't need to leave London, I wouldn't take this job. They might offer me twice the reward, and it wouldn't be enough to tolerate that arrogant, self-absorbed man! What makes him think he's better than the rest of us?"

Actually, she had to concede, she knew why he might think that. He had good reason. Most theater workers, especially women, were not members of the respectable classes. Performers were, on the whole, considered little better than street walkers, unfit to mix with polite Society outside the bounds of the Green Room. The gentlemen might enjoy their company. They might even set up a dancer as a mistress and give her a life of luxury and comfort. But they would never bring her into the world of their family and respectable friends.

It was one of the reasons Byron had been appalled at her decision to join the troupe last winter. He'd argued, shouted, threatened, forbidden her to do it. All to no avail, since Alice had had no choice, not after Madame Fournier had turned her off. It had been work in the theater or starve, and Alice had had enough of starving. Working in a shop, as she had done for seven years whilst learning her trade as a seamstress, had earned her enough to pay her rent, but little else. Sometimes she'd had to eke a day's food over two or three days, simply to make ends meet and keep from falling into debt. She would certainly never have made enough to save toward her own shop.

She'd been in despair when Madame had let her go. She'd wondered how she would survive. But then, she discovered she could earn more in a month in the theater than she would have seen in a year at even the most generous modiste's. And considering Madame had believed her a ruined woman anyway, unfit to sew the hems of respectable ladies when Alice had done nothing to deserve such judgment, well, baring her legs at the back of a stage didn't seem so bad when it meant she could eat every day and afford a room and have a little more. Wasn't that why most of them ended up here?

But not Benedict. He wasn't cut from the same cloth as the other actors. He came from a good family, that was obvious, since he was cousin to a nabob. One didn't rise from a tenement in St. Giles to become one of the richest men in England, and presumably, the rich man's cousin had had a respectable upbringing as well. Which left her intrigued as to how he came to be working in the theater in the first place.

Then again, as Byron was always quick to point out, Alice's family had not been embedded in London's stews for generations, either, yet she worked here. In some ways, it was stranger for her to be here than it was for him, for Alice's maternal grandfather was an earl. Not that she'd ever met him, nor did she wish to, for he had disowned her mother after she eloped with Papa. Alice could not fathom how a loving parent could do that to his child, and she'd hated him on Mama's behalf from the moment she knew about it.

Mama had always said it did not affect her to have lost him and the rest of her family. It had been easy for her, she said, because she and Papa were so blissfully happy together. But even so, Alice knew that every now and then, when she thought nobody saw, a sadness came into Mama's eyes, and she would take Grandfather's last letter, the one where he'd said she must never darken his doorstep again, and she'd reread the words, stroking her fingers gently over his spidery handwriting. Then she would sigh deeply, fold the ancient paper back into her box of treasures, and get on with her life.

Alice thought her grandfather rigid and uncaring, completely undeserving of a daughter as wonderful as Mama had been. In her estimation, the old man was a fool who had held priceless treasure in his hands and thrown it away for cold duty and sterile conformity.

She took the miniature of her mother from her reticule and held it so she could see the picture in the dim light. The painting showed a smiling young woman with hair the same shade of honey-wheat as her children's, and eyes the exact light blue Alice saw in the mirror. It gave her comfort to know that Araminta Buck had grown from that Society Diamond into an even lovelier older lady. Her face had been lined as she aged, of course, and her skin had become less bright, but she'd been happy, and that had shone from her, giving her a beauty the younger woman could not have competed with.

If only she and Papa hadn't died in the measles outbreak. How different things might have been. Papa had always earned enough to support them all, and he'd been able to control Byron's worst excesses, so all had been well with their family…until it wasn't. In a twenty-four-hour period, she and her brother went from being happy, cared-for children to orphans—penniless, homeless, without hope.

Alice, ever practical, had accepted her new lot in life and found work and lodgings quickly. Byron, who'd always been more proud of their lofty antecedents, resisted all attempts to make him do the same. Even now he had hopes that, one day, he would call on their grandfather, announce his identity, and be welcomed with open arms.

It had never been Alice's way to live in a land of fairy wishes. Life was real, and needed facing up to. But now, with three months' money soon to be in her pocket, and a collection of dresses to sell, all of them only slightly worn, she felt as if someone had waved a magic wand and granted her those wishes after all. With those riches, she could set herself up in a provincial town in northwest England, far from London and the dangers of men like Percival, and the grasping greed of Byron. She could build a respectable business. All for playing the role of a newly married woman for three weeks.

"I'll have my dress shop, Mama," she whispered to the miniature. "I'll make you proud of me. Three weeks in company with that odious man is tolerable to achieve that."

She closed her eyes. A picture of Benedict Summersby formed in her head. Tall, handsome, well-made, those moss green eyes, the dark curls…

Briefly, she wondered what he looked like beneath the beard. She'd never seen him clean-shaven, although Sally had. Sally had been with the troupe when he was last here, a year ago. She'd told Alice how Mr. Tate had cursed loudly when his star was lured away to work elsewhere, and how every woman in the chorus shed tears at his departure. Alice herself knew the excitement his return had caused. The dancers had been full of it, and even Mr. Tate had smiled.

"I would wish he didn't have that beard, though," Sally had lamented. "It hides the most delectable face, with wonderful high cheekbones, and a perfect chin!"

Alice wasn't certain what 'a perfect chin' might

look like, but that didn't matter. Sally was adamant Benedict had one, and that was that.

"And why should I be remembering that?" she asked the empty room. "Why waste my time thinking of him?" She huffed impatiently and fought to replace thoughts of him with plans for her future, before giving a growl of frustration at her inability to do so.

"This is ridiculous," she muttered. She didn't have time to waste on thoughts of him! Honestly! She was no better than Sally, mooning over his fine eyes and broad shoulders. If she didn't get herself under control, the next few days were going to be even more unbearable.

She lay down on the chaise longue and closed her eyes, willing her brain to quieten itself. Finally, she must have dozed, because she startled awake when she heard the clank of buckets and mops in the corridors. The cleaners had arrived, which meant it must be six o'clock. Not much longer to wait, and then she would leave here forever.

Chapter Seven

Alice avoided being seen by the cleaners, hiding behind the drapes when they came into the Green Room. They cleared away the leftover food, changed the tablecloth, swept and scrubbed the floor, then left for the next place. She breathed a sigh of relief and came out of hiding again. The fewer people who saw her here this morning, the less likely it was that Percival's men would be able to trace her.

She made her way to the dancers' dressing room, where she washed her face and straightened her hair, then sat to wait for Benedict to arrive. The dressing room door opened, startling her, and her spirits fell when she realized it was not him but Sally.

Her friend was as surprised to see Alice as Alice was to see her. "What are you doing here so early?" she asked.

"I—erm—" Alice's brain fought to come up with a convincing answer, before she went on the defensive. "I could ask you the same thing."

"I left my best coat here," said Sally. "I always do. I'm not leaving it where my landlord might get his thieving hands on it. But now I need to pawn it until payday." Which probably meant things had not gone well with Lord Greensborough.

Sally gestured at the bulging reticule on Alice's lap. "Looks a bit full," she said, too nonchalantly. Did she suspect Alice of stuffing it with goods stolen from the theater?

"Yes. I have a…"

She may as well be honest. After all, she'd packed the dress before she knew of the trip to Shropshire. Byron, and the men with him, would know she'd left her lodgings, too, so she had no need of secrecy about that. Besides, Sally knew about her troubles with Byron.

"I have a dress in here," she admitted, and she patted the reticule.

Her friend saw nothing untoward in that. "You're pawning stuff as well, are you?" Alice felt her cheeks heat, and Sally laughed. "Don't be ashamed, Al. We all do it. It's the only way to get by." She studied Alice for a moment and her expression became sympathetic. "Your first time? Well, don't you worry. We'll go together, and I'll make sure you get the best price. Come on." She grabbed her coat from the garderobe, then looked expectantly at Alice. "We can get there before there's too many people about."

Alice swallowed, hard. "I'm not pawning it."

"What? Then why are you wandering about with a dress in…" Sally frowned, suspicious. "You're leaving, aren't you?"

"Yes." Alice swallowed again. How could Sally make her feel so guilty over this? "Yes, I am."

"Leaving the theater? Or leaving London altogether?" She studied Alice's face for a moment, then nodded. "Leaving London. Because of your idiot brother?" She rolled her eyes. "Honestly, Al, I could swing for him. The things he's put you through. But why are you leaving? What's he done now?"

Tears threatened and Alice looked away. Sally sat

beside her and put an arm around her shoulders. "Never mind. I can guess." She pulled Alice into her so that Alice could put her head on Sally's shoulder. The warm wool of her friend's pelisse, the soft strands of her hair and the feel of her skin, still cold from the outdoor air, were reassuring. She smelled of violets and morning.

"I'll miss you," she said, quietly. Then she sat up and looked intently at Alice's face. "But if you're leaving London, why are you still here? Why aren't you at a coaching inn, getting on board?" Her eyes narrowed. "You're not going by public coach. You've got someone coming to pick you up." She chuckled when Alice looked away, flustered. "You dark horse, you."

Alice didn't even try to answer. She couldn't have come up with anything that made sense, anyway.

Sally could. "You're eloping." She beamed, ecstatically. "Who with? Do I know him? Come on, Al, spill it. Tell me who the lucky gentleman is."

"I am." The voice was low and deep and made Alice jump. Sally turned to the door and gaped at Benedict.

"You?" she breathed.

In his traveling clothes, Benedict looked every inch the wealthy, respectable gentleman he was playing. His coat was long and beautifully made, with two capes. His boots gleamed, and his top hat fitted perfectly. The beard was gone, too. Alice had thought him good-looking before. Now, she saw he was…beautiful.

Could a man be beautiful? He could now. On top of which, she had to admit, Sally had been right. His chin *was* perfect. It was firm and masculine without being too square, while his cheeks were flat, lean planes either side of a straight and perfect nose. The green of his eyes seemed darker this morning, but still mesmerizing. He watched Alice now, as if she was the only thing in the room he could see.

Mayhap he was searching for signs of whatever mischief she'd got up to after he left, she thought cynically.

"I never would've guessed," said Sally, bringing her attention back to where it ought to be.

Ben glanced at Sally, and Alice found she could breathe again.

"You never said a word," Sally continued, her tone accusing.

"No." It was the only word Alice was capable of forming in reply.

"All that time, when I was prattling on about him… Oh, don't you poker up, Benedict Summersby. You have to know some of us took a fancy to you."

Alice vaguely registered the stiffening of his shoulders and the rising color in his cheeks. He was uncomfortable knowing the dancers admired him? That was…rather endearing.

Which, in turn, annoyed her. She didn't want to find reasons to like this man. Not even a little.

Sally squeezed her arm. "I should be mad at you, love. But I'm not. Only because I can see how much in love you two are. Although I'm supposed to be your particular friend. You could've told me."

"We wanted it kept secret from everybody," said Benedict. His smile, together with the adoration on his face, was completely convincing. If Alice hadn't known the truth, she would have been fooled. He really was the excellent actor Fremont had pronounced him. "Didn't we, darling?" he asked.

Sally frowned. "And you couldn't wait any longer

before you scarpered? You've still got two more nights of this show." Understanding dawned on her. "You're haring off because of last night, aren't you? Because of that wastrel brother of yours."

There was the slightest narrowing of Benedict's eyes, an instant of surprise. Hadn't he known that Byron was her brother? Had he thought…?

Alice's lips thinned. Why should she be upset that he'd thought Byron was her lover? He'd made no bones about the fact he thought her a drunken wanton last night.

"I knew I should've thrown him out," continued Sally. "Always coming here, taking your money. Well, you don't want him spoiling this for you, so you get to Scotland before he catches up with you."

Ben smiled, all trace of surprise gone from his face. "We will. As long as nobody tells him."

"My lips are sealed," promised Sally. "Lord, this is so exciting. I never knew anybody what eloped before."

You don't know anybody now. Aloud, Alice said, "You won't tell a soul, will you, Sal?"

"'Course I won't. But you'd best be off. There'll be others here soon, and I can't vouch for their silence. Besides, it's a long way to Gretna Green. Go on, and let me get on with my business. This coat is not going to pawn itself."

"Put it back in the garderobe," Ben said, and he flicked a sovereign at her.

Sally caught it and looked at him, at first puzzled, then insulted. "You don't have to buy my silence."

"I'm not. I'm celebrating. I want to share my good fortune." When she continued to glare at him, he went on, "Under normal circumstances, I'm sure you would have been Alice's bridesmaid. Just because you can't be there doesn't mean you can't share in it. Buy yourself a drink and toast us."

The pair of them stared at each other for several more seconds. Alice could feel the tension rising. It made her uncomfortable, eager to leave.

"We need to get going," she said, as steadily as she could. Sally put the sovereign in her pocket and her coat back into the garderobe. Benedict held his arm out and Alice pushed hers through it. He was warm and solid beneath her hand.

"You are right, as usual, my love," he said. Then, without warning, he bent his head to hers and kissed her.

Alice knew the kiss was an embellishment, meant to reinforce their story, for Sally's sake. It was of no more consequence than that. And yet...

Benedict's kiss was gentle, a touching of his lips to hers that was soft, barely there. He was warm, his lips full, the skin around them already rough with new beard growth, though he'd only shaved in the last four hours. He tasted of coffee, and the mint of his tooth powder, and London's early morning crispness. He smelled of balsam and the starch in his cravat, the wool of his coat, and the musky essence of man. His arms went around her, enfolding her into his embrace, pulling her nearer. His chest was hard against hers, and her nipples tingled as they chafed on her cotton chemise. Her stomach did a funny little flip, and a strange, warm ache built between her legs, making her want to press against him, to somehow ease it.

He deepened the kiss, increasing the pressure, and...

His weight held her in place. She couldn't move, couldn't get away. He pawed at her, his fingers like claws, grabbing, spiteful. His mouth was on her, slobbering, biting at her like a vicious dog. He squeezed her face, pushing her cheeks in, hurting her. He tore her bodice away, pinched, pressed his fingers into her flesh…

Alice stiffened, fighting the panic that threatened to engulf her. She wanted to push him away, to scream for help, to run as fast as she could.

Benedict pulled back and let go of her. "Are you all right?"

Alice pushed a shaky grin into place. "I'm eager to be gone," she said. Even to her own ears, she sounded far too cheerful to be genuine.

He studied her for a moment longer, then gestured that she should lead the way.

Sally followed them to the stage door, where she embraced Alice. "I'm happy for you," she whispered.

Alice's return smile was bittersweet. Sally would be upset when she realized they'd lied to her. Although Alice herself would not be here to face her friend's anger, Benedict would be. She hoped his reputation didn't suffer, hoped he wouldn't be accused of jilting and abandoning her. He needed to work with Sally in the future, and she could make life difficult for him if she thought he'd done Alice any wrong. She would have to write to her friend and explain.

A comfortable but unremarkable coach stood at the stage door. It bore no crest, nothing to say whose it was, but it was well cared for, the lacquer on the woodwork shining and uncracked, the plush seats unsnagged, the windows clean. Alice looked furtively up and down the alley and satisfied herself that nobody watched her, then allowed Benedict to help her inside. He climbed in behind her and took the backward facing seat opposite her.

"Good luck," said Sally. She waved as the coach moved off. Alice's return wave was smaller and showed her nerves.

Benedict grinned. "Somebody enjoyed the idea of you and me leaving together," he said.

Alice shrugged. "Sally's a romantic. She still thinks an earl's going to come one day, sweep her off her feet, and marry her."

"It does no harm to dream."

Alice bit her bottom lip. "She might be angry, when you return. She'll think you left me."

He frowned, puzzled.

"I plan to stay in Shropshire when we are finished."

Benedict's face cleared, showing no emotion. "If that's what you wish."

"It is." Suddenly unsure of herself, she looked away, out of the window. They turned from the alley and onto the main thoroughfare. It was still early, and few people were about. The lamplighters had been and gone, extinguishing the street lamps, leaving the early morning sun to light the place unaided. A flower seller sat on the theater steps, her blooms surrounding her. A man pushed a handcart filled with produce, and a baker's boy carried a large basket of loaves. A gentleman walked along the street, two burly servants accompanying him.

That he was a gentleman, there was no doubt, although he looked the worse for wear at the moment. His coat was torn, his cravat skewwhiff, and his face battered, as if he'd been in a tavern brawl. Alice turned away, then did a double take when she realized it was Byron.

Alice gasped and pushed herself back against the

squabs, shrinking into the corner of her seat while she prayed he hadn't—and couldn't—see her.

****

Ben saw Al's sudden movement, and the fear on her face, and glanced through the window to see what had discomfited her. There was the dandy from last night, his face looking even worse in the harsh daylight. He was flanked by two bully boys, one tall and broad, his shoulders impossibly wide, his thick arms ready to burst from his coat sleeves. He had a craggy face with a prominent chin and a nose that had been broken more than once. His cauliflower ear suggested he'd spent time in the boxing ring where, if Ben was any judge, he'd probably inflicted a lot more damage than he'd received.

The second man was shorter and less powerfully built, but he looked as if he could take care of himself well enough. He had a broad chest and a strutting walk that reminded Ben of a cockerel in a farmyard full of hens. The dandy between them looked uneasy, to say the least.

Ben sat back, schooling himself to seem relaxed. When he spoke, he barely moved his lips, not wanting to draw attention to the fact there was somebody in the coach with him. "I take it that's your brother?" he asked, mindful of what Sally had said.

Al bit her lip and nodded. The dandy glanced at the coach, saw Ben and looked again. Ben gave him a disdainful look and hoped the man would think he had nothing to hide. The coach moved on, and the dandy's companions urged him in the other direction.

"My condolences," said Ben.

Al pursed her lips. He guessed that it stung, hearing a member of her family disparaged that way, but at the same time, she wouldn't feel able to defend him. Ben understood that. He felt the same whenever anybody spoke truthfully about his scapegrace father.

They turned onto a second road, which would eventually lead them away from the city's center. It was only when they had gone around the corner and there was no chance of her brother seeing her that Al relaxed. Her breathing steadied and her shoulders dropped, and her jaw unclenched.

"I don't believe he saw me," she said in a low, almost-whisper.

There, Ben could reassure her. "He did not."

"You are certain?" She bit her bottom lip, catching it under her two front teeth. It was not provocative, or in any way seductive, but it caused a strange sensation in his lower stomach. He clenched his muscles against it.

"I am," he answered her, then looked away. Outside, they passed tall buildings with porticoed doors where housemaids knelt, scrubbing steps. Delivery boys pushed carts laden with everything a thriving household needed, and liveried footmen with powerful shoulders walked delicate-looking dogs. A small boy ran along, rolling a hoop, and a nursery nurse struggled to keep up with him.

"Had your brother seen you," Ben continued, "he would have chased the coach."

She looked relieved. He didn't necessarily want to destroy that feeling for her, but at the same time, she should know her brother was not casually seeking her out, and was determined to find her. "He was at the theater last night," he said.

"Yes. And I thank you for making him leave. I should have said that before."

"You did, and that's not what I meant. He came back after I locked up."

Her eyes widened. She swallowed.

"He couldn't get in." That was one of the most useless statements he'd ever made. It wasn't even reassuring. "He rattled the door as if he tested the lock, but of course, I had secured it."

You're making it worse, idiot.

Her answer confirmed that. "I thought that was you." She bit her lip again. "And did he then kick it or hit it, or something?"

Ben didn't want to answer that, but she needed to know the truth. "Percival kicked it."

Al paled. For a moment, Ben thought she might slide from her seat into a faint. He braced himself to catch her, but she just closed her eyes and rubbed agitated fingers against her temples.

Al's brother clearly had business with Percival. Bad business, if the state of his face was any indication. That was his affair, and nothing to do with Ben. However, if his sister was involved, if she also had dealings with the gang boss, it became of significant interest to him.

"If this is likely to affect what we're doing, I need to know. What is Percival's interest in you?"

Al stared out at the passing landscape for several moments. Ben wondered if she would refuse to tell him. Or worse, was she concocting a lie? He needed the truth. If he didn't know exactly what difficulties he might face, how could he possibly deal with them effectively?

"Byron—my brother—gambles," she said, at last. The shamed blush told him it was the truth.

"With Percival?" Not just a dandy and a gambler, but a fool.

"So it seems. He's lost a great deal of money to him. More than he can hope to repay."

Ben was not stupid; he could read between the lines. Byron, her scapegrace brother, had run up a debt and Percival would take Al in settlement. The idea made Ben feel sick. An actress she may be, with however many lovers in her past and an elastic concept of morality, but even lightskirts deserved some respect. They should be paid for their work, and they should be *willing* partners in everything they did. Neither of those things applied here.

"Your brother agreed to Percival's terms?" He kept his voice pitched low and even, though his stomach roiled and his chest tightened. He clenched his hands and imagined the blackguard's neck beneath his fingers.

"He did." She raised her chin, defiantly, though he saw the sheen of tears and heard the soft tremble in her voice. "I, however, did not."

"That's why you were so keen to come to Shropshire?"

She swallowed again. "Yes."

Outside, the buildings gave way to fields dotted with cows and sheep and an occasional horse. Cottages replaced the brick buildings of the city. The traffic grew quieter. It made the rage inside Ben seem all the greater. That a man could do such a thing at all was disgusting. That he could sell his own sister to someone like Milton Percival was so far beyond the pale that it was out of the charted wilderness and into the area marked "Here be Dragons." Ben would have wanted to kill him for it, even if the sister was not known to him.

But Al *was* known to him. He had seen her about the theater, worked with her, spoken with her. For God's sake, he'd kissed her!

He could pretend he'd done that for Sally's benefit. They had said they were eloping, so it was natural they would kiss. But if Ben was honest—and with himself he must be, or all was lost—he'd wanted that kiss very much.

It had been a spur-of-the-moment act. He'd not thought about it consciously beforehand. He made no effort to build up to it, either, nor did he give her a chance to turn away or avoid him. He had swooped in and taken, like a falcon might take a mouse. He should be ashamed for that, but he wasn't. Not ashamed, and not sorry.

The kiss had been gentle. He'd had enough about him for that. It was the kind of kiss he would have given a virginal lady like Amelia, his cousin's new bride, rather than a loose-moraled actress. That had been instinctive. Oh, he could have pretended he was simply immersing himself in his role, treating Al as his lady wife the way he meant to carry on, but that would have been a lie. The truth was, he'd been gentle with her because he'd needed to be. *She* needed him to be, although how he could possibly know that was beyond his ability to explain.

The return kiss had been as virginal as he might have expected from the true Amelia. That surprised him. Al had been hesitant, though not unwilling, with a certain unpractisedness about her. If he didn't know better, he would say she'd never been kissed before. She'd tasted of apples and the sticky syrup of orgeat, and she smelled of violets and soap: clean, fresh, and honest.

There had been honesty, too, in her reaction to his kiss. She'd been mortified. Not by the kiss itself. She had, he would wager, enjoyed that. Her lips moved with his, and she let him taste her mouth, his tongue playing with the tip of hers, teasing, tormenting, tantalizing. It was what had come later that bothered him, how she'd reacted when he drew her nearer. She had pushed him away, her shoulders stiffening against him, a hitch in her breathing, and terror in her eyes.

Terror? Of him? He could not believe that. He'd done nothing to terrify her. A maiden might have been a little shocked at the unexpected kiss, but she would not have been unduly frightened by it. An opera dancer like Al should have taken it in her stride. And yet…

What had happened to make her act that way? Had the tirade she'd directed at that gentleman in the alley been a repudiation of his treatment of her? Had he…?

"If I'm not there, Percival will find another way to extract his money from Byron," she said now, bringing Ben back to their conversation. The tremble in her voice said she was unhappy, and more than a little frightened at that idea. "I hope he'll let him work it off. He could put him to work in one of his gambling hells. Byron would make a good dealer." She gave a half smile. "He's useless as a card player, but he'd know what to look for in other players. He'd be valuable to Percival in that role."

Ben did not disabuse her of the notion. Hopefully, when her idiot brother's body was fished from the Thames it would not be newsworthy enough to reach Shropshire, or wherever she went from there.

"Do you think he will give up the search for me?" she asked. She bit her lip, anxious.

Ben felt his stomach tightening again, and he looked out of the window, trying to ignore it.

"There must come a point when I'm no longer worth the bother, mustn't there?" she continued.

That depended on how much her brother owed, and how many people knew Percival had been thwarted by her. A man like that thrived only as long as his victims knew there was no escape. Thankfully, he had no idea where they were going, and he didn't have the manpower to scour the entire country for her. As long as Al kept away from London, she should be all right.

"I'd say so," he agreed, then crossed his fingers. He would rather misinform her than frighten her. And really, the farther they went, the safer they'd be, so there was that.

"We'll stop at Stevenage tonight," he said, more to change the subject than because it was interesting conversation. "Fremont has secured rooms for us there. Then we'll move on to Bedford, then Hinckley in Leicestershire, Birmingham, and finally Abberley, in Worcestershire."

Al smiled and her cheeks gained a little color, so perhaps he'd succeeded in damping down her fear.

"Five days on the road, then?" she asked. She watched the villages on London's outskirts give way again to the rolling greenery of the true countryside. Ben sat back against the squabs, closed his eyes and dozed.

Chapter Eight

The coach pulled into an inn near Shenley for nuncheon. Benedict secured a private parlor, where they ate a hearty meal of beef stew and dumplings with carrots and green beans. Benedict ordered a fine claret to wash it down, although Alice refused to take any. She had seen the effects of drink far too often to allow it to addle her mind. Instead, she asked for chocolate, which arrived steaming and beautifully foamed. It was not something she indulged in every day, and she savored every mouthful. Its luxurious warmth made her bold enough to ask the question she had pondered for the last couple of hours.

"Mrs. Summersby," she said. "Do you know her?"

Benedict nodded. "We've met."

"What do I need to know of her? So that I can play her to the best of my ability, that is."

He thinned his lips and held her gaze for a moment, as if questioning her motive for asking, although surely he saw the advantage of an authentic performance. Amelia Summersby might not be widely known, but there was always a slim possibility of meeting someone who'd heard of her. Society may well have speculated about her, especially if she'd married a nabob. It seemed sensible to learn about her, if Alice was to play her well.

After a moment, he nodded, obviously having reached the same conclusion. "Let me see," he said.

"She's the oldest of three sisters. I believe she's younger than you…how old are you, if I may be so impertinent?"

"I am three-and-twenty years old." Alice raised her chin, prepared to hear that he'd thought her older, that her lifestyle had left her haggard.

To her surprise, he simply nodded, his expression showing no reaction. "Amelia is almost nineteen. But you're close enough. And, to be honest, you could pass for it."

"Oh. Thank you." The compliment was unexpected and disconcerting, and exceedingly pleasing. Alice fought to keep her smile of appreciation from showing. "In the interests of fairness," she went on, trying to gain control before he saw how pleased she was at his words, "how old are you and your cousin?"

"We're the same age. Thirty." He chuckled. "In some ways, you know, you and Amelia are very alike."

Alice could not fathom how that could be. Amelia was the genteelly reared daughter of country gentry, brought up with every advantage and groomed to be a wealthy man's wife. Alice was raised in London's rookeries, albeit by a mother who'd been born a lady. Despite her mother's attempts at raising Alice well, the coarseness of the streets had inevitably battered her into a shape that fitted her surroundings, enabling her to survive.

Suddenly unsure that she could carry this off, and confused as to what Benedict meant by his remark, Alice tried to make light of it. "What?" She laughed. "She's an actress?"

"Everybody acts," he replied. "But no. I meant you both rush in where angels fear to tread. You have a propensity to jump into a situation, without thinking it through."

Alice bristled at the implied criticism. "I thought it through."

He raised an eyebrow, conveying his skepticism.

"Truly, I did. I'm a quick thinker." *One has to be, where I grew up.*

"I noticed. You are equally quick to make your decisions. Listen, Al—what is your name? I only know you as Al because that's what Sally called you."

"How very improper. We have not been introduced, sir." She inclined her head in her most ladylike way. "I am Alice Buck. *Miss* Buck. And you are Mr. Benedict Summersby."

"Ben," he corrected.

She nodded, once. "Ben," she repeated.

"As I was about to say, Alice—may I call you Alice?—this mission we're undertaking, you should know, it may not be the straightforward quest Lord Fremont made it out to be. I made some enquiries. Quick enquiries, I grant you. Nothing in depth. But my informants told me that, if he's involved, it may well be dangerous."

Alice sighed. "So is staying within arm's length of Milton Percival. And it wouldn't be the first time I've found myself in a dangerous or uncomfortable position. You forget, I walk home from the theater every night. I'm alone and unescorted when landlords throw the drunks out of their pubs, and the villains of London are creeping out of dark corners to attack the unwary and the weak. I don't live in Mayfair. I am not, as a rule, driven about in comfortable carriages, and I've never been followed by a big brute of a footman whose sole purpose is my safety."

****

Ben nodded. "Point taken. I apologize."

She smiled. It brightened her face, changing it from attractive to stunningly pretty. Her eyes shone the color of the sky on a summer morning, and a dimple played on her cheek. Today, not being on stage, she wore no makeup and he could see her roses-and-cream complexion was unmarked by the ravages of late nights and dissipation that robbed so many dancers of their looks before their time.

He cleared his throat and concentrated on pouring himself another glass of claret. He didn't want the drink, but it served as a distraction.

She was playing his wife. His *newly married* wife. He had to appear besotted with her, should anyone be watching them. He did not have to be enamored of her in reality. He needed to remind himself, *now*, that she was an accomplished actress. Hadn't he said that very thing to Tate when he'd asked him to promote her?

An *actress!* Not a blushing bride. Not a member of polite Society. An *actress.* An opera dancer. An experienced woman.

It made no difference that she could affect a cultured accent and walk in a refined way, or that she had pretty manners when she spoke with the landlord and the girl who brought their food. It was all a pretense. He'd seen for himself what she was underneath it.

She denied that she drank. Ben knew better. He was thankful she'd taken chocolate today, rather than wine. The last thing he wanted was for her to over-imbibe.

As long as she remained sober and did the job she'd been given, Ben would be happy. In fact, her carefully crafted air of fresh-faced innocence might prove an asset, distracting the men they needed to meet and making it easier for him to gather information. Other than that, she mattered to him not at all.

He sat back and stretched out, deliberately turning his mind to other things. The coach was comfortable, well-sprung and well-padded, but like most coaches, it was not designed for a man with long legs. He could not straighten them there as he wished, not without taking up far too much space and coming dangerously close to her. He did not want to offend her by encroaching on her. Nor did he want to encourage her by it.

If he'd felt he could justify the expense, he'd hire a horse and ride alongside the coach, ridding himself of all his problems at once. Alas, he could not do that. Fremont wouldn't appreciate that listed in the expense column.

Suddenly restless, he stood, strode to the window and pretended great interest in the scene in the yard. There was a farmer's cart there, the driver looking bucolic in his smock and flat-crowned, floppy-brimmed hat. He spoke with the ostler, and both grinned in the way men did when something risqué was said. A middle-aged couple came out of the tavern and climbed into a gig, throwing a coin at the young lad who held the horse steady. Another boy swept the yard, fighting a losing battle with hay stalks and mud and horse apples.

Behind him, paper rustled. Puzzled, he half-turned to find Alice hiding behind the newspaper that had lain on an occasional table near the hearth.

What was she doing? Did she think reading the paper was something ladies did? Ben supposed they might look at the Society pages, but Alice didn't turn to them. Which was hardly a surprise. She was, no doubt, pretending to read, and in that case, one printed page would be as good as another.

"Lord Liverpool has gone to the king," she said.

Ben blinked. Where had she heard that?

"Is an election a good thing or a bad at this time, would you say?" She looked at him as if she was interested in his answer.

"You know of the general election?" *What a stupid thing to ask!* Of course she knew there would be an election. She'd just mentioned it, hadn't she? *Pull yourself together, man. She's playing her part. You need to do so, too.*

"Only what I read in the paper," she answered his question, amiably. "I'm not well versed in all the arguments. But then, why should I be? Nobody will ask for my vote."

"You can read?" Incredulity made him blurt the question before he could think about it.

Her face tightened and the blue in her eyes turned from summer to winter. "Did you think I couldn't?" she asked, in a voice that was far too reasonable.

He said nothing. There was nothing he could say.

"Can your opinion of me go any lower, I wonder?"

"I didn't mean—"

"Yes, you did." She carefully folded the paper and put it back where she'd found it, then glared at him again. He felt as if he faced a firing squad. He tried to brace himself.

She didn't raise her voice. She didn't alter her tone. Somehow, that made it worse. "I may not be out of the top drawer," she said. "I may not languish on sofas, suffering from elegant megrims whenever there is a disaster, such as too much sugar being put in my tea, or a flower on my bonnet being crushed. But, I assure you,

I am not a complete heathen."

"I didn't think—"

"I can read. I can write. I can even figure out simple arithmetic problems." She smiled, too sweetly. He gulped. "I know which knife and fork to use with which course of a meal, and which glass should be used for which color wine. You've no need to worry on that score."

"I apolog—"

"But tell me," she interrupted his apology, which she dismissed with a languid wave of her hand. "Is it only me you think so poorly of? Or is it your opinion that all women are stupid?"

That was not a question he intended to answer this side of the next millennium, although the look on her face suggested she waited to hear what he would say.

"I'll pay the shot," he said, "and we can be on our way. We still have the better part of twenty miles before we reach Stevenage."

With that, he made a tactical withdrawal from the room and went in search of the landlord.

They reached the Castle Hotel at Stevenage as it grew dark. It wasn't a large inn, but it was a respectable one, and it was where Fremont had secured rooms.

Ben stepped down from the carriage gratefully and arched his back to relieve the tension in his muscles before he turned and offered his hand to Alice. He was relieved when she took it. She'd refused his help to climb in at Shenley, taking the coachman's arm instead and giving that man a smile that would melt ice. It had certainly melted Fremont's driver. John seemed to float to his perch afterward.

The landlord of the Castle was a bluff man, full of

bonhomie. "Welcome, Lord Fremont," he called, so everyone in the taproom turned to see. Alice lowered her eyes demurely as he added, "and Lady Fremont."

Ben opened his mouth to explain that, although Fremont's man had made the booking, it wasn't Fremont who would occupy the rooms. Then he decided that would probably cause too much confusion, and it didn't matter anyway. "You have rooms for us," he said, instead.

"Well," said the landlord, his smile slipping slightly. "The messenger sent to book your accommodation only arrived this morning."

Ben had a horrible feeling they would be turned away. He adopted the icy demeanor of a thwarted aristocrat and glared at the man, who swallowed and wiped his meaty hands on his apron.

"Are you saying there is no room for us?"

"No, my lord, I'm not saying that, at all. But, by the time the messenger came, we only had the one bedchamber left. As I'm sure you'll appreciate, my lord, I couldn't very well throw other guests out of their rooms, could I?" The way he said it made Ben wonder if he'd tried to do that very thing, and failed. Many titled people would have expected him to.

The man's grin brightened. "But then, I was told you was newlyweds, so I thought to myself, they won't object. They'll want to be together." He gave a very salacious wink.

From the corner of his eye, Ben saw Alice's face turn a deep crimson. He could almost feel the heat of it. An unaccustomed protectiveness came over him and he narrowed his eyes at the landlord, daring him to insult her further with his innuendo.

"The bed's comfy," confided the landlord, oblivious to the mood of his important guests. If it were possible, Alice's blush deepened.

"Is there another hotel in town?" asked Ben, shortly.

The landlord pulled a face that almost looked sympathetic. "Not with rooms to spare, my lord. I could have hired out your room three times over today. There's a...an event happening in the town tomorrow." He leaned in and spoke to Ben in a stage whisper that would have reached to the gods at Drury Lane. "It's a cockfight, my lord. Begging your lady's pardon," he said. Then he shrugged, nonchalantly. "There's not a room to be had in the whole town tonight."

Ben knew that was the truth. People would have come for miles to see the unfortunate birds rip each other to shreds, and wager large sums on the outcome. He'd never seen the attraction of it himself, but it always drew huge crowds. Which meant he and Alice could either collect the trunk of clothes Fremont had sent here for her, then make their way on, in the dark, with a tired coachman and exhausted horses, in hopes of finding somewhere else, or they could make the best of it here. It was the lesser of two evils, he supposed. He turned to Alice. "Do you mind awfully, my love?"

"No, of course not."

If he believed that, he'd believe anything.

The landlord must have sensed her unhappiness as well, because he quickly told her he had saved his best parlor for them, and his wife had their supper cooking even now, and she was the best cook in Stevenage.

Alice nodded, wearily. Ben felt crushed, as if this was his fault and he'd let her down. Which he knew was absurd. Not only was the situation beyond his control, but even if it hadn't been, it wasn't as if sharing a room with him would be as hard for Alice as she pretended it would be. It would not be the first time she'd shared her bed with a man, he made no doubt, and it wasn't as if he planned to ravish her. He didn't dally with opera dancers. Even if he did, he wouldn't tonight. Tonight, all he wanted was a meal and a good night's sleep.

"I tell you what," said the landlord, smiling at Alice as if he was about to offer her the world wrapped in a big, pink bow. "To make up for it, I can let you see the coffin for free. I usually charge a penny, and it's cheap at twice the price."

"The coffin?" Alice looked as alarmed as Ben felt.

"Henry Trigg's coffin," explained the landlord. "He used to own this place, before it was an inn. And he's buried…" He laughed. "I don't suppose buried is exactly the word. He's…*interred* in the rafters of the barn out back of the house."

Alice stared, wide eyed, at him. Ben was in complete agreement with her. It took him a full minute to find his voice while the landlord told them about the eccentric Henry Trigg and his unique resting place.

"Thank you," Ben said, at last. He gave the man what he hoped was a convincing smile. "It is a very kind offer, but we'll settle for a private parlor, a good meal, and a comfortable bed."

The landlord tapped the side of his nose to signal his understanding. "Right you are, my lord. Not really the thing to be showing your lady wife. We don't want her having nightmares." He directed a maid to show them to the parlor and ambled away to serve other customers.

"A coffin in the rafters," said Alice as she removed her bonnet and gloves in the parlor. Her lips twitched, and humor danced in her eyes.

Ben hoped the strange tourist attraction was enough to secure his forgiveness. It seemed as if she was talking to him again, at least.

"It's different." She grinned. "Let us hope everything else about this place is more in keeping with what we were expecting."

"I'm told your new clothes were delivered to the room," said Ben. "If you'd like a bath prepared, I can wait in here."

She nodded. "Thank you."

They studied each other for a moment. Ben wondered whether to apologize for insulting her earlier, but he didn't want to bring it to the fore again. He'd be more careful from now on, and hope that was enough.

"I would like a bath," she said. It put an image into his head of her, lying in water, her shoulders glistening with the wet, her breasts just hidden below the surface, knees on show. His thighs tightened.

"But where will you bathe?" Her eyes met his, and he could not look away. "I can…" She swallowed. "I can hardly leave the room once I'm ready for bed. I mean…" She colored again, a deep rose-pink that made her eyes bluer, and her hair shine like gold.

He felt that sensation again in his lower belly. He had to clear his throat before he could speak. "I'll use the stables." She bit her lip. He looked away, concentrating on the wall above her head. "I will…I'll tell the landlord you wish to soak after our long journey." The images of her in the bath returned. He sounded as breathless as he felt. His heartbeat sped up, and his breeches grew uncomfortably tight. He was going to embarrass them both if he was not very careful.

"Thank you," she said.

He cleared his throat again. "Won't you sit down?" *So that I can.* To his own ears, his voice sounded strained. He still had a whole night to go, sharing a room with this woman.

Hopefully, his bath in the stables would be cold.

Chapter Nine

Alice bathed, luxuriating in the warm water. It was bliss, and she stayed until the bath began to chill, alerting her to how long she'd been there. She wondered where Ben was. Had he realized how long she was likely to be? The man had surely had mistresses in the past, so he must have some idea of how long a woman might take over her ablutions.

In the past. Who said all his mistresses were in the past? Alice knew nothing about him, except that he was a handsome man who, presumably, never lacked female company if he wanted it. Unlike most of the men who worked at the theater, she'd never seen him flirting with the opera dancers, never heard naughty banter between him and any woman. He obviously kept his private life away from the theater, and his affairs discreet. Perhaps he loved his mistress very much.

There was a strange pinching sensation in her chest. It didn't take more than a second to work out it was envy. Envy of an unknown woman who had captured his heart and held it so fast he didn't even notice scantily clad women around him.

How absurd! She had no reason to envy any woman of his. Why, she didn't even like him! He was arrogant and judgmental, and dismissive. He thought her a guttersnipe, so far down the order of things that she couldn't even read!

Although wouldn't it be wonderful to know a man loved you so much he didn't even look at other women, no matter the provocation…?

She dried herself and wrapped up her hair in the bathing sheet, then reached for the nightgown she'd found in the trunk Lord Fremont had sent. The nightgown was made of plain white linen, with delicate smocking across the bodice and satin ribbons threaded at the neck and wrists. Crisp and clean, thick and warm, it was the nicest nightgown Alice had ever owned. 'Twould be a pity to sell it on when she established her shop.

Perhaps… She bit her lip in tempted concentration. "No," she told herself, firmly. "You will need every penny."

You will also need a nightgown.

She pushed the annoying thought away as she brushed her hair and plaited it, ready for the night.

By the time Ben knocked on the door and came inside, she was in bed, the covers pulled up to her neck. The fire in the hearth had died down, though it still gave off enough heat to make the room comfortable, and it filled the place with a deep red light that was reassuring, even though it made strange shapes of the furniture, turning hitherto unthreatening chairs into lurking monsters and making Ben little more than a very large silhouette.

As he drew nearer to the hearth, she saw his hair was still damp, glistening from his bath. He carried his waistcoat and coat, his neck was bare, and he wore just his breeches and shirt, untucked and open at the neck, the dark triangle of his throat and the top of his chest visible. She wondered whether that chest was smooth, like

Byron's, or roughened by a smattering of hair, as Papa's had been.

She pressed her lips together firmly, looked away from him, and tried to banish the thoughts. Ben's chest was no concern of hers.

He stoked the fire, waking the flames, then positioned a pillow at one end of the rush mat in front of it. "Might I be spared a blanket?" he asked, quietly.

Alice looked at him, puzzled. "A blanket?"

"It often gets cold in the middle of the night."

"Oh. Yes. I see."

It hadn't occurred to her that he would sleep on the floor. She'd assumed, since there was only one bed, that he would insist on sharing it, and she'd taken comfort from the fact that it was a large bed. Sharing a bed with a man—any man—was not ideal, of course, and the idea of it unnerved her, but, she'd told herself, Ben was not interested in her in that way.

A voice in her head had mocked her for that. *All men are interested in that way.*

"I'm certain he will be a gentleman," she had replied. But to be on the safe side, and to appease the voice, she'd pushed her knife under her pillow, ready to retrieve at any moment, should the need arise.

Ben was not planning to attack her. Indeed, he preferred to sleep on the hard floor rather than be too near to her. Alice didn't know whether she was relieved by that, or insulted.

He took a blanket and laid it on the rug, then pulled off his shirt in one, quick movement. Alice bit her lip. That was more to stop the gasp escaping than for any other reason. It certainly was *not* because of the beautiful example of masculine physique that was suddenly on display.

Although, she could not deny, Benedict Summersby was a fine figure of a man. She'd known that before, of course. Over the last few months, she'd seen him in a variety of costumes, and each one had showed off the broad shoulders she now tried not to stare at, the taut skin that glowed crimson in the fire's light, the well-shaped back tapering to slim hips and the firm buttocks encased in those snug-fitting breeches.

What was she doing? She turned to the wall and lay there, contemplating the plaster and trying to ignore the hungry ache in her belly, the tingling want in her nipples, and the feeling between her legs that she couldn't even begin to describe. She closed her eyes and saw him again, in all his glory this time, her imagination filling in details her eyes had not seen.

She snapped them open and stared, resolutely, at the wall, watching the shadows flicker.

He lay down and was still for a few seconds. Then she heard him move again. Probably trying to make himself comfortable, something that wouldn't be easy on those wooden boards. He shuffled again.

The bed was soft and warm, and wider than the one her parents had shared. It was roomy enough for two people to sleep quite chastely, with plenty of space between them. There was no reason, in fact, that two people sharing this bed should ever even touch each other.

They'd told everyone they were newlyweds. If the maid came in to light the fire in the morning, she would think it strange that a newlywed man slept on the floor and not in the same bed as his bride. Besides, Alice could not, in all conscience, allow Ben to lie there all night while she had such a comfortable mattress.

So she turned over and took a deep breath. Found she could say nothing. Tried again.

On the third attempt, she managed to squeeze out his name. "Ben?" She sounded like a mouse.

"Yes?" His voice was deep and low. It seemed to stir the air around her.

She cleared her throat. "Are you comfortable?" Thankfully, that sounded more like her.

"I've known worse."

"Nevertheless…"

He sighed. "Go to sleep, Alice. We have another long day of traveling ahead of us."

Seconds passed.

She couldn't leave him there. Her conscience would not permit her a wink of sleep if she did. "You need to sleep, too."

Ben sighed again, more heavily. "Yes. Good night."

"You won't sleep well on the floor."

"I won't sleep well in a chair," he retorted. It was true. The chairs in the room were simple ones with ladder backs and rush seating. Comfortable to sit upon for a short while. Never to sleep on.

Alice drew in a big breath and finally said what she really meant to say. "The bed is…it is…" The next words came out in a rush. "Big enough for two people."

The room went still. She couldn't see him move. Couldn't hear him breathe. Even the fire had stopped crackling. Then she realized what she'd said, and how he might interpret it, especially considering the poor opinion of her he'd already formed.

"To sleep in," she qualified. "Nothing more. So we can each get a decent night's sleep. We wouldn't…we…to sleep." *You protest too much, Alice Buck! Be quiet!*

Ten seconds went by. It felt like forever.

"You…" He cleared his throat and when he spoke again, his words sounded less choked. "You want me to sleep in the same bed as you?"

It made her feel a little better that he seemed as discomfited as she was. She smiled, trying to reassure him, then realized he probably couldn't see her clearly enough to know.

"Just sleep," she said. "Nothing more."

Her face warmed, though she couldn't say whether her blush was in shame at her own wantonness, humiliation that he thought she'd meant something else, or disappointment that he clearly didn't want that something else.

The long silence was broken only by the crack and pop of the fire. She'd tried, she told herself. She'd made the offer. One could lead a horse to water, as the old saying had it.

"Are you certain?" he asked, at last. His voice was gruff. It made her nervous, so that her "yes," came out in a high-pitched squeak. "In that case, I thank you."

There was a soft rustling which was, presumably, him getting up. She felt the weight as he spread his blanket over the bed, then the tip of the mattress as he climbed in beside her. She lay rigidly still, maintaining her distance, so it was several seconds before she realized he'd climbed on top of her blankets, covering himself only with the one he'd already been using. She wasn't sure if he was protecting her honor or his own.

Afterward, she lay for a long time, not daring to move a muscle. Her back ached from the rigidity of her position, and she longed to turn over, to relax. Her heart beat too fast and her breathing shallowed.

What had she been thinking?

What if he thought…?

If he decided…?

Slowly, she raised her hand, touched the knife under the pillow, and felt a little better.

Not that Ben seemed the slightest bit interested in ravishing her. Even now, when they were in the same bed, she could see she held no attraction for him. After only a few minutes, his body relaxed and his breathing evened out, becoming steadier, deeper. He snored, softly.

The tension left her. She'd barely slept at all last night, and it had been a long, tiring day. The warmth of the room and the steadiness of his breathing were soporific. Her eyes grew heavy, grit gathering in her lashes…

She was in a strange, slow motion, when her legs did not appear to move but she glided along through a landscape made up of her room in London, the alleys around the theater, and the backstage corridors. Byron leered at her, his sneering mouth disproportionately large in his face.

"What was I supposed to do, sis?" He laughed. "You're a fish on the line."

All around her worms wriggled on hooks suspended in the air. A monkey chattered and swatted at them, sending them swinging at her face. She held up her hands to protect herself. Someone grabbed her, and there was Milton Percival, his icy eyes staring, boring through her. His hands were on her, his weight holding her down, his mouth hot against her, his teeth bared like a ravenous wolf…

She jerked awake, terror making her breaths hard and sharp. Her mouth was dry, her throat sore. Every nerve within her was at attention.

The room was dark, just the soft glow of the dying fire giving any light at all. A heavy weight lay across her waist, holding her in place, and a warm draught touched her face.

No. Not a draught. Breaths. Someone was breathing, so close she could feel their soft exhales on her cheek, her neck, her ear…

Trapped, panicked, she fought the urge to scream. With every ounce of strength she could muster, she pushed him away and reached for her knife. She would not succumb without a fight! She…

"Alice?"

Ben's sleepy murmur brought her crashing back to reality. Percival was not here. He hadn't found her. Ben had rolled over in his sleep and embraced her in his dreams.

There was nothing to be frightened of. Truly. Nothing to be frightened of. She was not frightened. He would not harm her. All was well.

"Alice?" He sounded less sleepy now.

She lay absolutely still. Every muscle clenched. Every nerve taut. She closed her eyes and hoped he would believe she was asleep. Her pulse battered her eardrum. Her heart thudded against her ribs. Her stomach threatened to empty itself.

He removed his arm from across her body, and turned over. Her skin was cold where his warm breath no longer fanned it. She missed it.

She missed him.

No! That was wrong. She didn't miss him. She was

relieved that he'd gone. More, she was relieved that it had been Ben leaning into her, not the monster in her dreams.

It took her a long time to fall back to sleep.

****

She woke to find herself alone in the room, sunlight streaming through the window, bright enough to tell her it was later than she'd expected. She thought Ben wanted to be on the road earlier than this.

That thought made her sit up, shocked and alert. He wouldn't have gone without her, would he? Surely, he wouldn't abandon her here, forty miles from London. What would she do if he had? She had no money, no connections, nothing but a trunk full of clothes…

There was a knock on the door and Ben came in, his eyes lowered. "Are you decent?" he asked.

Alice held back the sigh of relief. "Yes."

He looked at her, smiled, and closed the door behind him. He was dressed impeccably, his shirt pristine, his waistcoat jewel-bright. His cravat was simply tied and held in place with a plain, gold-colored pin, and his coat fitted perfectly, showing off his shoulders. Shoulders, she now knew, that needed no padding.

"I'll leave you to get dressed," he said. "I've ordered breakfast in half an hour, to be served in our room, since another coach has arrived and the passengers commandeered the private parlor. As soon as we've eaten, we can press on to Bedford."

A moment later, he had gone again.

Alice yawned, stretched, and climbed out of bed.

****

The woman who waited for Ben to share breakfast with her was a revelation. Every inch a lady, she had exchanged her shabby dress and threadbare coat for a carriage dress in a dusky salmon taffeta, with a neckline that sat at the base of her throat, giving her the appearance of a very proper Society wife. At the neck and the cuffs, the dress was edged with dainty lace, and the tops of the sleeves were puffed and full. Ben was not especially *au fait* with women's fashion, but even he could see the dress was stylish, and expensive.

She sat, straight-backed and proud, nibbling daintily on a piece of toast. He served himself from the platters the maid had brought in: a hearty breakfast of ham, kidneys, liver and mushrooms that would fill him until nuncheon.

"Good morning, sir," she greeted him. The refined timbre of her voice and the cut-glass accent were in keeping with the picture she presented this morning, much more so than they'd been in the Green Room the other night, when she'd looked like the actress she was.

"You look well," he told her, and he tucked into his breakfast.

"Well enough to pass for the wife of a nabob?"

He glanced at her, realizing she was nervous. She wanted to do justice to this role, needed to know she passed muster. Well, he could reassure her of that.

"You look perfect," he said. "A lady to your toes."

She smiled, demurely, and a warmth filled his chest, a feeling of triumph at having won that from her.

Suddenly, he wanted more. He wanted to please her, to let her know how well she was doing, how authentic she seemed. So he continued, in an admiring voice, "I bet your own mother would scarcely recognize you today."

The smile dropped from her face and her eyes iced over, the summer-blue sparkle turning to frost. The transformation was so sudden and so complete, it left him reeling. And confused. What had he said to cause such a reaction?

"Actually, she would." Her words were filled with disdain. "My mother expected me to be a lady at all times and, which is more, she expected it to be obvious to everybody that that is exactly what I am."

Ben opened and closed his mouth, shocked. Was she acting the part of Amelia now? Or was she genuinely insulted by his remarks? He couldn't tell.

He wouldn't apologize. If she was acting, there was no need. And if she wasn't, well. The guttersnipe had a talent for aping her betters, but pretending to be a lady wasn't the same as actually being one.

Let her sulk. He'd told the truth. Alice, the opera dancer with the worn-out clothes and the rounded-out vowels of London's less well-to-do neighborhoods was a thousand miles from Amelia, daughter of a gentleman, and wife of a nabob. They would not be mistaken one for another. She needn't think he would pander to her airs and graces. He would, of course, treat her with respect, but he wasn't going to stand for any nonsense.

Alice rose from her seat. Automatically, he stood, the way he would have done for a real lady. Then again, it didn't hurt to do that. If he behaved in private the way he should in public, he was less likely to make a mistake.

She pulled on her coat, a burgundy pelisse edged with ribbon in the same shade as her dress. Then she put on a pair of kid leather traveling gloves and set a pretty bonnet over her curls before picking up a reticule that matched the coat.

"I expect you will wish to be gone as soon as may be, if we are to make good time to Bedford," she said.

Her matter-of-fact tone made it sound like an instruction more than an observation.

Ben cleared his throat. "Yes," he answered, then cursed himself for it. This was *his* mission. She was *his* assistant, the chorus actress whose only role was to enhance his, so why was he deferring to her?.

"I need to visit…" She waved her hand, vaguely towards the door, and her cheeks pinked.

Oh, she was good. A lady would be uncomfortable about telling a gentleman she needed the necessary. Alice carried it off with aplomb.

"The coachman is standing by to secure the trunk," he said. "By the time you return, we should be ready to go."

"Then I will meet you in the yard." With that, she left the room.

Ben took a deep breath and blew it out again, sharply. "I think I've just been put on notice," he murmured, before leaving the room himself.

Chapter Ten

A few minutes later, he stood in the inn yard, watching John secure the trunk full of Alice's new clothes to the back of the vehicle. She'd been clever in her negotiations, he realized now, although when she'd spoken to Fremont Ben had thought she was selling herself too cheaply. Three months' wages and a trunk full of clothes amounted to very little in the general scheme of things. Now, he saw he was wrong. The dresses packed into that trunk would fetch far more, even secondhand, than Fremont would have been willing to pay her in coin.

There was, Ben thought, more to this opera dancer than met the eye. Clever to the point of cunning, quick thinking, yet with a brother stupid enough to find himself in hock to Milton Percival, she was a mass of contradictions. She could read, and not ponderously, which suggested more than a basic education. Yet she made her living in a job that required little of her, intellectually speaking. With her abilities, she could have worked in a respectable shop, or as a lady's maid, rather than on the stage. So why didn't she?

Alice had clearly had dealings with people of a higher class at some point, been close enough to them to study them well, and she could confidently put into practice what she'd learned. Her refined accent was flawless, and there were lots of incidental details—the

123

way she stood or sat, the way she walked, how she held her hands.

All of which made him wonder: just who was Alice Buck?

Her brother dressed as a dandy, albeit one past his prime, his clothes from at least one Season past, and more worn than most gentlemen would tolerate. It was plain he was on his uppers, yet he spoke and acted as if he was, somehow, superior to everyone about him. That deepened Ben's curiosity about the entire family. Were they exceptionally talented mimics? Perhaps they were confidence tricksters, fooling the unwary into parting with valuables because they trusted the "Quality." Or were they members of the gentry who'd fallen on hard times?

Ben could not believe that. Not when Alice made her living on the stage. That was not a job any respectable lady from a genteel family would even think of, no matter how far the family fortunes had slipped.

Whatever the Bucks were, he sensed there was quite a story behind them. He would love to know it, although now was not the time to ask her about it. Mayhap that time would never come, he acknowledged. He might never unwrap the mystery surrounding Alice.

Which was fine with him. He had no especial need to know. In fact, he wasn't even particularly interested in knowing. Not in the least.

"As long as it doesn't interfere with the mission," he muttered. He almost believed it.

Another coach pulled into the busy yard. It was a nondescript vehicle, the kind a stable might hire to travelers without a coach of their own but who wished to avoid the public stage. It joined three or four other vehicles in a queue for fresh horses, making Ben glad they'd made their own arrangements with the ostler last night. The latecomers might be here for some time while the stable boys sorted out which animals were fit and rested enough to use.

John asked how far Ben hoped to travel before they stopped for nuncheon. "Obviously, we'll stop to change the team," he said, "but is there somewhere you particularly wish to use for a longer stop?"

Ben opened his mouth to reply, but before he could, a voice he didn't recognize called out to him.

"Summersby? Benedict Summersby?"

Every muscle froze. Every nerve tensed. Ben's eyes met John's, who looked as wary as Ben at this possible complication. Almost imperceptibly, Ben nodded at John, whose half blink conveyed understanding and compliance.

"We'll be ready to go whenever you like, my lord," said John, using the title the landlord and his staff knew Ben by. Hopefully, it would put off whoever had called to him.

"I say, Summersby! Don't ignore me!"

A hand touched Ben's shoulder. He whirled around, shaking the offending limb away from him, and glared at the man who had approached him. His heart stuttered and his stomach flipped, and it took all his acting skill not to show the slightest recognition as he faced Byron Buck. Alice's feckless brother. His eye was not as swollen as it had been, and the bruising around it had already changed from dark navy to a more purple shade, tinged with yellow. His nose was crooked, and his jaw misshapen, but he was healing well.

Behind him, Ben saw the two bruisers the dandy had

been with yesterday morning. Their clothes were of better quality today, but they still looked exactly what they were: villains for hire.

Ben needed to get away from them quickly. He needed to warn Alice not to come out here. He also must ensure, somehow, that she didn't meet with them inside the tavern. How would he do that, though? That certainly was the question.

Byron supplied the answer. He frowned at Ben as if he was suddenly uncertain. "It is you, isn't it?" he asked.

The last time Ben had encountered Byron at close quarters had been in the alley beside the theater. At the time, Ben still sported his thick beard. On top of which, it had been dark. The only other time he'd been close to this man had been in the backstage corridor, when he stopped him hurting Alice. That time, Ben had not only had his beard, but he'd worn a wig, with long curls that fell to his shoulders. He knew he looked very different without those things, which meant there was a chance he could deny his true identity and get away with it.

Silently, he prayed that this would work, then said, haughtily, "You have the advantage of me, sir. Did we know each other before I left for India? If we did, I apologize, but you are clearly much changed."

Byron frowned. "India? What the devil are you talking about? I saw you at the theater the other night. You were very funny, by the way."

"The theater? You mistake me, sir." *Just enough haughtiness to make your disdain known but not enough to turn it into the contempt you truly feel.* It was the first rule in deception. There should be enough detail to make the point, but over-explain and it exposed the lie.

It seemed to work. Byron was completely

nonplussed. Ben gave him a final, withering look, then turned away.

"You're Benedict Summersby, the actor at—"

Ben turned back, quickly, wearing what he hoped was a mask of horrified insult. "An actor?" he said, his voice dripping contempt. "How dare you?"

The other men came forward. They didn't look happy, though whether their displeasure was aimed at Ben or Byron, he couldn't say. He tensed, preparing himself for a fight.

"Oh, come on," argued Byron. "I wasn't born last Tuesday. Where's my sister?"

Ben's heart banged hard and fast against his ribs now, and his muscles trembled as he put every effort into his act. He half expected a meaty fist in his face from the bigger of Percival's men at any instant. All he could do in his defense was to give the best performance he could. So he sneered at Byron the way a *ton* pink would have done. "Your sister? Run off with the hired help, has she?"

Byron peered into Ben's coach. Ben thanked God it was empty.

"Where is she?" demanded her brother, hands on his hips and an expression of thwarted fury on his face.

"I haven't the faintest idea where she is," said Ben, injecting languid boredom into every syllable. "Nor do I care."

The two villains exchanged uneasy glances. Ben hoped that was a good sign. Beside him, he felt rather than saw John tense, ready.

"But you must know!" blustered Byron. "That strumpet at the theater said you'd eloped with her."

Damn Sally! She promised not to say a word.

Ben continued his act, more in hope than expectation now. "As I have said, sir, you have mistaken me. I am neither an actor nor a seducer of women. I'm a happily married man. And, whilst I do hope you find your sister before she is completely ruined, I cannot help you in this matter. Good day to you." He turned to John and said, "Be ready to leave in two minutes. I'll go and pay my shot, and then we'll be off."

"Very good, my lord." John touched the brim of his hat and climbed up to his perch.

Ben turned to go into the inn, not to pay the cost of their night there but to warn Alice and try to spirit her away before Byron saw her. However, he'd taken just one step before the man grabbed his sleeve.

"I'm not falling for your game, Summersby. I know who you are. I want my sister back. Now!"

Ben gave Byron a look that said he was so far beneath him, he was hardly worth noticing. Then, his voice frigid, he said, "If you are trying to prevent the ruination of a lady, I'd suggest accosting strangers in a public place is not the way to do it. Pull yourself together, and unhand me before I call a constable. I suggest that instead of attacking me, you find your actor and persuade *him* to give you your sister. Using a quieter and more temperate tone."

"Now, see here…"

The bigger of Percival's men grabbed Byron's shoulder. That his grip hurt, Ben made no doubt, for the dandy winced. The henchman pulled Byron back, unbalancing him. Byron let go of Ben's sleeve.

"Sorry to bother you, my lord," said the big man. He had a nasal twang, presumably because his nose had been badly broken at least once in his career. "The gentleman's a little overwrought, as you can probably understand. We'll make sure he doesn't bother you again."

He pulled Byron back another step. Ben nodded at the big man and murmured a thank you, then went into the inn, leaving Byron to protest that the man he'd been talking to was, most definitely, Benedict Summersby, he had Alice, and why wouldn't they listen to him?

"You're causing a scene," said the second henchman, through gritted teeth. "Shut up. Now!"

Sound advice, Byron. Ben made good his escape.

Inside the inn, other travelers talked about what they had witnessed in the yard. His spirits sank. This wasn't what he wanted, and it would not be to Fremont's liking, either. It would make people suspicious of Ben, and, therefore, make it harder to find the information he sought.

"You all right, my lord?" asked the landlord. The jolly, outgoing man who'd greeted him last night was quieter now, filled with concern at the offense caused to a prestigious customer.

"Yes, I thank you. The gentleman was clearly overwrought."

"Aye." The landlord nodded. "It's what you get from the likes of him, I'm afraid. Too much time on his hands and too much booze in his veins, if you ask me."

"And a certain anxiety for his sister," said Ben. "Most men would be upset if they were worried about a female relative. That might make them act in unseemly ways."

"Very gracious of you to be so understanding, my lord. Even so, I hate to think this sort of thing has happened at my establishment. I'll refuse to serve him.

Tell him to move on."

Ben shook his head, an idea forming. "On the contrary," he said, finding a golden guinea and slipping it, surreptitiously, to the landlord. "We are just leaving. My wife is already in the coach, and I just need to visit…" He gestured toward the back of the inn. "If you could see your way clear to delaying that man…give us…two hours, perhaps?"

The landlord winked. "I'll make certain he doesn't follow you, my lord. Don't you worry." He pocketed the guinea and returned to the bar. Ben headed to the back door.

He found Alice outside, her face ashen.

"You know, then?" asked Ben.

She nodded. "I saw Byron, so I came out here to hide. I didn't know what else to do."

"You did the best thing you could."

"But what now? I can hardly stay out here until he leaves. Somebody's bound to see me. And what if he needs the necessary?"

"I agree, you can't stay here. Worse than that, though, I can't get you into the coach while it's in the yard. I suspect he will watch me leave."

She bit her lip. He had the urge to run his finger along it, to caress away the effects of the bite and make sure she had not marked herself. Which was absurd. There was no reason for him to do that. She hadn't even bitten herself hard.

He was simply worried for her, that was all. Concerned at her distress. Nothing else.

Trying to distract himself from the uncharacteristic way she made him feel, Ben looked around the tavern garden. It wasn't large, but it was tidy and well cared for, the grass short and neat either side of a graveled path, in which grew no weeds. A few bushes were dotted here and there in a pattern that looked random and was probably anything but. To one side, there was a small vegetable patch and, beyond that, three gnarled apple trees. They were in full leaf now, the first tiny fruits just beginning to show.

A small building in the corner housed the privies, and a fence marked the edges of the property. Beyond the fence was an area of woodland, the trees growing close enough together to form a screen, but not so close one could not walk between them. That people did so was evidenced by the little wicket gate that broke up the line of the fence, and by the pathway that meandered between the trees. It was probably a shortcut to another part of the town, which meant there'd be an opening to a road on the other side of the wood. He hoped so.

"I'm sorry to ask this of you when you are dressed in all your finery," he said, "but needs must. Go through that gate and into those woods. The path looks as if it goes in more or less a straight line from here to…" He shrugged. "I believe it will come out of the woods onto a road that is at right angles to the main highway."

"That makes sense," she agreed.

"I'll leave in the coach to put Byron off the scent. The landlord has promised to delay him so we can leave without being pestered. I'll follow the road around and wait for you on the other side of the trees."

"And if the path doesn't go that way?"

"If it doesn't, I'll return here when your brother's gone. All will be well, I promise."

"All right," she said, gamely, and gave him another facet of her personality to admire.

She is an opera dancer. An actress. The reminders were growing less effective. If he was not careful, Ben could find himself in real trouble here.

He watched her go through the wicket gate and into the trees, until she disappeared from sight, before he turned and made his way back to the coach.

Byron and his companions were now inside the inn and, Ben noted with satisfaction, he was not endearing himself to his host or anybody else.

"My friends and I need a private parlor," he said. His tone suggested it wasn't the first time he'd demanded one.

"As soon as it's free, you shall have it." The landlord's voice was dangerously quiet. Anyone with a modicum of sense would pick up the warning in it.

Byron did not have a modicum of sense. "How long is that likely to be?" he asked, testily.

The bigger of his two companions moved closer to him. "Mr. Buck, the ale and the food will taste no different here than they will in there." The man sounded reasonable and agreeable. If Ben hadn't known who he worked for, he might have liked the fellow.

"If you'd rather not eat in the public bar, sir," said the landlord, face impassive, "I can rent you a bedchamber. You can be private, and the girl will serve you your food."

"I don't want to pay for a bedchamber," objected Byron. "Why should I? As a coaching inn, you have private parlors, so people like me don't have to endure the riffraff while we eat."

The room fell silent. Every eye was on Byron. The innkeeper stood straighter, adding inches to his height. His eyes hardened. Byron's companions grimaced.

Byron, however, didn't seem to notice the change in the room's atmosphere. "I probably outrank the people you gave the parlor to," he whined.

Ben rolled his eyes, both at the outrageous claim and the stupidity of the man making it.

"No," said the innkeeper, flatly. "You do not."

That incensed Byron. "Do you know who I am?" His companions groaned.

This could become interesting.

"I don't care if you're the Duke of bloody Wellington," retorted the landlord. "The people in my parlor bespoke it first. In this house, that means they outrank you. I'm not in the habit of putting out my guests on the say-so of other travelers." He took a deep breath and pushed a smile onto his face, behind which, Ben could see, he had clenched his teeth. "Now, then," he said. "Your cattle have been taken out of the shafts, and put into my stables. I'm told you've driven them hard, and none of my lads'll put them back before they've had a good rest. So your vehicle, and by extension, you, are stuck here until such time as we find fresh horses for you. Whether your stay is one you remember with fondness is entirely up to you."

Someone in the bar said, "Hear, hear."

"Excuse my companion," said the smaller of Percival's men. "As you may have guessed, he imbibed rather more than is good for him last night, and the effects are still to wear off."

At the same time, the bigger man took Byron's arm in a none-too-gentle grip and pulled him to a table in the corner, where he shoved him into a seat.

With the entertainment at an end, the hum of conversation in the room picked up again. The landlord watched the three men settle themselves, then turned away from them. As he did so, he winked at Ben, who fought to suppress his grin. He went out to his coach.

Moments later, they left the yard and headed for the rendezvous with Alice.

Chapter Eleven

The sun barely penetrated the canopy of branches and leaves, which meant the woodland was less brightly lit than the tavern garden had been, and the ground underfoot was softer, although the air was no cooler. Ferns sprouted, the green of their new growth jewel-bright against the fawn skeletons of last year's fronds and the dark brown of the earth. The path was much used and easy to follow, which made Alice feel better since, she reasoned, if the inn's local patrons used this path often enough to keep it from overgrowing, it must lead somewhere and was unlikely to go on for miles. She certainly hoped so.

While she walked, she thought about what had just happened. Thank God she'd needed to use the necessary, otherwise she might have been out in the yard beside Ben, in full view of Byron and his companions.

That did not even bear thinking about.

How had he discovered them so quickly? She was certain he hadn't seen her in the coach yesterday morning, so even if he had recognized Ben inside the vehicle, he'd have had no reason to follow him, no reason to suppose Alice would be with him. On top of which, he couldn't have known where Ben was going. Ben could have been going to an address in the city, for all Byron knew. Or he might have been headed for Dover and the continent, or east to the fens, or down to the West

Country…

Byron had followed too quickly and too accurately for his arrival to be a lucky guess.

The only people who knew she and Ben were heading north were Lord Fremont and Sally. Lord Fremont was unlikely to have told anyone. Which meant Byron must have learned of it from Sally.

"Oh, Sally, Sally, Sally," she murmured, despairing. "What were you thinking?"

She frowned, perplexed. Something wasn't right. Alice had trusted Sally with her secrets before, and her friend had never betrayed her. Sally liked a cozy gossip as much as the next person, but if she was asked to say nothing, she stayed silent.

She also did not like Byron. She would not willingly tell him anything. What had she said?

You don't want him spoiling this, so you get to Scotland before he catches up with you.

Why would she say that, then tell him where they'd gone? It made no sense.

Not that the why and how of it mattered. The fact was, Byron had traced them, and they needed to get away from him as soon as they could.

She slipped on a muddy patch and threw her arms out, righting herself before she ended sprawled in the dust. It would be just her luck to land in mud and dirt and skeletal leaves when she wore the most exquisite traveling dress she'd ever had. The lower branches snatched at her bonnet and, more than once, she needed to stop and free it from their spiteful grasp. Her feet balanced precariously on ruts and ridges carved into the ground, which made her soles ache and threatened to turn her ankles.

By the time she reached the kissing-gate on the far edge of the wood some fifteen minutes later, she was hot and bothered, and feeling decidedly careworn and dowdy. Not at all the well-put-together lady she'd been at breakfast.

"Which, I suppose, serves me right," she muttered, "for being so proud of my appearance."

Once she was through the gate and onto the lane, she found Ben's coach easily enough. John had pulled up just past the gate in a small clearing between the road and the wood. It wasn't exactly hidden from view, but it would have been difficult to spot until one was almost upon it.

Ben climbed out as she approached, lowered the steps for her, then offered her his hand. She took it to climb in. Even through their respective gloves she felt the sudden tingling in her fingers at his touch. It jolted her, leaving her nonplussed, and a little scared.

"I'm sorry you had to walk so far," he said as he climbed in behind her. He closed the door while she sank into her seat and arranged her slightly soiled skirts. Now that she'd stopped walking over the rough terrain, her feet ached more. She tried to curl her toes inside her boots, but there wasn't enough room to make much difference.

"Couldn't be helped," she answered. It was true. And a walk through the woods was infinitely preferable to an encounter with Byron and whoever was with him, she knew that. "However," she added, "I am grateful to sit here for the rest of our journey."

The coach lurched as they set off.

"Drink?" Ben held out a hip flask that he'd pulled from his coat pocket. It was a small pewter flask with a leather top, the kind in which gentlemen sometimes carried brandy. Alice narrowed her eyes, first at the flask, then at the man offering it.

Ben sighed. "It's water, from the well at the Castle. I am assured it is clean and fresh, for the well is fed by an underground stream that flows speedily through."

Not altogether convinced, but thirsty after her walk, Alice took the flask and sipped at it, tentatively. It *was* water. It *was* cold and refreshing, with the crisp, clean tastelessness that water should have.

Her surprise must have showed on her face because Ben scowled, and looked insulted. "I do not lie, madam," he said. "Nor have I ever felt the need to ply a woman with drink."

"I beg your pardon," Alice apologized. "Although, I'm sure you'll agree, there are men, seemingly respectable man, who would do so. Nevertheless, I should not tar you with the same brush, and I am sorry."

Ben put the flask away and stared at the passing countryside, leaving her to feel awkwardly guilty.

Ten minutes later, the coach rolled to a stop and John climbed down from his seat. Ben put down the window and leaned out to see what was wrong.

"Begging your pardon, sir, but I was wondering what you want to do now?" asked John. "To avoid the rum un and his friends, I mean."

Alice's heart skittered. "He will try to follow us." It wasn't a question, although she hoped against hope that one of the men would answer her with a no.

"He will," confirmed Ben.

"He thinks you're eloping, miss," said John.

Ben's face creased with deep thoughts. "That could work in our favor."

Alice could not see how. "He won't take an

elopement well. He'll be all the more determined to catch up to us if he thinks that's happening."

"Yes," agreed Ben. "But he'll head for Scotland, directly north. Whereas we will be moving west, toward Shropshire. We'll take different roads to him and, by the time he realizes we're not for Gretna Green, our trail should be cold."

"I would add an extra layer of precaution," said John. He pulled on the end of his nose as he thought. "It'll mean forgoing the inns and hotels Lord Fremont secured for us, and finding out-of-the-way places in small villages and such, but I think we should avoid all the main roads, and any large towns, until we reach Abberley. If we encounter as few people as possible, the, er, gentleman is less likely to find anyone who can point out our direction." He shrugged. "It'll add a day or so to the journey, but…"

"It's a sensible plan," agreed Ben. "What say you, Alice?"

"Amelia," she corrected him.

"Excuse me?" He raised his eyebrows.

"You should call me Amelia, even when we're alone. And I should call you Joshua. If we do that at all times, we are less likely to make a mistake when we're in company. And as for taking side roads and back ways, I am happy with that, so long as I don't have to walk for miles to meet you again."

Both Ben and John laughed at that, then Ben said, "Josh."

She frowned, not sure what he meant.

"My cousin is never called Joshua. Always Josh."

"I see." She nodded. "Fair enough. Josh."

A minute later, John climbed back to the driver's

seat and they set off once more. Alice leaned back against the squabs and closed her eyes.

"Do you always do that?" asked Ben.

She opened her eyes and stared, blankly at him. "Do what?" She could think of nothing she had done that might have caused him to ask.

"Become the role you're playing. Insist your fellow actors call you by your character's name, even when you're not actually performing."

Alice scoffed at that. "I'd hardly say so. Third dancer, back row, doesn't exactly fall from the tongue with ease, does it?"

He grinned. "They could shorten it. Miss Third Dancer, for example."

"I suppose they could." She thought for a moment. Two could play this game. "Do they call you Primo Uomo? Or just Primo, for short?"

Benedict looked bemused. Alice thought she knew why.

"I suppose you're surprised that I know the Italian for 'leading man,' " she said, deciding it was better for her to say it aloud than him. "Or do you feel I have besmirched your character in some way by calling you that?"

He shrugged. "Primo Uomo does not have the connotations that Prima Donna carries. That term might mean 'Leading Lady,' but it also describes a woman who is difficult and demanding. Primo Uomo doesn't have the same effect."

"No, it doesn't." She smiled, sweetly. He looked wary. As well he might, she thought, as she continued, "Primo Uomo carries different connotations entirely since, for at least the last hundred years, the position in an opera has gone exclusively to castrati."

He swallowed, cleared his throat, shifted in his seat. Cleared his throat again. Alice felt the triumph surge within her. It served him right.

"I can assure you," he said, at last, "I am no eunuch."

She fought the grin that threatened to break out. "I'm sure the ladies in your life have been very grateful for that."

He turned to the window, his face a dark red. She thought he murmured that no one had ever complained, but she couldn't be sure, and she was not about to ask him.

****

Ben watched the landscape and pondered his traveling companion. Alice Buck was a puzzle, with many more layers than he'd thought. It irked him that he found her so difficult to understand, and so intriguing.

It should have been simple. She was an actress, a back row dancer in a third rate theater, with an eye to the main chance that would keep her on the straight and narrow—provided he kept her from strong spirits, that was. Except…she hadn't drunk strong spirits at all. Hadn't shown any desire to do so. Indeed, she'd been suspicious of the flask he offered her. That did not fit with the person he'd thought he knew.

She had adapted immediately and seamlessly into the role of lady. Not only her accent but her mannerisms, her whole being: she presented herself as a person born to it. She'd also behaved modestly. She had not deliberately flaunted her figure at him, had dressed herself away from his sight, and had made it known he was not welcome in the chamber while she bathed.

True, she'd invited him to share the bed last night,

but there was nothing venal in the invitation. It was clear it was so he could sleep. Nothing more.

Thinking of the other women at the theater, Ben could not imagine one of them who would have made such an offer for the same innocent reasons. Alice's friend, Sally, for instance, would have used the opportunity to ingratiate herself with him, and to further her career.

Thoughts of Sally led him to another puzzling aspect of Alice: her connection to Percival. He understood that her brother owed the man money and, if he couldn't get the cash from him, he would take it in a different form, but Ben had to wonder if that was all there was to it. Was Alice an innocent victim? Or had she brought Percival's wrath down upon herself?

Ben needed to know. Not simply to satisfy his curiosity, although it had been piqued. He also had to know what he was up against, and how likely it was to adversely affect this mission.

"Until the night before last..." he said, trying to sound unthreatening. He had the feeling she would not respond well to a harsher interrogation. "I wasn't aware you had a brother."

"Why should you be? You didn't even know my full name, so you were unlikely to know aught else."

Touché. "I sense you're not close to him?"

She gave an unconcerned shrug of her shoulders and looked out of the window. Her face was impassive, her manner disinterested. The only hint that she was bothered by his observation was the slightest tensing in her body.

"He owes money to Milton Percival," Ben persisted. She swallowed, but said nothing and did not leave her study of the countryside.

"He owes money, and he's traveling with two of Percival's employees. Which must mean your brother's journey has been sanctioned by his creditor."

"It would seem so."

Ben narrowed his eyes, but kept his voice low. "Why does Percival want you so badly?"

She glanced at him, then returned to staring out of the window.

"He has a stable full of whores. Why would he spend resources chasing one across the country?"

This time, her look was sharp. "I am not a whore."

"You will be, if Percival gets his hands on you. But why is he so keen? What makes you so important to him?"

She looked as if she would answer, then snapped her mouth shut and turned back to the window.

There was more to this than her brother's debt. Percival would take that out of the man, in lumps and bruises. Or, if the amount was too high, he'd kill him. So why...? "What did you do to upset him enough to send men after you?"

Her eyes filled with angry fire. "Someone pursues me, so it must be me who's at fault? Is that what you think?" She huffed, humorlessly. "How typical of a man. Always blame the woman. Whatever happens, blame her."

"I didn't—"

"And why shouldn't you? After all, it's been happening since Eve was first blamed by Adam." She mimicked a whining man. "I'm sorry, God. It wasn't me, it was Eve. She forced me to eat that fruit." She scowled. "Nothing changes."

A minute passed. Ben said nothing. What could he say? She was right. He had jumped to conclusions, and the logic behind them was less than sound. There could be any number of reasons for Percival's continued attempts to retrieve her.

"I apologize."

She gave him a look filled with frustration. It made him want to give her comfort, to reassure her. He leaned forward and reached for her hand. Once again, the touch of her sent a strong jolt through him, even though their gloves prevented skin meeting skin.

More was the pity. He wished to touch *her*, to feel the warmth and vibrance of her. Would her hands be soft, like that of the lady she portrayed? Or would there be callouses that spoke of hard work, and harder times?

Unnerved by his own response to this most innocent of touches, Ben cleared his throat and sought to deny the emotions her nearness evoked in him. "It's just...I... Will his pursuit affect what we're doing?"

He knew it was a mistake as soon as the words left his mouth. Her jaw tensed. She pulled her hand away as if his touch burned her.

"No." This time, when she turned to the window, she put her back to him. He leaned against the squabs, knowing there would be no further conversation between them at this time.

An hour passed. They changed horses. She did not look at him. Back inside the coach, she sat rigid, staring at the countryside as if fascinated by it. Ben tried to watch it through the other window but his attention constantly wandered back to her.

He was in the wrong. He knew that. She didn't need to have done anything to attract Percival's attention. If that man decided he wanted something, he would be relentless in his pursuit of it, to the point of insane obsession. Especially if what he wanted was denied to him. Percival did not take no for an answer. Ben knew that.

Ben also knew that his own interest in this went beyond what was good for his mission. Somewhere between London and wherever they were now, he'd come to worry about the feisty little woman who played his wife. He wanted her safe from Byron, Percival, and all others, not because it helped him, but because she deserved to be.

That was a new sensation for him. He did not, as a rule, concern himself with the lives of the dancers and actresses surrounding him. He paid no attention to their romances and their trysts, and the troubles such alliances brought on their heads. If they encouraged the gentlemen, he reasoned, they could pay for it.

Only, in this instance, the troubles were not because she'd encouraged anybody. They were not of her making. Alice needed support and protection from those who wanted to use her for their own ends. She needed his help.

He cleared his throat. She ignored him.

"Al…Amelia," he said. She turned and gave him an icy stare, which made him want to retreat and hide from her ire. He took a deep breath and did what he must, not only to restore harmony between them, but because it was the right thing to do.

"I apologize. I know a man like Percival doesn't need a reason to…" He gestured with his hand. "I'd like to help. Won't you tell me why he has fixed his desire upon you?"

She glared at him a moment longer, then stared out of the window again.

He sighed. "Are you going to give me the silent treatment all the way to Broseley?"

She sniffed.

"Al—Amelia?" He reached out. She flinched from him and he held up his hands in surrender as he sat back in his seat. "I'm sorry."

She did not respond.

Another minute passed. Two. Slowly, it dawned on him that her reactions were not quite right. Yes, she was angry, and that made her prickly and defensive. But there was more to it than that. He felt...fear. She was frightened. *Of him?*

He'd given her no reason. He had behaved as a gentleman throughout their brief acquaintance, hadn't he? He'd never in his life attacked any woman. Yet she shrank from him as if he was a monster, and even now, she sat stiffly, as if ready to repel him.

They were headed for Shefford, where they would stop for nuncheon. Cows, sheep and horses grazed in fields broken by copses of trees and bordered by dry stone walls. Fields and woodlands and hills stretched as far as he could see. In the distance, sunlight glittered on a slow-moving river. They were a long way from London. But not, it seemed, far enough.

"You are in danger," he said. "I see that. But it isn't from me."

"No," she acknowledged, wearily. "It is not from you."

"Then let me help you. Tell me what happened."

She closed her eyes for a moment. Her cheeks pinked. He held his breath, anxious but hopeful. Would she confide in him? Let him help?

When she opened her eyes again, she had steeled her resolve. "It has no bearing on what we're doing for Lord Fremont," she said.

It was the last straw. "The devil it hasn't! I've been accosted by your brother and forced to change both the route we are taking and the plans we've made. Instead of going to Bedford and the decent rooms Fremont has secured for us there, we are making our way, on dubiously made and poorly maintained back roads, which will lead us, so John said at our last change of horses, to the much smaller town of Olney. I don't even know if there is an inn at Olney, or if that inn is respectable, or has vacant rooms."

"I am sorry for your loss of comfort," she retorted.

He waved his hand, dismissively. "That's by the by. You and I are supposed to be newlyweds, happy, and without a care in the world. It's a difficult image to convey when the bride is constantly looking over her shoulder for her pursuers!" She opened her mouth to say something, but he held up his hand to stop her. "This jeopardizes everything. It's clear to me that your brother spoke with Sally, and she told him where we were. No, don't argue. He said something that confirmed the information came from her."

She looked shocked at that. Ben took a deep breath, his anger cooling, although he still needed to spell out his concerns.

"Your brother—and I'm sorry to insult a member of your family, but it is the truth—your brother is an imbecile. Milton Percival is not. He knows that the actress he wants—you—is eloping with the actor, Benedict Summersby. Me. Once he learns that said eloping couple has disappeared, how long do you think it will take him to learn that their disappearance coincided with the arrival in this area of my honeymooning cousin Josh? At which point, he could—probably will—ruin everything."

Alice stared at him, her face ashen. For a moment, he wondered if he'd gone too far, terrified her too much. Then she rallied. "Broseley is hundreds of miles from London," she said, defiantly. "There comes a point when even Percival must cut his losses."

Ben shook his head. "You're not that naive." He sighed. "He—Byron—staked you in his game, didn't he?"

Alice swallowed and nodded.

"You knew nothing about it?"

Her face reddened. Her eyes sparked. "Of course I knew nothing about it!" The fury in her made her tremble, and turned her fingers into gloved claws. Instinctively, Ben pressed back in his seat, putting distance between them, and she sneered at him, contemptuously. "I am aware of your opinion of me, Mr. Summersby. I have no idea why you should have taken me in such dislike, but it has been obvious from the start. I care little for your opinion. Ordinarily, I wouldn't even think twice about it. But since we must work together, let me clarify. Byron did what he did, without my knowledge or encouragement. Certainly without my participation. I was not there to stop him, although if I had been there, I doubt I could have stopped him anyway. Byron goes his own way, without regard to my—or anybody else's—feelings. He will do whatever it takes to benefit him. Always has done, and, I dare say, always will do. He doesn't care who is hurt by his actions, as long as he is all right. In that respect, he is like all other men!"

Ben bristled at that. "That's unfair."

"Is it?" She raised an eyebrow in challenge.

"It is. I would never do something as crass as to put up a woman as collateral for my losses."

"No. You would just blame her for the situation she found herself in as a consequence."

She turned fully away from him, signaling that the conversation was, for her, finished. Her shoulders moved up and down rapidly, betraying her agitation.

"Alice—"

"Do not speak to me. I wish no conversation with you." The rigid spine she showed him, and the finality in her voice left him in no doubt that she meant it.

An hour passed. The silence grew awkward, then oppressive. The only sounds Ben could hear were the whirring, grinding of the wheels on pebble-strewn roads, the thunderous beat of horse hooves, and John's occasional yell. Alice sat, staring at the scenery with an intenseness that must make her head ache, even if the rigid straightness of her body didn't make her back hurt. She never once looked at him.

He was in the wrong. He'd known it from the first, but the silence gave him time to ponder it, until it grew in importance, magnifying his guilt. He should not have assumed she'd done anything to attract Percival's attention. The man needed no encouragement, and Ben had no right to blame her for his actions.

His reasons for blaming her weren't difficult to work out, but they were hard to admit, and they did him no credit. He found he could not like them, or himself, very much at all.

He'd thought the worst of her, simply because she was an opera dancer. He'd decided, as most people no doubt did, that an opera dancer encouraged attention from men. True, many did—it was how they supplemented their income. But "many" did not mean "all," and he had no evidence that Alice was one of the "many." Instead of jumping to conclusions, he should have given her the benefit of the doubt.

Now he knew what he must do. There was no getting away from it. He must step up and be a man about it. On that thought, he cleared his throat, and said, "I apologize."

If it were possible, he thought her spine stiffened even more.

"I apologize," he went on, "for what I said earlier. The assumptions I made. They were very wrong, and unworthy."

She did not move a muscle.

He took in a deep breath, blew it out, and tried again. "I was insensitive and unthinking. I will try to do better as we go on."

She sat, immobile. She might as well be made from marble.

"Forgive me?"

She ignored him.

He willed her to turn to him, even if it was to shoot ice-fire from those blue eyes and drip venom from her bow-shaped lips. He longed to hear her say something, anything, in that low, husky voice of hers.

Time went by. The road changed to a better-made surface as they approached a town, and the whirring grind of the wheels became a dull roar on the tarmacadam. There was a metallic ringing in the thunder of the horse hooves. The whip cracked the air and John shouted, "Hah!"

Alice didn't move.

"Your brother should be horsewhipped for what he's done," Ben said.

That did make her turn, but if Ben thought she would thank him for his sentiments, she soon disabused him. "Telling me what should happen to Byron is not helpful," she said. "For your information, I agree with you, but again, that does nothing to bring about his punishment, or my salvation."

Her words, and the withering stare that accompanied them, made him feel two inches tall.

Chapter Twelve

Alice was being churlish when she could not afford to be. But it had stung when this oaf had accused her of bringing misfortune down upon herself, of deserving whatever may come. He'd actually felt the need to ask if Byron had sold her with her consent! She'd wager the value of all the gowns in that trunk he would never have asked such a thing of the real Amelia Summersby. With Amelia, he—and every other so-called gentleman— would be horrified for what she'd suffered, and would have assured her of his continued belief in her innocence, regardless of the fact they had no more proof of that than there was proof of Alice's guilt. Then, each and every one of those men would have stood ready to do battle in her name, to rid her of the blackguard who tormented her.

But Alice…Alice was a different kettle of fish.

It wasn't because she was an opera dancer. That didn't help, of course. She knew what people thought of those who kicked their way across the stage, wearing as little as the Lord Chancellor would allow. But Alice had been a seamstress before she worked in the theater, a respectable woman working in a respectable shop, and that had afforded her no better protection. She'd been accosted, propositioned, leered at, and followed, and she'd had no recourse. Even the law, had she appealed to it, would not have helped. The constables would have taken one look at her, ascertained her class, shrugged their shoulders, and turned away.

They wouldn't have protected her from Percival's vicious attack, either, had she reported it. Never mind that several gentlemen of quality might have testified on her behalf. The fact was, in the general scheme of things, women like Alice didn't matter.

This job for Lord Fremont was her chance to leave that life behind. With the assets gained from playing Amelia, Alice would finally be able to open her shop, moving from unprotected employee to respected business owner. But only if she earned the fee. Which meant playing the happy bride to Ben's nabob. She couldn't afford to sit here sulking, refusing to speak to him.

So she pushed a smile onto her face and turned to him. "Enough of me," she said, as sweetly as she could manage. "You are certainly what they call a dark horse, are you not?" She gave the tiniest laugh. This should turn the tables on the man. "Who would ever have guessed that you, a man who seems nothing more than an actor on the London stage is, in truth, working as a…what would you call it? A covert investigator for the government?"

He tensed, then shrugged his shoulders, deliberately relaxing them. "I'm not."

"Lord Fremont may beg to differ."

Ben shook his head. "This is a one-time deal."

Intriguing. "Why?"

Her question clearly startled him. His eyes widened and his eyebrows rose, though he quickly recovered. "Because that is what Fremont and I agreed."

"Could be lucrative work."

"It's dirty work," he murmured. Louder, he explained, "I don't wish to be one of Fremont's operatives more than this once and, if you asked him, he'd probably say he doesn't particularly want me, either."

"That's not what I asked," she protested. "I wasn't asking why you wish to do only this one job. But why, if you're not one of his operatives, did he come to you? Because you resemble your cousin? Are there no other men, besides your cousin, who might draw the attention of those we seek?"

"Possibly. The thing is, I look enough like Josh to have fooled his own father for a time. And I'm an actor. I'm used to taking on a persona that's not mine." He smiled, sadly. "And, unlike the other men you mention, should push come to shove, I'm expendable."

That was not a comforting thought. It also didn't marry with what she knew of him. The man had connections. That had to count for something, did it not?

"Surely, your family connections provide us some protection in this quest? Whatever else may happen, Lord Fremont wouldn't want to explain to your wealthy and presumably influential cousin that he put you into unnecessary danger?"

Ben chuckled, but there was no warmth in it. "Don't rely too heavily on my 'family connections.' Josh Summersby may have given me leave to use his name for this venture, but I doubt he'll shed many tears if anything happens to me."

She frowned. "You're not close?"

"We are not." A shadow passed over his face and for a moment he looked bleak. Then it was gone, and he was as impassive as he'd ever been.

Alice studied him, wondering what might have caused such a breach between them that the one would not care if the other died.

"I know all about family disputes and estrangements," she said, thinking of the way her mother's family had turned its collective back on her and her children. Then, not wanting to elaborate on that piece of her history, she continued, "with a brother like Byron, how could I not? But you talk as if the rift in your family is deep. May I ask what happened between you to make it so?"

Ben looked away, uncomfortable. Long seconds passed. She thought he wasn't going to answer. And really, why should he? His family business was not her concern, even if she was playing the wife of one of the antagonists.

Finally, though, he did speak, although he seemed to address the floor of the coach, rather than Alice, his eyes lowered, head bowed, shoulders slumped.

"I did something stupid," he whispered. She could hardly hear him above the sounds of the coach, and yet, every word was, strangely, clear. "Something that nearly cost Josh, his family, and Amelia their lives." His face darkened with shame. She felt the heat emanating from him.

Alice said nothing. In truth, she could think of nothing she could say. He'd told her something, and nothing. She knew little more about him now than she had before. Had whatever he'd done been the result of reckless hijinks? The product of youthful wildness that had almost led to tragic repercussions?

Or had there been malice in his behavior toward his cousin?

"I...became involved with people I shouldn't have," he said. "I didn't know what I was a party to until it was too late, but that's no excuse. I *should* have known. I should have delved deeper before I..." He sighed. "I'm lucky I didn't hang for it. Others did. Or they will."

"Hang?" She stared, open-mouthed. Of all the things he might have said, that was not one she'd expected.

"Yes. I could have been hanged. I was given a second chance, though I didn't deserve it. This mission for Lord Fremont is how I pay for the clemency I was shown. And, hopefully, how I redeem myself."

"But...hanged!" The word was little more than a soft breath. She could not have said it louder if her life depended on it. Whatever he'd done must be bad to carry such a penalty.

She did not realize she'd spoken her thoughts aloud until he answered her.

"It was." He took a deep breath, pushed his shoulders back and, much as she had done earlier, threw off the despondency the conversation had brought. "It's in the past. You may rest assured, I will never be so foolish again. Now, let me tell you a little about Josh and Amelia, so you may give a decent performance."

He told her what he knew of Amelia Summersby as they moved through the Bedfordshire countryside, and she did her best to retain the information. The woman sounded like someone Alice would like, and that would help her performance immensely.

It was a lovely day, the latest in a series of hot days, warmer than usual for this time of year in England. The sun shone in a flawless sky, making the colors of the country bright or, sometimes, blocking them with a blinding light that made one squint. The only breeze was the draught created by the coach as it bowled along, rippling the leaves on hedgerows and the tall grasses of the verges as they passed. Even with the heat, though, the air inside the coach was fresh and bearable. In London, it would be muggy and heavy, made so by the closeness of the buildings and the narrowness of the streets. The smells of the city would be magnified too: unwashed bodies, waste and refuse, sewers and rats, the dank waters of the Thames. By contrast, the cleanliness of Bedfordshire was close to heavenly.

Over the last two years the weather had been awful—cold and wet, stormy and dark. Indeed, the year before last, 1816, had been widely called "The Year Without A Summer" and was referred to, not altogether jokingly, as "eighteen hundred and froze to death." 1817 hadn't been much better. Those bad years had caused much hardship. The nasty weather decimated crops, which led, inevitably, to famine, starvation, and mass desperation. By contrast, these days of sunshine seemed like a new dawn, reviving spirits and pushing back despair.

Not that the couple Alice and Ben were impersonating had likely suffered too much in the worst of it, she thought, with a bitterness she was not proud of. Josh and Amelia Summersby would never have wondered where their next meal would come from, the way too many other people had. Their estates may not have made the profits they were used to, but they wouldn't have been destitute. The children in their families would not have been hollow-cheeked and miserable, their eyes too large in their faces, their bellies distended for want of food.

That realization set her thinking once more. Ben was

an actor. He wasn't bad at his craft, although he wasn't in the same league as Edmund Kean or William McCready. And, as Byron had pointed out to Alice many times, people from good families did not go into the theater.

Unless their "good" families completely rejected them, as hers had done.

She understood that Josh Summersby would not wish anything to do with Ben if he'd committed capital crimes, especially if Ben's actions had almost caused the deaths of Josh and those he loved. But she had the impression those had been recent events. They'd come about *because* Ben was not part of the family's inner circle. Why wasn't he? Why hadn't Ben been living in a way that fitted his family connections? He clearly knew his cousins personally, for he'd given Alice information that only personal acquaintance would have revealed. And yet…

"If your cousin is so wealthy," she said, unable to hold her curiosity, "how is it you are making your living as an actor?"

He raised his eyebrows, surprised by her question.

"I suppose what I mean is, if you'd been in the bosom of your family before all the—shenanigans, might it have prevented the crimes that were committed against them?"

"Possibly." He shrugged in a nonchalant fashion, but the hard glitter in his eyes said he was anything but relaxed about this. "It might have prevented my part in it, perhaps. I was hired to impersonate him, which would have been difficult if I'd already been known to everyone. But, as you probably know, ifs and ands are not pots and pans."

"That's true." She bit her lip, then asked, "Do you resent him? For his wealth?"

Ben seemed genuinely perplexed. "Why should I?"

"Some people—"*Byron*—"might believe a rich relative should take care of them."

He bristled. "I am not 'some people.' The money is his, not mine. He earned it, and he's entitled to it. He doesn't owe me a penny."

A minute went by. She asked nothing more. Whatever his relationship with his cousin, he clearly had regrets, and he did not wish to talk about them. A fact made more obvious when he suddenly grinned in a way that made her very wary. "But what about you? You called me a dark horse. Yet what do I know of you?" He held up a hand and counted on his fingers. "You have a brother who's not worthy of the name. You are intelligent and have clearly had access to an education." He held up the three fingers he'd extended. "Other than these things, I know nothing of you."

She folded her arms tightly across her chest, which pulled her reticule around in front of her, so that it acted as a shield. Her knees and ankles pressed closer together.

"There's no reason you should," she said. Her voice was calm and quiet, at odds with the tight, roiling, panicked sensations inside her. She didn't like to talk about her people. They were of no consequence to her, and shouldn't matter a jot to anyone else. If anything, they were a liability, for were their existence known, many of her neighbors would immediately be suspicious of her.

"No reason at all." She heard the defensive curtness in her voice and made an effort to relax.

"Seems a little one-sided, don't you think?"

"No." She swallowed. "I need to know about your family in order to carry out my task for Lord Fremont. All you need to know about me is that I'm capable of playing Amelia."

"True," he conceded. "I don't *need* to know." He grinned again. It made him look boyish and mischievous. "But I am interested."

Her throat tightened and her mouth dried. The mischief she'd seen in his face now took on a sinister bent. His curiosity was too much. It made her cheeks heat with prickling color, and her spine stiffened.

There was no reason not to tell him what he wished to know, of course. There was nothing in her background of which she was ashamed, but she was less than comfortable sharing it. Some people might think the story reflected badly upon her mother, the disobedient and disrespectful daughter who had ruined herself and blighted her family for at least two generations. But in Alice's opinion, her mother was not the one to blame. To her mind, the person who should be ashamed was her maternal grandfather, the Earl of Ely. Unfeeling, unbending snob that he was. Alice had never met him, never intended to, and unlike Byron, her connection with him did not make her proud. He and the rest of his oh-so-noble family had cast off Alice's mother without so much as a penny and shown not the slightest concern for her well-being from that moment on, simply because she'd fallen in love with a man whose position did not benefit the family fortunes. Their cold-bloodedness and willingness to sacrifice Mama for their own gain disgusted Alice and put them beneath her notice.

Oblivious to her thoughts, Ben continued with his questions. "For instance," he asked, "is Byron your only relative?"

"My parents are dead." Alice could not say more than that, not without lying.

"I'm sorry. And you have no other siblings?"

She shook her head.

"Aunts? Uncles?"

"I know none." Again, it was not exactly a lie. She knew they were there. She'd never met them, so she didn't actually know them.

"It occurs to me you must have…friends, among the higher echelons of society."

That puzzled her. "Why would you think that?" Alice's friends were, almost exclusively, working people from the area where she'd grown up. They were shop workers, seamstresses, actresses, dancers, even a soiled dove or two. None of them were part of the Mayfair set.

"Your accent is…convincing," he said.

Was that a compliment? Or an insult? Did he not think her acting skills up to the task of appropriating an accent? He didn't think highly of her, he'd made no secret of that. This seemed to be another example of his low opinion of her. Well, she had had enough.

She adopted the roughest cockney accent she could manage, and asked, "Wot? You fink I coutn't manage to toulk proper unless I fahnd someone wot could show me 'ow?"

He winced and his cheeks darkened. *Good. He deserves to be embarrassed.*

"I meant it as a compliment," he said.

"Oh, I can see that." she nodded, sagely. "I am, of course, as common as muck. So if I am able to sound…convincing, was that what you said? If my performance is 'convincing,' then I must have learned it from my betters." The urge to shock him grew. She smiled sweetly and added, "Would those betters be my 'gentlemen friends' when I was flat on my back underneath them?"

"Don't be coarse."

She laughed. "Coarse? When *you* think *me* a whore, it is understandable and acceptable. When *I* call *you* out on your assumptions, I am coarse."

"I didn't mean—" He gritted his teeth, exasperated. "I was, truly, paying you a compliment."

She kept her glare fixed on him, and raised one eyebrow to denote her disbelief.

"You are an accomplished actress," he said. "Better than 'third dancer, back row' would suggest. You have a talent for the different accents of London. It isn't easy to go from one to another, but not only can you do it, you can do it credibly."

Alice watched him through narrowed eyes, certain there would be a sting in the tail, something to negate his words of praise. Of course, if he knew both accents came naturally to her, he would not be so impressed by her "talent." She'd grown up in a household where one accent was exclusively used, but it was in a neighborhood where everyone else used the other. She'd had to move between the two in order to survive.

Not that he needed to know that.

"Just as long as I can convince the men we're looking for," she said. She would do the job, collect her payment, and disappear into her new life in the north Midlands, where hopefully she'd be far enough away from the draining scourge of Byron and the threat of Percival, as well as leaving behind the theater and Ben Summersby.

Chapter Thirteen

They spent the next five days traveling across the country, using lesser known routes between towns and villages that rarely, if ever, saw a coach from one week's end to the other. Most of the roads were little more than tracks, often no more than a single carriage width winding between meadows, where this season's baby animals played next to their patient mothers, and fields planted with half-grown crops. Most of the tracks were uneven, with deep ruts either side of the mound which ran down the center. Sometimes, the coach's bottom grounded on the highest and most pronounced of these mounds, making an horrendous graunching noise that was harmless, but alarming nonetheless, and which forced them to slow to a walk at the worst points. Other roads sported huge potholes which tested John's driving capabilities to the limit as he swerved around them, trying not to jolt his passengers too much while, more importantly, avoiding broken axles and buckled rims. Wet mud splattered the coach, and poor John had to clean this off at every stop. Alice marveled at how hard he must work, for no matter how dirty the vehicle was upon arrival, it invariably gleamed when they set off again.

The inns they found varied in quality, though none were so base that she felt uncomfortable staying in them, and the best was not so high in the instep that she was tempted to curtsy to the landlord. All were clean and warm, and most served good food. The worst had a menu that was passable, and all were sensibly priced.

They booked their rooms under a variety of names, taken from characters in stage plays. If Byron and his friends should double back and scour the countryside for them, they didn't want him hearing the name Summersby, and picking up their trail that way. They knew they'd be remembered—a well-dressed couple in a private coach, staying at inns that saw little traffic, was bound to be remarked upon—but, hopefully, their invented surnames would be enough to throw pursuers off the scent.

On the fourth night, Ben announced that, from this point on, they must be Josh and Amelia again. They were close to their destination now, close to the people they hoped to fool, so they could no longer risk using any other name. Alice hoped Byron had lost their trail by now, if he'd ever picked it up. If they were truly lucky, he would have given up completely and gone back to London to face the music for himself, though she knew this was highly unlikely, unless it was forced upon him by his traveling companions.

Then again, the prospect of her brother finding them was not the part of the journey that caused her the most consternation.

To Alice, the most troubling part of their dash across the country was the accommodation that Ben booked each night. Because they had not used the inns Fremont had picked for them, Ben had had to lay out more money than he would otherwise have done. It would be some time before he could reclaim these expenses from the viscount, so naturally he did what he could to save funds.

In most places, this involved cutting the number of rooms they rented.

They always hired the private parlors, of course, but, whereas they would usually have had a bedchamber each, now they shared one—not something that the upper echelons of Society did, as a rule. As they were supposed to be newlyweds, it raised fewer eyebrows than it might otherwise have done, and they made sure to bill and coo like a pair of sickeningly amorous twits, so nobody was in the least surprised that this particular couple wanted just one room.

But, although it made sense economically, sharing a room with a man, night after night, left Alice discomfited and filled with nerves.

It was not Ben's fault. He behaved as a perfect gentleman and made no attempt to take advantage of their situation. He left the room while she bathed, and when she dressed and undressed, and he took care to disrobe himself discreetly, behind the modesty screens when he could.

Alice had to admit, if only to herself, that she wasn't certain how she felt about this. On the one hand, she was grateful that he treated her with respect. She knew what he thought of her—and she could hardly blame him. Being an opera dancer left her open to that kind of judgment, no matter how unfair it might be. Many men would have regarded being in her company in a room containing a bed as an opportunity. That Ben did not was a fact that raised him in her estimation.

At the same time, it was lowering to know her charms were so easy to resist. Ben wasn't the least bit tempted by her. Other than when they acted the loving couple for the benefit of onlookers, he hardly glanced at her at all, and when he did, there was no more emotion in his eyes than there was when he spoke to John.

Not that she wanted him to feel anything more for her. She didn't want him to desire her, or anything of the sort. She was more than happy with their arrangement: a business transaction that enabled him to do the task he'd been set and allowed her to escape to her new life. Anything more would complicate and spoil things.

Still, an occasional look of appreciation for the way she looked in her new clothes, and with her hair done to varying degrees of perfection by the maids the inns supplied, might have been nice.

But it didn't matter. Truly, it didn't.

Having allowed him to share the bed in the Castle Hotel, she'd decided it would be churlish of her to deny him that comfort in subsequent inns. It was unfair to expect him to lie on the floor, or to sit all night in a chair, while she got a decent sleep. He was always respectful, and left at least one layer of blankets between her body and his.

Which didn't stop her feeling the nearness of him. The weight of him beside her, especially in some of the smaller, narrower beds, was at once reassuring and disconcerting, and his warmth against her body both comforted and alarmed her.

They began each night as far apart as the bed would allow. She lay on the edge of her side, tense and stiff, making herself as narrow as possible. Ben was not a small man, and he took up a lot of space, even though she suspected he, too, tried to minimize the room he used.

But no matter how far apart they started each night, by the time they woke in the mornings, they had found each other. In sleep, they would both roll to the middle of the mattress, and they would wake face to face, inches apart. Usually, his arm rested across her body, the weight of it anchoring her in place, although she no longer felt trapped by it, as she had that first night. She knew Ben would not hold her against her will. She only had to push him away and he would let her go, even in his sleep.

On the second morning of their journey, his nearness had panicked her. He was so big and heavy, and so much stronger than she was. It had threatened to overwhelm her; the musky scent of sleeping male had combined with the rough rasp as his morning stubble caught on the linen pillowcase and sent her heartbeat into a frenzy, while her breathing shallowed and terror scratched her throat, urging her to scream.

It had taken all she had not to do so. For a moment, she'd been back in the alley, Percival pressing her against the wall, rough bricks pulling at her hair till her eyes watered, his hot breath, his hands, his lips, his teeth…

Swallowing her fear, she'd stared hard at the man beside her and told herself, over and over, he was not her attacker. This was Ben, and he was a gentleman. He wouldn't hurt her. He would never force her. She had no need to be afraid.

While she willed her terror to subside, she watched him in the half-light. In sleep, he looked younger, less harsh, his mouth relaxed. The stubble on his lower face was dark and thick, and she could see, should he wish to grow it back, his beard would soon be as abundant as it had been last week. His hair was tousled and curled and his eyelashes were impossibly long, fanning in half circles against the skin under his eyes. His cheeks had the tan of a man who'd spent time out of doors. His breathing was even, unsteady, unthreatening. She began to feel better.

It helped that their animosity had lessened. He didn't seem so inclined to judge her harshly, while she'd lost her prickly defensiveness and her willingness to take offense at everything he said. As a result, their conversation became more polite and measured, almost friendly. They even shared a joke or two, smiled at one another, and laughed with affection and humor rather than with bitterness and suspicion.

On the third morning, she woke without any feeling of fear and realized she had not had her usual nightmare about Percival. It gave her hope. For far too long, that night and the things that monster had tried to do had loomed far too large in her thoughts. The fear had dictated every move she made, everything she did. Perhaps, she could now begin to put him behind her.

There'd been no sign of Byron, nor of Percival's men. Not since that morning at the Castle. Her brother had clearly believed she and Ben were heading for Gretna Green and, although she'd been upset that Sally had betrayed their confidence, she now thought it was good that she had. Not that it made her less angry with Sally; her friend had believed Scotland was their true destination and had told Byron, regardless. But it might have worked to their benefit.

Gretna Green wasn't the only place north of the border where couples could wed over the anvil and thwart the stricter rules that governed marriage in England. It was the most well-known place, presumably because it was the first town most people came to. Hopefully, when he found no trace of them there, Byron would feel obliged to check on some of the other villages thereabouts. With luck, by the time he returned to England, this job would be completed, she and Ben would have parted company, and her trail would be too cold for her brother to pick up. Especially if she changed her name.

There was just one thing about that scenario that gave her pause—what would happen to Byron when he didn't find her? She had no doubt that Percival would punish him for failing to deliver her. He'd probably beat Byron until he was black and blue. There may even be broken bones. But then, as her father had often said, if one lay down with dogs, one rose with fleas. Byron had willingly slept among the dogs, so he could blame nobody but himself if the fleas now bit. Plus, she thought, hardening her heart against the desire to protect him, he'd not cared a whit what would happen to her. To be honest, a beating might do him good in the long run.

She pushed away the guilt she felt for thinking that, and focused her gaze again, only to become aware that Ben was gazing back at her. His eyes, usually more green than brown, were dark in the half light, and regarded her steadily. How long had he been watching her? Had he been studying her all this time, as she gathered wool?

They were close, their faces inches apart. She saw the dark lashes rimming his eyes, his eyebrows, straight and clean and even. His breath was warm on her skin, carrying the faint smell of last night's tooth powder. It mingled with the crisp starchiness of the sheets and pillowcases, although they'd been softened somewhat by having been slept upon. The faint hint of pine cones came from the banked fire, and his skin smelled of balsam, from his soap and his cologne, together with that morning heaviness that was all him.

If she moved, just slightly, if she leaned toward him by the merest fraction, their lips would meet. Dare she?

They'd kissed just once before, when they'd needed to convince Sally they were in love. It had been her first proper kiss—she would not grace Percival's effort with the name—and it had been magical. She'd wanted more. More of the kiss. More of the strange sensations on her skin, in her chest, her stomach, between her legs…and then she'd panicked, pushed him away, acted the outraged miss.

Her cheeks heated now at the memory of it, and of her reaction to what had been no more than an act on his part. His bewilderment at her behavior shamed her. He had plainly thought her, at best, a tease. At worst, he probably saw her as a hypocritical harpy, someone who'd use him for her own ends and make no effort in return. An impression she had probably reinforced over this journey, considering her attitude toward him for most of the way.

She should kiss him now. Catch him off guard. Press her lips to his and take the heat of his mouth, feel again the way her body responded, and relish the taste of him, so she could store it in her memory for when he was gone. If she started it, then she could end it. It would be hers to control, and she would permit it only so far as she wished it to go…

No! That was exactly what Alice would do if she was the kind of woman he believed her to be. But she wasn't that kind of woman. She never would be. And she was damned if she'd give him any reason to reinforce his opinion. So she pulled away, climbed awkwardly out of bed, and wrapped her robe around her before going behind the modesty screen to use the chamber pot.

****

Alice had been going to kiss him. Ben was convinced of that. He'd woken to the sound of her soft breaths, felt them on his skin. She smelled of tooth powder and chocolate, and beautiful woman.

For she was beautiful. Alice had none of the world-weary hardness that so often marked women in the theater. Nothing in her suggested the cynicism or larceny one so often found there, nor did she seem to have an eye to the main chance—the speed and ease with which she'd insinuated herself into this job notwithstanding. And, much as he'd objected at the time, Ben had to admit she'd been right on that subject. She saw, long before he did, that it would benefit him to have a wife traveling with him.

It startled him to realize all his objections to her had gone. More than that, he was actually enjoying her company.

He hadn't done, at first. There'd been animosity and distrust, offense taken and received, but he was honest enough to accept that had been as much his fault as hers. *More* his than hers. He'd assumed she would be a burden, demanding and unreasonable, milking the job for everything she could get. He'd expected her low morals to show through, putting everything in jeopardy, or, if she did manage to keep her skirt hems down, that her lack of breeding, intelligence and education would give her away.

None of those things had happened. So far, she'd played her part to perfection and, in doing so, had left him confused, intrigued, and pondering just where she came from. He couldn't help but ask himself what her true background was, for one thing was clear to him—this woman might live in the stews, she might be poor, in need of work, and none too particular about how she earned her money, but she was also much, much more.

When they had set out, he'd thought her a whore. She might still turn out to be one, although he didn't believe it any more. If she was, she was clever about it. On this trip, she'd thrown out no lures, batted no lashes. She did not hold her head just so, in the practiced way coquettes did when they tried to tempt a man.

True, she hadn't baulked at offering to share beds with him along the way, something no real lady would ever have contemplated, but even as she'd made the offer, her intentions were plain: the only thing Ben would be getting in those beds was sleep.

Whatever else she might or might not do, Alice Buck did not sell herself cheap.

This morning, Ben had realized, by the cadence of her breathing, that Alice was awake before him. So he'd let his own eyes open slowly and carefully, just a little at first, trying to see her through his lashes without letting her know he, too, had woken. It hadn't taken long to determine that, although she looked straight at him, she didn't see him, and her attention was not on him. She was deep in thought, so deep, she didn't notice when his eyes fully opened and he stared at her.

Myriad thoughts flickered on her face. They made her frown, though whether because they troubled or puzzled her, he couldn't say. She grimaced, then her lips twisted. Her cheeks darkened, her eyes softened, and she licked her lips with just the tip of her tongue. It was, at once, seductive and wanton, and yet the most innocent gesture he'd ever seen. He would wager Alice did not even realize she'd done it.

Parts of him were always inconveniently hard when he first woke. This morning, though, watching the desire, the temptation and the uncertainty on her face, he was harder than ever. He felt the restlessness in his stomach, the strange ache in his chest, the bristling hairs on his thighs as his muscles tightened.

She was going to kiss him. He could feel it in the air, which seemed to vibrate around them. He saw it in the way her eyes explored his mouth, hungry and wanting. She smelled of arousal, heightening his.

Ben did not dare move. He didn't want to frighten her before she came closer to him, before she let their mouths join. He wanted that kiss so badly, he could see, feel, taste every part of it as if it were happening here, now.

It would be soft, tentative at first, the touch of her lips to his no more than the brush of a butterfly's wing. Then she would press a little harder, and he would kiss her back, using his tongue to encourage her to open for him, to let him inside…

Then, everything changed. The desire left her eyes. In its place…horror. Shame. Mortification. The emotions passed over her face in quick succession and then were gone, but he was left in no doubt as to how she felt about him, about kissing him. She'd clambered from the bed as if it had caught fire, wrapped herself tightly in her robe, and retreated behind the screen, while the wants and desires of a moment ago dived behind the mask she now wore and would wear for the rest of the day.

Left alone in the bed, Ben closed his eyes and willed his body to behave. As soon as it did, as soon as he could move without embarrassing himself and frightening her, he would get up. And then he'd go out to the yard and wash himself, at least twice, in the stone cold water of the horse trough.

****

It was the final part of their journey. They'd reached Worcestershire, a land of undulating hills rising from the valleys around wide, slow-moving rivers. Sheep grazed in fields between rocky outcrops and villages built in honey-colored stone with roofs of dark slate.

"We should reach Abberley Manor by about noon," Ben told Alice, as they left another hamlet in their wake. "We'll be the guests of Lord and Lady Abberley." She swallowed, nervously, and he smiled, hoping to put her at her ease as he continued, "The Abberleys are newlyweds. I've met Catherine, Lady Abberley, a few times, since her parents live near my cousin. But Adam will be a new acquaintance for me as well as you." Ben had already left his cousin's home and returned to London before Adam Mason, Baron Abberley, had arrived in the Rotherton district of Sussex so, of course, their paths had never crossed.

"I wonder that they desire our company, if they're so recently married," said Alice. "And I'm surprised they so readily open their home to strangers."

"That's at Lord Fremont's request." Adam, Ben knew, had been an operative of Fremont's until his marriage. With a wife to support and an estate to administer, the recently elevated baron would no longer take an active part in Fremont's missions, or so the viscount had said when he'd discussed the logistics of the trip with Ben. Apparently, though, the former agent was happy to offer hospitality.

"It will allow us to prepare for the job Fremont

wishes us to do," Ben continued. "The rest of your clothes will be there for you, too."

Alice nodded and caught her bottom lip behind her top teeth. It was a sign of nerves, but it sent heat shooting straight to Ben's groin. He swallowed, then crossed his legs to hide the evidence of what she did to him, and looked out of the window so he did not stare at that delectable mouth. He had the sense he should say more, tell her what to expect, try to put her at ease. At the moment, though, there wasn't a single coherent sentence he could have uttered.

And deep in his brain, the words of his mantra beat like a tattoo, over and over again, reminding him, cautioning him, *I don't dally with opera dancers. I don't dally with opera dancers.*

Chapter Fourteen

The Abberley estate was not large, but it was imposing. The coach turned off the road, through an open gate flanked by stone pillars which had suffered from exposure to the winds coming in from the Marches, together with a certain lack of upkeep. The gate itself was tall, intricately shaped wrought iron, but its paint was marred by large rust spots, and it sagged on its hinges so that one corner of it dug into the ground, while long grass and nettles grew around its base. Alice suspected the baron could not have closed it if he tried.

By contrast, the driveway through the park and gardens to the house was smooth and even, as if it had been repaired very recently. Sheep were dotted about the park, grazing happily, and a small herd of deer meandered through, feeding and watchful. Here and there were trees—elm, oak, a copse of silver birch. They looked as if they had grown randomly; Alice suspected they had been specifically and meticulously placed. To one side of the park was a small building, a folly, which looked like a cross between a miniature mediaeval castle and a Greek temple.

After the park came the formal gardens, with flower beds and box hedges, a maze and a fountain. The gardens had an air about them, as if they, like the gates, had been left to their own devices for too long and were only now being restored and brought back into control.

The house was about a hundred years old. A square stone building with what looked to be a flat roof, it boasted a double door in studded oak, flanked by Corinthian columns which held up a gabled portico. Rows of windows, each uniform in size and regimented in distance from each other, gleamed orange in the reflected noonday sun.

As the coach turned in a wide arc at the top of the driveway, the house doors opened and a young couple stepped out onto the shallow stone steps that led from door to drive. The woman, whom Alice surmised was the new Lady Abberley, was slender and elegant, with thick chestnut hair and a healthy glow to her cheeks. Beside her, Lord Abberley stood, tall and well-built. His short, spiky hair reminded Alice of ripe wheat, and his cheeks and jaw were sharply defined. He was a handsome man, striking, though he couldn't hold a candle to Ben's masculine beauty. The baron had his arm around his wife's shoulders in such a relaxed and affectionate manner that Alice was put at ease immediately.

The coach stopped and a footman opened the door and lowered the step. Ben climbed down, then helped Alice to alight. Lord and Lady Abberley came forward, smiles welcoming.

"Summersby," greeted Lord Abberley, and he bowed to Ben, who bowed back. The bows were proper, but not stiff. A casual observer would have seen friends greeting one another.

Lady Abberley was not so formal. She stepped forward, arms outstretched, and took Alice's hands in hers. "Amelia," she said. "It is so good to see you again."

They were ushered into the house and offered tea while their luggage was unpacked. "Of course, most of yours is already done, Amelia," said the baroness, who had whispered, "Call me Catherine," during their initial greeting. "So clever of you to have it sent on. You didn't want that weighing you down. I wish I'd thought to do that. But then, you always were far more practical than I. Ah, Peabrooke, could you arrange for tea to be served? Thank you. But come through, because I'm dying to hear all your news. How is your Mama? And your sisters? Are they well?"

The door closed, leaving the four of them inside a large room with a high ceiling. Striped blue-and-cream wallpaper covered the walls, and blue floor-to-ceiling curtains were tied back at the windows. The chairs were a mixture of blue and cream, and there was a plush, sky-blue chaise longue to one side of the window. Occasional tables were dotted about, some bare, ready for plates and cups, while others held porcelain figures. An ormolu clock sat on the mantelshelf, over an unlit fireplace.

"We'll wait for the tea, then get to know one another properly," said Catherine, in a quieter voice that was more real than the happy greeting had been. She turned to Ben. "As long as you know, Mr. Summersby, Adam will advise and assist you, but he'll do nothing more than that."

"So I was informed," Ben agreed.

"As was I," said Adam, a smile playing over his lips. His wife gave him a narrow-eyed look, and he returned it with an expression of overdone innocence. After a moment, Catherine sniffed and looked away, clearly having decided to ignore him.

As they sat together over tea, Alice found herself thinking that this lady was as gifted as any actress on the London stage. And, for all she'd been at pains to insist on her husband's non-participation, Alice got the impression that Catherine was enjoying every minute.

After tea, they were shown to their suite, which consisted of a bedroom each, a dressing room each, and a sitting room. A maid hung the gowns Alice had brought with her into a garderobe already stuffed with beautiful clothes. Then, she promised to have a bath prepared in the dressing room and left Alice to settle in.

The bedroom was beautiful, and vast. It was bigger than the entire set of rooms her family had rented when she was growing up. The walls were painted a light shade of green that reminded Alice of peppermint, and the carpet, curtains, and bed hangings were a dusky pink. Lace-covered cushions filled two easy chairs and a couch, while a large dressing table matched the garderobe, as did the frame of the cheval mirror.

A quick check through the dressing table drawers revealed a vast collection of shifts, chemises, petticoats, night rails, gloves, stockings, and unmentionables, all made from the finest lawn. To wear such garments next to her skin would be heavenly.

But the collection in the drawers paled into insignificance when she opened the garderobe and looked closely at the gowns Lord Fremont had provided for her.

The viscount had taken the job of clothing "Amelia Summersby" seriously. The gowns were all of a quality that was more than fit for a nabob's wife, made in a variety of materials, from muslins to cottons, satins and silks to fine wool. There were morning dresses, walking dresses, carriage dresses and promenade dresses. She saw after-nuncheon gowns, dinner gowns, theater and opera dresses, at least two evening gowns and a ball gown, and two riding habits with smart frogging. The clothes were arrayed in different colors: blue, lemon, primrose, violet, red, pink, ivory, cream, gold, silver, midnight, and white.

"If we worked on this job for a year, I wouldn't wear all of these," she whispered, running her fingers lovingly over the fabrics. If she used these gowns to stock her shop, she would likely be well established and making a tidy profit before she ever had to invest in more clothing, or more fabric to custom make any.

"I will be the best nabob's wife in the country," she vowed. Lord Fremont had paid her well. She would make sure he received value for every single penny.

****

Ben met Adam in the billiards room, where they indulged in a friendly game over a rummer of brandy. Unsure what Adam had been told about him, Ben was wary at first, but his host seemed keen to put him at his ease.

"Your cousin spoke well of you to me," he said. He hit his ball with a sharp thwack. "He said you helped thwart the conspiracy and saved lives." He lined up his follow-up shot.

Ben sipped at his drink and said nothing. What could he say? If he agreed with Josh's interpretation of the events, he would be less than honest, claiming an innocence he didn't own. If he contradicted his cousin, he could lose the goodwill of a man whose help he might need in the near future, and with it, all hope of succeeding in this quest.

"I have to say, the resemblance between the two of you is incredible." Adam stood back from the table so Ben could take his shot. "You're not identical, but you're close enough that you might be fraternal twins."

"Even the viscount was uncertain when I first turned up." Viscount Frantham was Josh's father. "Although, to be fair, he hadn't seen his son in fourteen years, so that's not as unlikely as you might think."

"And now Fremont is using it against you." Adam grimaced his distaste.

Ben was uncomfortable at the accusing tone Adam had used. Fremont was an opportunist, it was true, but he was not a villain. And Ben did need to make reparations somehow.

"Be wary of him," Adam warned. "The man's good at his job for a reason. You give him an inch, you can be sure he will squeeze the mile from you."

"This is a one-time job." Ben bent low over the table, squeezed his eye shut to line up his shot, then hit the ball. It made a satisfying clack as it cannoned into the next ball.

"Does Fremont know that?"

"I certainly hope so." Ben straightened, picking up the warning in Ben's tone. "Does he still hound you?"

"Not so far." Adam grinned. "I don't think he wishes to try the patience of my lovely wife, to be honest. He is probably well aware that, in her, he would meet his match." He examined the table and decided on his next shot. "Seriously, you and I are different kettles of fish. I am a peer of the realm, financially independent, and recently married. All of which strengthens my hand. You, however…"

Ben nodded. "Point taken." Even as he said it, though, he wondered if working for Fremont would be so bad. Being a government agent might not be deemed completely respectable by members of the *ton*, but Ben did not, as a rule, mix with members of the *ton*. The stigma the job brought to the likes of Adam did not touch Ben, who was considered beneath the notice of Society anyway, thanks to both his career on the stage and his status as a poor relation.

In many ways, working for Fremont might be an improvement on his current lot. It would provide him with a better, steadier income and allow him to use his acting talents in a way he'd find preferable. Playing second fiddle to clowns wore thin after a time. On top of which, he'd no longer need to worry about the theater being controlled by someone like Milton Percival.

There was, as far as he could see, only one disadvantage to working for Fremont. "He does play his cards close to his chest, does he not?" he said. "I've agreed to carry out this task for him, but to be honest, I'm not altogether certain what I'm supposed to do. It's like taking to the stage without a script and being expected to perform a perfect play."

Adam turned to Ben, one eyebrow raised in surprise.

"Oh, I know some of it," Ben continued. "I know I must go to Broseley to look at investment opportunities that would interest a wealthy man. I suppose there are many, considering the industries around that town. But I have no idea which ones I should pay more mind to and which ones I should be indifferent about. A man as wealthy as Josh Summersby would not have become as rich as he is by investing indiscriminately, and if I show any lack of discernment, the people I seek will surely smell a rat."

"Damn Fremont and his secrets!" Adam took a large swallow of his brandy. His mouth was set in a straight line, and his eyebrows lowered. "He'll get you killed.

Ours is not a profession where ignorance is bliss."

Ben noted that Adam had called intelligence work "*our* profession." He might claim to be retired, but his speech gave the lie to that. Ben hoped that meant he could count on his practical support, should he need it.

Adam leaned back against the billiards table, his cue held in one hand, its end resting on the floor like a medieval castle guard's pike. "Let me see if I can enlighten you," he said. "There is, it seems, some sort of fraud happening in this area. I hesitate to call it clever, but it's certainly well thought out and planned. It may have been going on for some time before it was spotted, and even though people like Fremont are now aware of it, they've been unable to identify the perpetrators or to garner much more than the basic details. It came to light by chance, and it would seem to be very rewarding for the villains, considering the number of victims it appears to have had." He picked up his glass from the cushion of the table and took a drink. "It centers around the industry in Broseley."

"Which one?" There were several. Timber, cotton, iron, slate, granite, the Potteries. Those were the ones Ben could name quickly. There were others.

"I don't know." Adam moved his fingers and the cue twirled in his hand, its end spinning on the plush carpet. "There are, as you may imagine, plenty of legitimate and respectable business investments to be had in the area. A man could become rich indeed, if he has the blunt to stake himself and chooses the right scheme to invest in."

Ben grinned. "If it were that easy, everybody would be doing it."

"Quite. And the schemes that are, shall we say, not such good investments, can be indistinguishable from the lucrative ones."

"So how do you tell?"

"That, my friend, is the question. From the investigations Fremont's agents were able to do, it seems clever. Nothing promises too much. Nothing seems too good to be true. And thus, nothing stands out to alarm anybody.

"No one can tell from the losses the investments make, either," Adam continued. "As I'm sure you know, investments can rise or fall on a whim. There's no easily discernible rhyme or reason to it. Perfectly good ideas fall and fail through nobody's fault, and things that should, by rights, collapse catastrophically, do well. Which is why, for every fortune that is made, a hundred other men lose their shirts."

Ben nodded. "I can see that."

It was always the same, no matter where money could be made. Some rose to the top, others sank without trace. His cousin had become wealthy beyond belief in India, but many others had not done so. There was skill, judgment, and intuition involved, of course, but all of that was leavened with a large helping of luck, of being in the right place at the right time, and having the courage to act when the outcome was not certain.

"In this instance," said Adam, "there's more to be lost than your shirt. Which is something Fremont should have warned you about before he encouraged you to give your service."

Ben frowned. "You're saying it's dangerous?"

"Yes, it is. Since they began looking into it, Fremont's men have discovered a higher than usual mortality rate amongst the moneyed gentlemen coming into this area."

That was not a comforting thought. Not that Ben would have refused the job, even if he had known of the dangers, although he might have taken greater precautions. He would also have fought harder to keep Alice from joining him. Risking himself was one thing. Putting her in danger was quite another.

Then again, he doubted he could have done much to change her mind. Alice had been very persuasive when she talked to Fremont, and Ben's objections, vehement as they had been, had fallen on deaf ears.

I could have tried to keep her safer.

He knew, the minute the thought came, it would have done him no good. Alice would merely have pointed out she was already in danger. Traveling to Shropshire might put her in the line of fire of a different set of villains, but staying in London was not safe for her either.

"Is it not possible to discover what the dead men invested in?" he asked now.

"If it were just that easy." Adam stood up straight, drained his rummer and offered Ben another drink, then crossed to the tantalus. "We know the deceased gentlemen invested large amounts—in some cases, ruinously large amounts—into projects around Broseley. We know this because all of them had, shortly before their untimely deaths, met with their bankers, or with wealthy family members, and secured funds. They all said they would use the money to invest in something that had hopes of growing significantly in value. Alas, none of them were forthcoming with the details."

"People gave them funds without knowing what for?" Ben could not imagine that nobody had been alarmed by this.

"Apparently so." Adam rubbed his thumb, and the index finger of his right hand across his forehead, as if massaging it. "Greed is a powerful motivator. Show a man the prospect of a large enough return and his common sense and discernment fly out of the window."

It was a tale as old as money itself. Hold up the plausible opportunity to grow a man's wealth and you had him eating from your hand.

"Some did ask," Adam said. "But the investors either said they were sworn to secrecy, or they out-and-out lied about what they intended to use the money for. Then, armed with the funds, they set off to make their investment, and…" He shrugged.

"They died."

"In random ways that cannot immediately be connected." Adam counted them down on his fingers. "Highwaymen attacked them. Footpads dragged them into alleys and beat them to death. Carriage accidents with no survivors. One or two disappeared and were suspected of absconding with a rich relative's money. All in all, the end result is the same. They are dead, or gone, the money is nowhere to be found, and there's no trail to follow."

Ben took another sip of his brandy. It was smooth and fruity, a fine blend of superior cognacs. If he didn't know better, he might have assumed liquor of this quality was run. But Adam had recently worked to smash a smuggling ring that was a front for treason. He was unlikely to buy contraband after that.

Adam returned to the billiards table and lined up another shot, pocketing one of the balls.

"Basically," Ben summed up, "I'm looking for somebody who encourages me to invest, perhaps not too heavily, but enough to be significant, who will only take cash, leaves no paper trail, and insists on absolute secrecy."

"Secrecy is not, in itself, a cause for alarm. Many investment opportunities are kept quiet until the last minute. Nobody wants a rival to steal his thunder." Adam hit his ball again.

Ben nodded. "At least I have some idea of what I must do now." He put his glass down on the tantalus and played a shot. "Why Fremont couldn't have explained all this a week ago is a mystery. I still would have accepted the job, if that's what he was worried about."

Adam blew out a heavy breath of sympathetic exasperation. "I have long since stopped trying to fathom the workings of Fremont's mind. The man takes the concept of secrecy to a level most of us could not imagine. Though, in his defense, in this case his hands may be tied. I hear there are wealthy and influential families potentially caught up in this. They won't want every Tom, Dick, and Francis to know they've been gulled."

"I can understand that." Nobody wanted to be a laughingstock. And whether it was deserved or not, the victims would be mocked by those who believed they would have known better.

"There's probably a favor being pulled in here, because this is not the sort of work Fremont usually involves himself with. He's more often to be found chasing down French spies and treasonous conspirators, rather than fraudsters and thieves. Those investigations, by necessity, involve secrets and subterfuge. He may just be carrying on the habits of a lifetime by keeping all of this so quiet."

Ben groaned. "I sincerely hope this does not involve French spies and Bonapartists. I've had enough of those to last a lifetime."

"You and me both." Adam slapped Ben's shoulder in a gesture of camaraderie. "You will be pleased to know there's no evidence to suggest their involvement. I would think Shropshire a little far north for those who'd conspire with the French anyway." He grinned, mischievously. "Of course, I can't guarantee there's no plot by the Scots or the Welsh. No love lost between them and us. Sometimes, I think they hate us more than the French do."

They played on for several minutes, concentrating on the game.

"Your Amelia is very good," said Adam, when he came to the end of a run of shots.

"Yes, she is." Ben saw Alice in his mind's eye. Her hair was swept up in an elegant chiffon, the way it had been for most of this week. The gown he imagined her wearing was modest and of good quality rather than the coarse, sequined outfits she wore on stage. His fantasy Alice looked every inch the lady she played, with no hint of the dancer beneath.

"She has just the right amount of spirit, mixed with gentility." Adam studied the balls as he spoke. "I would love to know how you persuaded a lady of her caliber to agree to this charade."

Lady of her caliber. Adam's belief that Alice was a lady of quality was both alarming and reassuring. On the one hand, she had proved herself adept at the role, so Ben needn't worry she wouldn't be convincing when it mattered. On the other hand, he was all too aware that he'd brought an opera dancer, a woman who was little better than a streetwalker, into the very proper home of Baron Abberley, and had then introduced her to the peer's wife. Most men would be outraged. Ben could not blame them. What he'd given Adam and Catherine by bringing her here was nothing short of the gravest insult.

"I didn't persuade her," he said, and decided he should make a clean breast of it. Chances were, he would probably need to confess the truth about her anyway, for Fremont wouldn't hide it should the topic arise when he met with Adam. *Might as well get it over with. I hope Adam allows the breach in societal protocol for the good of the mission.*

"She volunteered," he said aloud. "I didn't want her, but Fremont overruled me." Quickly, nervously, he explained how Alice had come to be part of this job.

He needn't have worried. Far from being upset by her presence in the same house as his wife, Adam merely seemed impressed with her talent. "An opera dancer," he marveled. "I never would have guessed."

Ben narrowed his eyes, suspiciously. "You don't mind her presence here?"

"Not in the least. Why should I?" Adam shook his head at him. "Because she's a dancer? Mr. Summersby, I am shocked at you. I do believe you are a snob."

"A snob? No, I…" That was not something Ben had ever been called before. Usually, he was on the receiving end of any snobbery. It galled him to think he was now behaving in a way he had always found abhorrent in others.

Adam laughed. "I'm teasing you," he said,

Still the doubts lingered. Ben had been ready to apologize for bringing Alice into this house. He'd judged her and found her, not only wanting, but unworthy. The realization did not sit well with him.

"Neither Catherine nor I are so high in the instep that we'd look down our noses at someone for making an honest living. And, having met her, I'd wager your opera dancer *is* an honest woman. There's a certain quality about her. A...*je ne sais quoi*, as our French friends say. She could, quite easily, pass for a true member of genteel Society. I'd go so far as to say there are titled ladies who cannot match her for elegance, sophistication, and respectability."

Which mirrored Ben's thoughts about her over the last few days. She had grown up in one of the roughest areas of London, and her family was not, by any stretch of the imagination, well-to-do. Yet her brother dressed as a gentleman, albeit one who'd hit hard times. His coat was worn and his shirt probably darned, but Byron Buck acted as though he was owed deference. Where had he come by such an attitude of entitlement? Was it in the same place that Alice had learned the qualities that made her a lady? For that was what she was. Ben could see it now.

He wondered about the mystery surrounding her. Why a woman like her, filled with a class and quality that came naturally, would have been playing the part of third dancer, back row.

Why do you want to know?

There was no reason for him to know. As long as Alice did the job she'd been hired to do, Ben should be happy to act opposite her, and let that be that.

However, what he *should* be doing was not the same thing as what he *wanted* to do. He wanted, no, *needed!* to understand Alice. He needed to discover her secrets.

Not because he was interested in her in a personal

way, of course. Not as a friend, or a lover, or anything like that. He was merely satisfying his own curiosity. Alice Buck did not make sense and it was perfectly natural for him to ponder on that, especially when he thought in terms of where they were, and why. He wanted no surprises that could impact the task he had been set. There must be nothing that could cause him to fail, or put him, or anybody else, in danger.

Otherwise, he wouldn't care a fig about her history. Truly, he wouldn't.

A pair of well-shaped eyes, the color of the sky on a sunny winter's morning, filled his mind's eye. A smile, not quite mischievous but not too proper, flashed through his memory. He fancied he smelled violets in the air, and tasted the warm plumpness of her lips pressed against his—soft yet firm, full of promise and temptation but strangely chaste and untried.

Untried. That was, he realized with a shock, the way he now saw her. An innocent maiden, who made a man revel in the idea that his were the first lips she had ever kissed.

Which was nonsense, of course. He had seen her himself, swaying drunkenly. Had heard her yelling at an unwanted admirer, as loud and common as any Haymarket whore.

And yet…

He cleared his throat, took a breath, drank his drink. He didn't have time to think on the enigma of one talented opera dancer. He had a job to do.

Chapter Fifteen

Alice and Ben spent almost a week at Abberley, playing the part of a honeymooning couple pausing in their travels to spend time with old friends. It was, for Alice, a respite from the daily hardships of her ordinary life, and a glimpse into a world she could never have sampled otherwise. She rose late each morning and wore gowns of a quality she'd previously dreamed of. She luxuriated in baths of hot, scented water she hadn't needed to fetch herself, and her hair was dressed by a maid who knew exactly how to style it for the best effect. Every meal was served without her having to lift a finger to help, and the food was of the finest quality. She was, in short, being thoroughly spoiled, and enjoying every minute.

Catherine was wonderful company. She knew Alice was an opera dancer and didn't seem to mind at all. Alice had arrived expecting to be sneered at, the baroness's nose wrinkled, as if a bad smell had invaded the room. She might not receive a Cut Direct, since Adam and Catherine would not jeopardize the mission Fremont had sent Alice and Ben to carry out, but she didn't expect the warmth and friendliness to continue in private. However, there'd been no airs and graces about her hostess, and Catherine would never know how much that meant to Alice.

"I think there's rather more to you than an opera

dancer who can play a lady," Catherine said on the third morning of their stay. The two women sat in the morning room, enjoying a pot of tea and a plate of Marie biscuits. Catherine worked, rather reluctantly, Alice thought, on a piece of embroidery. The stitches were tight and labored, but not so much that it wasn't a passable piece of work. Alice darned her elderly shift. She might have numerous new garments to wear for now, but when this job was done, she would need every one of them to stock her shop. It made sense to mend her own clothes while she had the time.

Catherine watched her set the first few stitches, amazed, she said, at how practical sewing seemed so much more interesting than the flowers she decorated her handkerchief with. "I've always hated sewing," she confided to Alice. "I have neither the talent nor the patience, and what I am expected to do seems such a prodigious waste of time. This handkerchief," she held up the offending scrap of cotton, "will do the job whether it has a rose on it or not." She gestured at the shift in Alice's hands. "That looks much more satisfying. A useful application of the skill."

Alice grinned. "A necessary one, for most."

"I might enjoy sewing if it was necessary." She stabbed her embroidery needle into her handkerchief again, forming another long stitch in the petal she was making.

"Or you might hate it even more because you had no choice."

"True." Catherine sat back in her seat, the embroidery in her lap. "Lord, I am spoiled, am I not? Don't argue or try to deny it, for it is true. I am a rich man's daughter, and a rich man's wife. The least I can do is acknowledge my privilege." She watched Alice set more stitches across the darn. "I do have another hoop here, should you need it. If the local ladies come to call, it's probably as well they don't see the nabob's wife darning her underwear."

The local ladies were, of course, bound to call once they heard that the extremely wealthy Summersbys were staying. Women who would have twitched their skirts away to prevent contamination by touching Alice the opera dancer were only too eager to make the acquaintance of Amelia the nabob's bride. When they called, she would smile and simper, act happy to make their acquaintance, and tell them, in a vague, I-know-nothing-really way, that her husband sought investment opportunities in the area, then hope they would go home to their husbands and encourage the connections.

Alice didn't know if any of the ladies were likely to be connected to the fraudsters Ben looked for. In fact, she thought it highly improbable. She'd always imagined that if a man was a villain it would be obvious when one encountered him, in the way Milton Percival's villainy was obvious to all who crossed his path. He gave off an air of menace that made one watch him carefully and instinctively try to keep a distance, if that was possible.

But then, Percival was one type of villain. He dealt with people who needed to know he was dangerous, so he had no reason to hide his true nature. The men involved in this scheme, by contrast, would wish their victims to see them as harmless and respectable. Trustworthy.

Which meant Alice could trust nobody. Certainly, she could trust no outward signs of respectability. And if she forgot that appearances could be deceiving, she only had to look in the mirror to be reminded, for hers was the most deceitful facade of all.

Something Catherine was curious about. "There's more to you," she'd said. Alice ignored it, but Catherine was persistent. "Where are you from?" she asked, between nibbles of a biscuit.

"London."

"Whereabouts in London?"

"I grew up in Spitalfields."

"There are worse addresses, I think." Catherine pulled a face, self-recriminating. "I'm sorry. I am being rude. I am far too curious."

"Understandably. You've opened your home. You must wonder about the strangers making free with your hospitality."

"You've given me no cause for concern. I am simply being inquisitive. It is, I suppose, an occupational hazard for the idle classes. We have nothing better to do than to investigate every facet of the lives of others. Of course, we also provide endless sport for those around us. My neighbors doubtless call me a Cit's daughter whose father bought her a title she did not merit."

"That is not true! Why, anybody can see yours is a love match. You love your husband, the baron, but I believe you would have loved him if he'd been a barrow boy."

Catherine's smile was rueful. Alice frowned, wondering why that should be, but Catherine immediately changed the subject, thrusting the limelight away from herself.

"And you?" she asked. "Have you known Mr. Summersby long?"

"A matter of months. He'd taken a hiatus from the

theater, presumably to play his cousin, when I first joined. And even when he returned, we were not well acquainted." She set another stitch in place. "Ben is a character actor. He often takes leading roles, or at least, roles where his presence is noted. I am an opera dancer. If you look very carefully, you may see me in the line with the other dancers. Unremarked, unknown, and not missed if I am not there."

"As different in your spheres as a farm laborer might be from a duke?"

Alice pulled a face to say it wasn't quite the same thing. In the theater, the lines were more easily crossed. "A cat may, at times, spend time with the king," she said.

"And, likewise, the king may spend time with the cat."

"If he has a mind to."

Catherine grinned. "I think he does. I see it in his eyes. Besides, if he didn't wish to spend time with you, he would not have chosen you for this role."

Alice felt her cheeks heat. She lowered her eyes and concentrated on her sewing. The sting of tears pricked at her nose and eyes. She didn't wish to tell Catherine that Ben had not chosen her, that she'd been forced upon him, and he'd objected, strongly. Telling her how Alice had pushed her way into this job might lead to other confessions too, other things she did not wish her new friend to know of her. It was refreshing to be accepted by this lady, and Alice did not wish to see condemnation— or worse, pity—shadow her eyes.

She could not, however, leave Catherine with the impression that there was anything between Alice and Ben beyond the professional. Even if, in the privacy of her own thoughts, she wished there was. And that was more dangerous than all the rest of it put together.

****

Over the next few days, Alice and Ben were introduced to members of the local society. They attended two dinner parties and a soiree, and met with people in other, less formal settings as well. In all places, Alice joined Catherine in charming the ladies while Adam and Ben spoke to their husbands of industry, innovation, and investment. As he'd hoped, Ben was made aware of several opportunities he might wish to take advantage of. Some were sensible, steady ideas that made him wish he truly had money to put into them. Those ventures would grow slowly, but steadily, and in the long run would provide a comfortable income, though he doubted any of them would make him wealthy. They were not ideas to be suspicious about; the rewards were too modest to tempt gulls, and they were not shrouded in secrecy.

He was offered a share of a slate quarry, a coal mine, a manufactory, two shops, and a proposed canal. None fitted the criteria which would have made them suspicious. Nobody insisted that any transactions be done only in cash.

Then there were ideas which raised his eyebrows, to say the least. One man dreamed of a tunnel between Liverpool and the east coast of Ireland. Another hoped to build huge glasshouses where he could grow cotton without fear that the cold English climate might destroy the crop.

"Cut out the shipping," he said, in a clipped way that suggested he was afraid of wasting time on fully formed sentences. "Reduce slave labor. The one cuts costs. The other keeps the ladies' sensibilities at bay." He winked at that, as if he was sharing a great joke. Ben agreed to think about his idea.

"He thinks he can adapt his glasshouses to grow wine grapes as well," he reported to Adam over a late-night drink when they returned home. He mimicked the man's fast, no-nonsense way of speaking. "Make our own brandy. Cut taxes. Cut smuggling. One in the eye for the French."

Adam saluted with his glass. "I'll drink to that."

Ben sat back in his chair and crossed one leg over the other. "I need to broaden my horizons. You've given me useful introductions, but I think we're too far from the center of the scheme to find much here. From all you've said, plus my research and Fremont's initial comments, the scheme we seek is perpetrated in the area around Broseley and the Ironbridge. So that's where I'll have to go."

"Fair enough," said Adam. "My uncle's farm is near Much Wenlock, which is five miles from Broseley. Catherine and I need to visit him, so why don't we travel together? We'll go on to my uncle while you stay in Much Wenlock. You'll be near enough to cast your lures, but not so central that anyone might suspect your motives. You can secure rooms at the Swan and Falcon. I'd say that's the best inn in the town. And may you have good fortune in your quest."

It took the better part of a day to travel from Abberley to Much Wenlock. Catherine and Adam continued their journey to Adam's uncle, promising to return in a few days, while Alice and Ben took rooms at the Swan and Falcon. A small coaching inn on the town's High Street, the inn had a genteel air, although it was not particularly grand. A two-story timber-framed building with a modest yard, stables and barns at the rear, it had thick oak doors and mullioned windows, and a fine Jacobean staircase, which the landlord, Mr. Burton, was keen to point out to them.

"Finest staircase in the town," he said, proudly, before directing his lad to "take the lady's and gentleman's luggage to their rooms." He rubbed a soft cloth over the newel post.

"It's beautifully crafted," observed Alice, in a voice that told Ben she was as bemused as he was at having their attention drawn to a staircase. Burton clearly missed her tone, because his proud smile grew wider, before he showed them into the private parlor. It, too, retained the look and feel of its seventeenth-century origins, with oak-beamed ceiling and whitewashed walls, stone floors covered in ancient rugs, and a plain oak table, set before a fireplace large enough for a man to stand within.

"We have lamb stew or leg of mutton today," said Mr. Burton. "Both cooked by my lovely lady wife, so they'll be done to perfection." They both chose the mutton, and he hurried away.

Ben watched Alice pull off her gloves and put them into her reticule, before she sat at the table, close enough to the fire to feel its warmth but not so close it would burn her. Although they were coming into summertime now, and the weather was far more clement than it had been over the last two years, it still was not hot here, in the open lands of Shropshire. There were hills and escarpments to temper the winds, but the rural landscape and the nearness of two large rivers cooled the area more than might have been the case in more urban areas. As well as which, the stone walls and floors of this room leached from it a lot of the heat and left a decided chill.

"Well," she said, "we are where you wanted us to be. Now what?"

That was a good question. Ben knew the real targets of his enquiries were to be found at Broseley, five miles from here, or at the settlements growing up around the Ironbridge, rather than in this tiny market town. However, he hadn't wanted to insert himself into those places in a way that might be too obvious. He'd thought, and Adam agreed, a honeymooning couple would not want to stay in the midst of industry. A newly married man did not upset his wife by making her trip all about his investment, and five miles was not an onerous journey.

"We'll settle in today, and spend some time appreciating the charms of Much Wenlock, just as we would if we *were* traveling for leisure," he said.

"Is there much to see in this town? It seems very small to be at the center of anything other than farming, and I cannot think farming is the secretive investment we seek."

She was correct. Nobody, with the possible exception of a peer facing bankruptcy, would need secrecy for deals involving farms, nor would those deals need to be done in cash only.

"There's a limestone quarry nearby," he said. Although that, too, was unlikely to tempt the gulls. "And there's the Buttermarket, which will prove a diversion. I don't expect to meet our real prey here. Our sightseeing here is more about doing the pretty, so anyone observing us can be certain we are on our honeymoon, and any business deal I might land is, therefore, incidental."

They fell silent as the door opened and a maid

brought in their food. A mouthwatering aroma rose from the platters of roast meat, potatoes, vegetables, and thick, dark gravy, which the maid set down on the table. Behind her, a youth with long skinny limbs and acne carried a bottle of claret and a tiny boat filled with mint sauce. He put the boat on the table, poured the wine into Adam's goblet, then looked nonplussed when Alice asked for lemonade instead.

"My wife does not drink wine," explained Ben. The boy bowed and went to fetch the soft drink, though the look in his eyes told them how strange he thought she was.

They ate in comfortable silence. The food was as good as Burton had proclaimed, the claret excellent, the air warm and relaxing.

After they had cleared their plates, Ben held up the lemonade jug in a gesture of offering. Alice gave a small nod and stood, with a scrape of chair legs over stone flagging. He reached for her cup at the same moment she did and their hands met. A zing of electricity shot through him. It had happened several times now, but it still took him by surprise. He no longer pulled his hand away in shock, however, but let the feeling flow through him. It was not entirely unpleasant.

He was gratified to see that Alice did not jerk back from him. When their journey began, she'd been prickly and suspicious of every touch, however innocent or inadvertent. She always left him with the impression she thought he was far too near to her, even if he stood on the opposite side of the room. That she no longer shied away and glared at him seemed to Ben a victory, and he savored it.

Now, she withdrew her hand, and placed it firmly in

her lap. It seemed to him the air around her cup grew colder for the lack of her.

Lord! Wasn't that the most idiotic statement he had ever heard? He'd seen better prose than that in Caroline Lamb's book, *Glenarvon*, and he hadn't had the will to finish reading that.

He cleared his throat and poured her drink. She waited until he put down the jug before she picked up her cup and sipped daintily from it.

"Shall we visit the Buttermarket today?" he asked, trying to sound nonchalant.

Alice nodded, but she did not meet his eyes. He sat down, feeling strangely bereft, as if something precious had been lost to him, although he could not have said what it was.

Ten minutes passed. They sipped their drinks and made small talk, the sort one would expect of a new acquaintance. The friendliness that had sprung up between them in the coach seemed lacking now, replaced by an awkward distance that confounded him, for he could see no reason for it. Alice avoided his gaze and concentrated on her drink, or on the flames in the fireplace, dancing merrily over a large piece of wood. Now and again, the wood cracked sharply as the fire reached in a little farther. Once, the log collapsed slightly, giving the flames better access to the heart of it and sending up a shower of sparks.

"Shall we go?" he asked when she'd emptied her cup. He moved around to take her chair for her. She pushed back as he reached forward and, suddenly, he could not have said how, they were face to face, bodice to chest. His hands were on her upper arms, his grasp gentle, steadying her rather than possessing, although he didn't feel in the least bit steady inside. His heart drummed, loud and fast, until he thought she must hear it. His mouth dried, his breath caught, and his thighs tensed as his body hardened. Her hand rested on his chest, her fingers scorching him through the layers he wore.

She made no attempt to push him away, just stood there, close to him. The air was filled with the violet scent of her, the mint sauce she'd eaten with her dinner, the fir cones burning behind the log in the fire. He saw strands of her hair around her face, and the long, long lashes around her eyes. Eyes that looked up at him now, imploring him, yet filled with innocence, too, as if she hardly knew what she was asking for.

He'd thought her eyes a clear blue, solid like the endless expanse of the summer's sky. Now he saw they were, in fact, a kaleidoscope of colors, light blue and darker, with flecks of silver and navy and grey. Her skin was satin-soft, her lips full and pink and moist, and he could no more resist kissing her than he could fly to the moon.

The first touch was gentle, barely there. She tasted of roast lamb and sharp lemonade, of soap, and fresh air. He kissed her again, a little firmer this time, felt the plushness of her mouth, the small swallow of trepidation, heard the tiny mewl of pleasure. It sent his own need soaring.

His hands moved from her arms to her shoulders, to her back. He held the nape of her neck in one palm and the soft strands of her hair tickled his knuckles. His other hand roved across her back, down her arm to her waist, then up again, over her ribs until he found her breast, round and heavy. He imagined it freed from her bodice, nipple at attention, the dark areola standing out against the pallor of her skin. His fingers touched her nipple and he felt it grow, begging for more of his touch.

He ran his tongue along the seam of her mouth, encouraging her to open to him. When she did, he pushed inside and felt the dance of her tongue against his, the exotically gentle scrape of her teeth, the heat of her desire, building, higher, higher…

Suddenly, it was gone. She pulled away, fighting him, pushing at him, squirming in panic. She clamped her teeth together hard, and he cried out as she bit him. He staggered back, his hand over his mouth, a fingertip tentatively touching the tip of his tongue, cooling the sting. He glared at her, ready to curse her, to tell her exactly what he thought of her shenanigans.

Then he saw her. His anger, his frustration, the insults he'd meant to hurl at her faded away.

Alice was pressed against the wall next to the fireplace, her body folded into a cringe, a look of terror on her face. Her eyes glistened with tears and she trembled like a captured bird.

This was more than the reaction to a man taking a liberty. This was…what? He didn't know. He intended to find out.

"Alice?"

She didn't answer. She seemed to have withdrawn, deep into herself.

"Alice?"

Slowly, she came to. Her breathing steadied, and color flooded into her too-white cheeks. But still she trembled. Still she cringed.

And Ben finally realized what should have been obvious to him all along.

"Who hurt you, Alice?" He fought to keep his voice gentle and kind, when he felt anything but. Somebody had done something to this lovely young woman. They'd terrified her. The rage that knowledge caused within him was like a ball of white hot flame, ready to burst forth and consume the evil that had dared such a thing.

An evil that was not here, he reminded himself before he exploded. He couldn't reach the villain who'd hurt her, couldn't wring the blackguard's neck. All his fury would do now was frighten her even more.

So he took a deep breath, willed himself calm. Took another. And another. The red mist of anger that had fallen over him began to burn away.

Alice was still pressed against the wall, her eyes fixed on the door behind him. She was probably weighing the chances of reaching it before he could stop her. Not that he would stop her, although it was plain she didn't know that.

He wanted to yell, "I'm not the one!"

But somebody was. Somebody had hurt her. And suddenly, the truth of that was the most important thing in the world. He must know. Nothing else mattered until he did.

"Who hurt you, Alice?" He almost whispered the question, so determined was he not to shout.

A minute passed. Neither of them moved. The fire crackled and hissed. In the inn beyond the door, a murmur of voices was broken by the bark of masculine laughter. She shrank again.

"Somebody hurt you. Who was it?" *Please tell me. Trust me.*

Emotions flitted across her face, one after another, too quick for him to interpret them. He kept his own gaze steady, willed his own face to remain impassive.

Finally, she spoke. In the quietest, tiniest voice imaginable, she said, "Milton Percival."

Chapter Sixteen

Alice hadn't meant to say anything. She'd intended to stay silent, refusing to answer his questions until he gave up and walked away. Alice needed him to walk away. He was too close, though the width of the room lay between them.

He was between her and the door; he'd cut off her escape. Although, what escape was there? She could hear half a dozen men, laughing in the public bar, men she'd have to push past if she was to get outside...

Out of the frying pan...

No! This was Ben. He wouldn't hurt her. Lord knew he'd had more than adequate opportunity to do so. They'd been cooped up in a closed coach for the better part of a week, slept side by side in the same bed every night, and he'd done nothing to alarm her.

And yet... Benedict Summersby was...too much. Too big. Too virile. Too...everything. He stood now, feet apart, his shoulders broad, jaw tight. His expression was carefully neutral, but he could not hide the anger in his eyes. He was furious. With her?

Alice shrank against the wall, its cold hardness settling her, helping her to feel a little more in control, although she knew that was an illusion. She could not hope to best him in any way.

Cautiously, his steps steady and unhurried, he moved away from the door to the window, where he stood, hands clasped behind his back, staring out at the High Street. It took Alice a moment to realize he'd moved deliberately. He'd cleared her escape route, letting her know she was free to leave.

Knowing that she could, she no longer wanted to. The tension within her reduced. The muscles in her neck and shoulders were no longer knotted, and her nausea subsided. She moved from the wall to sit at the table, where her fingers fiddled with the edge of a placemat. She fixed her eyes on the old wood of the tabletop. The log in the fire cracked. It sounded like a gunshot. She jumped.

"What did he do?" He spoke just above a whisper but still, Alice flinched.

She didn't want to tell him about that night. About all the times before then, when she'd seen the gang boss watching her, felt his hard stare upon her like a physical touch. She didn't wish to think about the times Sally had whispered a warning to her.

"He's got his eye on you," her friend had said. "Watch your back."

Alice had shuddered. "I'm not interested in him."

"You think that makes a difference? Keep your head down, Al, but keep your minces peeled." Sally had used the East London cant, warning Alice to pay attention at all times. "He's a nasty cove, and no doubt."

Sally had the right of it there. Milton Percival was the nastiest, most brutal man Alice had ever come across. He held most of the streets in their part of London in his hand, and he ruled without mercy. Shops and businesses paid him to keep them safe, knowing if they didn't, not only would he not protect them from random attacks, but he'd ensure those attacks happened. Prostitutes handed over a sizable portion of their earnings to him, even if they already had panderers. Barrow boys and costermongers, flower sellers and chimney sweeps, even the lads who swept the road at crossings, all of them paid tribute to Milton Percival.

It was rumored he wanted to spread his influence. He'd taken over several other areas of London already, building his "manor" while the previous holders of power had nasty accidents. He owned gambling hells and brothels, and she'd heard he wanted to take over some of the theaters.

Having spread his presence as far as he could across the city, he'd moved into other areas, too. He ran the activities in a sizeable part of Essex, and even up into the Fen country to the northeast. He'd made inroads into Hertfordshire and Buckinghamshire. The latest stories had him involved in smuggling on the coasts of Sussex and Kent, although Alice thought that was a long way for him to try to reach. Then again, he was nothing if not ambitious, so perhaps it was true.

Alice had hoped that building this vast empire would divert his attention from her. That the women who answered his call willingly—well, perhaps not willingly, but without demur—might be less troublesome to him than one who was not interested.

She'd been wrong.

Ben moved across the room again and took a seat at the far end of the table. He rested his forearms on the tabletop, his body language relaxed and unthreatening, but even so, she tensed.

"Alice?" His voice was soft, friendly. He was asking her to tell him, but he wasn't demanding it. If she chose not to say anything to him, she knew, instinctively, he would not insist. It was that knowledge, that freedom to choose, which finally persuaded her to tell him.

"He was everywhere I went," she said. Her voice was flat, totally devoid of emotion. It was the only way she could hope to get through this. "It started when I worked as a seamstress. He saw me leave the shop one night and he…he watched me all the way along the street."

His eyes had been hard, and cold, and intensely terrifying. She had felt them on her, and had to fight the urge to run and hide. When he'd been outside the shop again for the next three days in a row, Alice had started leaving by a different door, though it involved a convoluted route through dark corridors and into a neighboring business.

From then on, she'd tried never to leave the shop alone. She never spoke to him, never looked at him, never gave him reason to feel encouraged. At that point, he hadn't tried to speak to her, but she knew there'd come a time when he did. She could only hope to make her disinterest so obvious to him he would transfer his attraction elsewhere.

It was the worst thing she could have done.

Shortly after she'd tried ignoring him, Alice had been pestered, repeatedly, in the street by two men. They leered at her and called out lewd suggestions, followed her, frightened her. When her employer heard of this, there had been no concern for Alice's safety, no sympathy for an unprotected female. Madame Fournier's only worry was that her clients might think she ran a house of ill repute, and Alice had quickly found herself unemployed.

With hindsight, she realized Percival had set the

tormentors on her, and then encouraged Madame to turn her off. He'd thought the desperation of being without a job would bring Alice to heel. She couldn't prove that, of course. She had no evidence of it. Indeed, she hadn't even suspected it until Sally explained it to her. She'd been so naïve.

Then again, that naivete also meant it never occurred to her to admit defeat, the way, she made no doubt, other women had done before her. Alice had simply swallowed her pride and taken a job in the theater, a job she would not have considered before.

"A few months passed, and I never saw him," she told Ben now. She still spoke in the dull monotone, delivering her tale as if it meant nothing to her.

Ben did not move. He sat, relaxed and quiet, and let her speak without interruption. Alice was glad of it. If she stopped telling the story now, even for a moment, she would never have the courage to take it up again.

The candle in the center of the table sputtered and fizzed as it reached the low point. The fire burned, its merry flames and hearty crackles at odds with the atmosphere of the room. The pits in the tabletop stood out, dark scars gouged by hundreds of knives and spoons on the otherwise smooth, grey surface. The scent of burning cones mixed with the clean balsam of Ben's cologne, freshening the air. The edge of the placemat frayed under her busy fingers. She curled her hands and forced herself to stop touching it.

"I truly thought he'd gone away," she said. "Lost interest in me. Until that night."

She told Ben what had happened outside the theater, the terror she had felt, the pain, the brute strength of the man against her, his fingers pressed hard into her face, bruising her and forcing the insides of her cheeks between her teeth until she tasted blood. The rasp of his tongue on her skin, the nip of his teeth, the smell of sweat and grime, and the dirt of the alley. The rescue by Fred and the Green Room Galahads, and the weeks and months of nightmares, both when she slept and while she was awake. She told him how she always looked over her shoulder now, hugged the walls as she walked, listened for every sound, was aware of anything out of place.

"I know he didn't actually…" she said, when she'd told him everything. "He didn't…"

"He did enough." Ben's voice was low and gravelly. His jaw was tight. A muscle jumped in his cheek, and there was a murderous glint in his eye. "Dastard," he muttered. His face shadowed, as if he, too, felt the impact of that night.

"I'm sorry," he said after a few seconds. "I didn't know. I…"

"No reason you should." Alice swallowed, hard. Tears stung the back of her eyes and humiliation burned her cheeks. She didn't want his pity. She could tolerate anything but pity.

He must have sensed that, because his sympathy turned to renewed anger. "And now," he said, his words cut into shards by his gritted teeth, "your brother has promised you to him." He ran his hand through his hair in a gesture of frustrated rage. "I don't know which of the two I'd like to kill first."

"Neither of them." She folded her arms across her middle as if, somehow, she could hold herself together for just a little longer. "They aren't worth hanging for."

He mumbled something. She didn't catch the words

but she thought he said, "For you, they are." Which could not be right. He'd probably used a curse word she didn't know.

It was gratifying to know he cared enough to be angry on her behalf. Fred had been upset when he'd run to the rescue, of course, as had the Galahads, but only inasmuch as they would have been outraged by any woman being so ill-used.

Ben was angry for *her*. He wanted to avenge *her*. And while she did not wish him to do anything, and would be horrified if he did, it was still comforting to know he cared enough to want to do it. Her heart melted a little and her stomach untightened. There truly were good men in this world.

And then, he spoiled it all.

"He affected you badly," he observed. "I'm guessing you haven't been with any man at all since that night, have you?"

Alice straightened. She felt her shoulders go back, tensing her spine. White anger filled her chest and stiffened the muscles in her face.

How dare he? She had just bared her soul to him, told him more even than she'd told Sally. She'd believed he understood, was sensitive to her pain, respectful of her, accepting of her innocence. And all the time, he thought her the lightskirt he'd first taken her for.

Well, Alice had had enough of being judged and found wanting. It was time to put him straight.

She raised her chin and glared down her nose at him, in a way that would have made a dowager proud. "I would have you know, Mr. Summersby, that I have *never* been with a man in the way you mean. Ever."

One of his eyebrows raised a little. The supercilious

prig!

"Don't look at me like that, sir. It is the truth."

His eyebrow smoothed back into place, and he gulped. "I'm sorry. I…"

"No, you're not." She was not in the mood for halfhearted apologies. Not this time. "You are not sorry in the least," she accused. He had the grace to look shamefaced. "I will allow that you are shocked, perhaps. A tad disbelieving. More than a tad, because you know what you know of me, and this puts the lie to all you have assumed."

She took in a deep breath. Another. Her chest rose and fell. Her throat tightened until it ached.

He stared at her. Wisely, he made no attempt to speak.

"Let me tell you, Mr. Summersby, just so you can know the truth, whether you choose to accept it, or not." She strained to keep her tone reasonable and even. She would not give him the satisfaction of hearing her screech like a fishwife, or sob like a child. She was a sensible, rational, grown woman and, by God, that was what he would see and hear. "I am a respectable woman," she went on. "I am not a whore, or a lightskirt, or whatever it is you call me. I do realize that my profession has given you a certain impression of me. That, I cannot help. But just because you believe it doesn't make it true."

She clamped her lips closed and breathed in and out through her nose. She could feel the flare of her nostrils, the fury in her clenched jaw, the sparks of anger shooting at him from her eyes. He lowered his own gaze, suddenly finding the tabletop fascinating. His cheeks were dark red, his mouth a narrow line. He was thoroughly discomfited. Good. It was past time that he should be.

"Moreover," she continued, "there are three things you should bear in mind before you rush to form your sanctimonious opinions. Number one." She held up her hand with her index finger extended. "I am an opera dancer. That much is true. I dance on stage in clothes I wouldn't normally choose to wear, and which, perhaps, show more of me than I like. I sing with the chorus, and yes, I kick my legs. I kick them. I do not open them."

He glanced up, looked as if he might say something, then changed his mind and lowered his eyes again.

"Number two." Alice extended her middle finger. "I became a dancer for the simple reason that I needed a job and the theater offered me one. Happily for me, it happens to pay far better than working in a shop ever did. Which brings me to number three." She extended the third finger on her hand.

"As I've already said, before I became a dancer, I worked as a seamstress. A respectable profession for a respectable female, I'm sure you'll agree. But being a respectable seamstress did *not* protect me from the unwanted attentions of so-called gentlemen, in addition to those of Mr. Percival. A working class girl, it seems, is a working class girl, and to far too many respectable gentlemen, she is fair game, wherever she makes her living.

"And, when she is cornered, and pestered, and yelled at, and worse, it doesn't matter that she pushes him away and refuses his attentions, or that she has done nothing wrong. It doesn't matter that she has not encouraged him, and has, in fact, done all she can to discourage him. To polite Society, whether that be in the form of respectable employers and their respectable clients, or the honorable ladies who twitch their skirts away as they pass her in the street, or supercilious *gentlemen*," she curled her top lip contemptuously at him as she said the word. "To all those people, all she is, is a woman whose morals have been questioned and found wanting. And when, faced with such censure, she has no option but to take a job they find objectionable, they pat their own backs and congratulate themselves on having been right about her all along."

He swallowed and opened his mouth to speak. She did not want him to speak. There was nothing he could say that she wished to hear.

"If you'll excuse me, I'm going to my chamber, where I can sit in my wanton shame and low character, undisturbed." She stood, head high, and walked toward the door.

Ben stood, too. "Alice…"

"I do not wish to speak with you at this time, sir," she said. She was proud, and not a little amazed that her voice sounded so strong and steady.

She swept from the room and made her way along the corridor, up the stairs, and into her chamber, every inch the proud, unbending lady. Only once she was safely inside with the door locked did she allow herself to burst into tears.

****

Ben sat for a long time after she had gone. How could he have been so stupid? Worse than stupid. He was a blackguard of the lowest kind.

He'd known it as soon as he'd said what he said. His words were crass and boorish, and she'd been right to attack him for them. If he had insulted a man the way he'd insulted her, he would be meeting him at dawn.

Although, he thought, with more than a little admiration for her, she had skewered him with her tongue as effectively as anyone with a blade might have done.

Idiot! He deserved everything she'd said. His words were unforgiveable. They weren't even what he'd meant to say. Truth to tell, he didn't know what he'd meant to say. She'd been in shock, lost in her memories, suffering all over again. He'd wanted to end that, to move the conversation on. If he'd been thinking straight—if he had been thinking at all—he would have said something else. Anything else.

Or nothing at all. That would have been preferable. Instead, he…

He was no better than Percival, and all the others who had abused and belittled her. He was worse than them, in fact, for he *knew* her. He should have known better.

He'd made assumptions about her weeks ago, and they'd proved difficult to dislodge. He'd been sure he had seen her, a drunken slattern, yelling at a clearly embarrassed gentleman. Then again, he'd seen her in the corridor, arguing with what he thought was a persistent lover, and that had turned out to be her wastrel brother. Had he also misinterpreted the scene in the alley?

Ben put his head in his hands. He'd been in her company for over two weeks now. In all that time, she'd acted the lady, never letting him down, never giving him a moment's doubt.

Because she *was* a lady! There was no denying it any longer. Alice was genteel and respectable, a lady through and through. It wasn't an act. The actress of dubious character, the drunk he'd seen in the alley, the high-kicking chorus girl—those were the acts. They were personae she put on, like a domino at a masquerade.

Underneath, at her core, Alice was a lady. And Ben owed her an apology.

He should go up to her now, speak to her, beg her forgiveness. But what if she didn't give it? He had insulted her and hurt her. She might not open her door to him at this moment, let alone listen to him groveling to her.

And what would he say anyway? How could he broach the subject without insulting her all over again? *'I'm sorry I thought you were a lightskirt?'* That was definitely not something a man would say to any respectable woman, let alone the woman he loved. It was not…

He froze. Stared, dumbfounded into the fireplace. *The woman he loved?*

Ben swallowed at the thought. It was not true. He did not love Alice. Did he?

Images paraded through his mind. Alice, high-kicking across the stage with the other dancers. One of the group, but standing out to him, as charismatic as any leading lady.

Alice in the corridor after Ben had seen off her brother, her blue eyes clouded with worry.

In the coach on the journey here, laughing at something he'd said.

At a dinner party in Abberley, charming every gentleman at the table, yet also managing to endear herself to their wives.

With Catherine, talking and smiling together, the best of friends.

With Ben, looking at him with happiness in her eyes,

so innocent, yet fit to drive him mad with desire. Kissing him. Confiding in him.

His beautiful, wonderful, many-faceted Alice.

The woman he loved.

The woman he had wronged.

Ben closed his eyes, despairing at his own behavior. He deserved her anger for the way he had treated her, not just today, but all along. If she ever thought of him again with kindness, it would be more than he deserved. Oh, he knew she would be civil, play the part she'd been hired to play. She would act the besotted bride, as she'd promised Lord Fremont she would. But it would all be for show, a performance for the benefit of others. When the curtain came down and there was just Ben and her…

The parlor was suddenly too small and stifling. He needed to get out, to walk the streets of the town, feel fresh air on his face. He needed a breeze to blow away the self-pity threatening to engulf him. Mayhap then, he could think more clearly, see a way to win her forgiveness, and begin afresh.

He grabbed his gloves, left the inn, and stalked along the High Street toward Barrow Street and the heart of the town.

The road was filled with shoppers, making the most of the market or moving between shops. Some stopped to talk to neighbors. Young women admired a friend's new bonnet, while lads pushed and shoved at each other, playfully. Older men sat outside a pub and sipped from tankards. Carts rumbled along the street, and men on horseback maneuvered around them. Chickens in cages cackled complaints and flapped their useless wings in a display of affront. Sheep bleated in their pens. Ben smelled the waxy earthiness of their fleeces, the moldiness of the chickens, the sweet-sourness of horse apples, the perfume of a passing woman. An urchin approached him and said something, but he must have been put off by the scowl on Ben's face, because he scuttled away to find surer pickings.

So lost in his misery was Ben, he almost didn't see the man. In fact, he looked at him twice before he registered any recognition.

The man was tall and broad, his shoulders wide, and his thick arms looked ready to burst from his respectably tailored traveling coat. His face was craggy, with a prominent chin and a nose which had been broken multiple times. Below his hat, his cauliflower ear stood out. He lumbered through the crowd, but he didn't use his size to intimidate, or push his way past. Instead, he moved around people, stepping into the road if he had to, making a polite request for them to excuse him if he couldn't get by any other way. A gentle, well-mannered giant.

And a traveling companion of Byron Buck.

Chapter Seventeen

Alice cried until her eyes were hot and swollen and her cheeks sore. Her head ached and there was a lump in her throat the size of an apple.

How could Ben have been so cruel? After all they had done, the time they'd spent together, the things they'd said, she would have hoped he knew her better. She'd bared her soul to him, told him everything, and still...

It had not been easy, telling him all that had happened to her, all that Percival put her through. She hadn't told anyone before, and it had weighed on her, bowing her down. She hadn't realized that until she'd spoken of it, explained everything, holding nothing back. Afterward, she'd felt...lighter. As if a huge boulder had been pressing on her soul, and telling her tale had shattered it into a million tiny pebbles, sharp and nasty, but easy to brush away.

And then he'd said...

A hiccup escaped her. It acted as a clarion call, bringing her from the depths of her misery and making her look at the situation with dispassionate commonsense. She couldn't change Ben's mind, not when it was so firmly made up. He had looked at her and seen what he saw, and nothing would change that. No use to cry about it.

Alice would just have to go on as if nothing had

happened. She'd do the job Lord Fremont was paying her for, collect her fee, then begin her new life as a provincial dressmaker. She would, at least, be away from London and the danger of Milton Percival. Away from the endless whining demands of Byron. Away from Ben.

But oh! his judgment hurt. She would swear she'd felt her heart crack when he said…

She stood and brushed her hands down her skirt, determined and firm, as if she pushed away her feelings with the creases. She would *not* dwell on his words. She would *not* think about the way he'd made her feel.

"What does it matter what he thinks?" She sniffed and moved to the dressing table where there was a pretty patterned wash bowl and a matching ewer filled with water. The water was fresh and still warm, though not hot, having been delivered to the room at the same time as their luggage. It would do.

Alice poured some water into the bowl and used the edge of a drying cloth to dab at her eyes and cheeks. The water soothed but did not, yet, lessen the effects of her crying. Even the cold cream in her vanity bag would struggle to take them away completely.

Hardly surprising, when all she wanted to do was cry again.

It was so unfair. How could the man believe…?

"It doesn't matter," she repeated, more forcefully. There was no reason why it should. Ben was not the first man to think such things of her, and he wouldn't be the last. She had always ignored such men in the past. Their good opinions meant nothing. So why should his?

The answer came to her in a blinding flash. Because she loved him.

Alice had gone and done the most stupid thing

possible. She'd fallen in love with Benedict Summersby.

Idiot! She washed her face again, splashing water over her cheeks and eyes and letting it drip down her chin. *How could you be so silly? What right have you to be falling in love?*

Falling in love was all very well, if one was a lady, who had the luxury of giving one's trust to a man who returned it. For a woman like Alice, falling in love was a disaster. To fall for a man like Ben Summersby, a man with wealthy and powerful connections, a man who could have any woman he wanted, and who'd certainly never want Alice...

He did not want her. That had been made plain by his reaction to her story. He'd listened, and been outraged by it in the same way he'd be outraged on behalf of any woman who'd been attacked. The fact that the victim was Alice did not weigh with him at all.

I'm guessing you haven't been with any man at all since that night, have you?

There had been no malice in his statement. He hadn't been sneering, implying everything was her fault. In fact, he'd been trying to sympathize, to condole with her about the aftereffects of her ordeal. And in his attempt to do that, he'd told her exactly what he thought of her.

Alice would survive his opinion. She had survived the deaths of her parents, come through the loss of her employment, the need to work as a dancer. Percival's attack. Byron's casual betrayal.

Any one of those things might have destroyed her. But they hadn't.

Nor would this.

From now on, she would do her job, tolerate Ben's

company, and play the role of his loving wife for as long as she was needed. After that, she'd collect her fee and move away, start anew. And nobody, least of all Ben, would ever know he had broken her heart.

Having washed away as much of her crying jag as she could, she patted her cheeks dry and applied cream to them, soothing and smoothing her skin, building her armor for when she must leave this chamber and face him again.

She was almost ready to return to the parlor when there was a knock on her door. Her breath caught and her heart did a strange pit-a-pat in her chest. Had Ben come looking for her? Would he apologize for what he'd said? Alice hoped not.

Not unless he meant it.

She took a deep breath, and opened the door.

It was not Ben.

Byron pushed past her as if he owned the place, and closed the door behind him. The swelling at his jaw had gone now, and the bruising had disappeared but for a slight yellow tinge around his eye. He looked, more or less, respectable.

"Hello, sis." He sounded jovial, as if he hadn't a care in the world. The way he did when the cards favored him.

Alice rushed to the fireplace and grabbed the poker. It was short, barely a foot long, and would be of little use if it came to fighting him, but it might hold him off long enough for her to scream for help. In a pinch, she thought she could deal him a hard enough blow to give her time to escape.

"Don't be so dramatic," he drawled.

"I'm not returning to London with you." Her voice was gratifyingly firm and steady.

Byron shrugged. "Fair enough," he replied. "I'm not going back myself. I have better plans. I will say, though, it was badly done of you to send me on a wild goose chase to Gretna Green."

"I sent you nowhere."

"You told that dancer that was where you were going. We went miles out of our way. Lost days. Spent a good deal of blunt on rooms and board as well, before we realized the truth and turned back. You ought to reimburse me, you know. And don't tell me she made the story up, because I know she didn't. She got it from you. Percival questioned her himself, and he gets the truth." Byron shuddered. "Don't like his methods, I confess, but they are effective."

Alice felt the blood drain from her face. Her heart missed a beat and her stomach turned over. "What happened?" Her voice was a whisper. She hoped he hadn't heard her question. She did not really want to hear his answer.

Byron pulled a face. "I'd rather not recall it."

"He hurt her badly." It was a statement, not a question. Sally had had information Percival wanted. He would not have been gentle.

Byron looked away, unable to meet Alice's eye.

She gasped and covered her mouth with her hand. "He killed her." The words were so quiet, she was not certain she'd said them until he answered.

"It was the kindest thing for her, by then."

Hot bile rose to the back of Alice's throat. She swallowed. Swallowed again. Her stomach churned. It took all she had not to bring up her nuncheon.

"Concentrates the mind, when you know the price of failure," said Byron, as if he discussed the weather.

He lay down on her bed, his head on her pillow, boots hooked over the bottom board. "You'll do everything he wants, the way he wants it done, as quickly as you can."

Pain lanced her chest, hard and sharp. Sally was gone. Percival had killed her. With Byron's help.

"What kind of man are you?" she spat. "Did you hold her down while he killed her?"

"I say! Cut line! I did nothing."

Tears fell. "No. You did nothing. You let him murder that poor woman, and you did nothing. And now, you want to give me over so he can do the same to me!"

"I do not!" He stood, pulling the quilt askew. "I don't *want* to take you to him. I never *wanted* it. I just…I didn't have a choice." He pulled out a silk handkerchief and offered it to her. "Don't cry, Al." His tone changed to cajoling. "I hate it when you cry. Besides, there's no need. I've sorted everything."

Alice ignored his handkerchief and washed her face in the bowl instead. She had thought Ben had broken her heart earlier. She knew now she'd been wrong. That had hurt, yes. But it was nothing compared to the pain now.

Sally was dead. She'd been tortured and killed. And it was all Alice's fault. If only…

So many if onlys. If only Percival hadn't hounded Alice from her job and forced her into the theater. If only Byron hadn't lost to Percival. If only he hadn't used Alice to pay the debt. If only she hadn't hidden in the theater and overheard Ben talking with Lord Fremont. If only she hadn't butted in. If only Sally hadn't needed to pawn her coat. If only, if only, if only.

And now, Sally was dead.

Alice knew it was unlikely Percival would pay for killing her. Not only was the gang boss virtually untouchable in London, but nobody in authority would bother to investigate the murder of an opera dancer. Nobody would deem it worth the manpower, and even if they did, they'd find no witnesses. Nothing to secure his conviction.

Nothing could be done for Sally. Not now. But Alice was damned if she'd fall victim too.

"I'm not going with you." She picked up the poker again and brandished it at Byron with all the menace she could muster. "You got yourself into trouble with that monster, you can get yourself out of it. I won't pay your debt for you."

"We are in complete agreement." His cheerful tone sounded obscene in the wake of the news he had delivered. "You'll be pleased to know you don't have to."

What did that mean? Alice was not daft enough to believe he'd decided to make a stand on her behalf. Nor did she think him willing to return and face the music himself.

"I'm working on something that will sort everything," he said, as if he'd heard her thoughts. "Biggest opportunity of my life has fallen into my lap, at just the right moment. With the rewards I expect it to bring, I'll be able to pay Milton Percival off completely and set myself up for life. That's what I came to tell you. You and your paramour don't need to lay false trails all over England anymore, because we're all going to be free and clear of Percival, very soon."

"How?" Suspicion filled her. Nobody ever got free and clear of Percival, unless he permitted it. And anyway, where would Byron find the money he'd need to do that? He wasn't a good enough card player to win a fraction of what he owed.

"Honestly," he said. "That's how. And I'm not gambling for it. I've foresworn all that. Chump's game. No one but the House wins. Took me a while to learn that, but learn it I did."

He sat back down on the bed. The ropes creaked under his weight, and the pillows collapsed into a pile in the middle of the mattress. "I always thought London was the place to go to make one's fortune. Streets paved with gold, and all that. But London's small time. Do you have any idea how much money a man can make in this area?"

"What do you mean?" Anger changed to wariness, suspicion to a nagging fear. What had Byron done now? Would a new set of nasty individuals soon be ready to chase him from this place? Or, worse, would he swing for what he was planning this time?

"Shropshire is bursting with raw materials, did you know that?" The wonder at his new knowledge was clear in his voice. "There's coal, and iron, granite, and, I can't remember all the others, but it's a gold mine." He grinned. "Literally. I'll be rich beyond my wildest dreams. And aside from what's *in* the ground, there's all the industry one can invest in. One could become as wealthy as Golden Ball, if one had a mind to. Wealthier."

Something in his words, and the way he said them, stopped Alice. He was too pleased with himself. His face was animated, and there was an unholy gleam in his eye.

Oh, Lord, no! "Be careful, By," she said out loud. "Not every investment opportunity brings great rewards."

"I know. I'm not a fool." She did not argue with his self-assessment, but he must have seen her thoughts anyway. "I'm not a fool," he insisted. "I know what I'm doing." He sighed. "It is galling to hear your opinion of me. No, don't pucker up at me. I know you didn't say anything. You didn't need to. It's in every line of your face." He pouted like a child. "You always assume I will fail."

Because you usually do. "I'm concerned for you."

"You have no reason to be."

Alice had a strange intuition that she had every reason to be. She and Ben were in the area searching for 'investment opportunities' that were, at best, confidence tricks, and at worst, death traps. And much as she abhorred the man Byron had become, she did not wish him to fall foul of the criminals Ben was seeking.

At the same time, she couldn't tell Byron of her suspicions. The information was secret, and she was not at liberty to share it. Especially not with Byron. He was just the sort of man to talk in his cups, alerting the villains to the danger. He was also the kind of man who would sell the information. At the very least, the mission would fail. At worst, Ben could be killed.

"It's not just me who thinks this is a good investment, Al," he said, drawing her back to the conversation. "Hawkins and Dirk think it's a sure thing, too."

"Who?"

"Hawkins and Dirk. They work for Percival. He sent them up here with me."

They must be the men who had been with him at the Castle Hotel. Not exactly people whose judgment she would trust.

"They're putting up the blunt. I don't have to lay out a single penny." Byron looked pleased with the deal he'd struck. "My contribution is to make the connections. They'd never pass for the caliber of investors the businessmen in this area want. But me? The grandson of the Earl of Ely? That's worth a third share of the profits to anybody."

"The *unacknowledged* grandson of the Earl of Ely," she pointed out.

"Doesn't matter whether he acknowledges me or not. The old man can't deny the truth of it. Why, I even look like him. And my uncle, for that matter."

Alice groaned. She wished he would forget his obsession with their mother's family. They were not wanted there. If only Byron could accept that he would, she made no doubt, be happier in the long run. Not that he'd listen to her on that any more than he would on anything else.

"Where did your friends get the money for this 'investment'?" She wasn't really interested, but she needed to keep him here until she could alert Ben. He'd know what to do. He might be able to save her brother from himself without endangering everything else.

"They borrowed it," Byron said. "Percival gave them cash for the journey."

Her eyes widened. "They've stolen Milton Percival's money?"

"They've stolen nothing!" Byron looked insulted. "They were given the money to use while we were away from London. Percival didn't say what they might use it on. And besides, they'll pay him back. Out of our profits."

Alice was so shocked by his stupidity, she couldn't answer.

"Anyway," he went on, "he's only himself to blame.

If his employees were happier, they'd be more loyal, wouldn't they? Happy workers do not look for ways to escape an employer. He treats them like skivvies, you know. He doesn't pay them anywhere near what they are worth."

She thought, but didn't say, that Percival paid them exactly what they were worth.

"Percival will have his money back in short order," continued Byron. "He'll be none the wiser about that, and he'll be happy that I've repaid him as well. And we—that is, Hawkins, Dirk and me—will live as gentlemen of independent means for the rest of our lives."

Which isn't likely to be that long.

"You should be celebrating, too, you know. You benefit. Because of what we're doing, Percival won't be able to demand I hand you over to him to redeem my debts. Everybody wins."

This was moving from bad to worse. Was there nothing she could say to make him think again? "What if the scheme doesn't provide the income you're expecting?" she tried.

"There you go again," said Byron, sounding like a petulant boy. "Doubting me. I know what I'm doing, Al. This scheme is a sure thing."

"Byron! Remember what Papa taught us? There is no such thing as a 'sure thing.' " Alice tried to rein in her temper. If she shouted at him, he would dig in his heels and the situation would grow worse. Instead, she tried, once more, to reason with him.

"Let's say, for argument's sake, that you do strike it rich. What then? I'll tell you, shall I? Milton Percival will learn of it. Not only is he not a forgiving man who'll know you stole his money for your stake in this scheme, he's also a shrewd businessman. If he doesn't kill you outright for taking his blunt, he'll certainly demand a cut of your profits. And he won't take no for his answer. What will you do then?"

Byron dismissed her argument with a languid wave of his hand. "By the time he discovers we made the deal, it'll be too late for him to do anything. We're going to take our profits and leave the country, do you see? As soon as we have the cash, we'll head for the Americas. There are great fortunes to be had in the Americas, Al. Greater even than this. Not only that, but it's safe. He cannot reach that far."

"*You'll* be safe. I'll still be here. I don't want him coming to 'question' me like he did Sally." Her voice broke on her friend's name. It took a moment to compose herself before she could continue. "I won't let him hurt me for your sake, By."

"You could come with us, I suppose."

She despaired. Everything she said had landed on deaf ears. The ache behind her eyes, begun by her tears, sharpened. A heavy weight pressed on her chest. This could not end well.

Unless…mayhap there was a way to save him. If she could learn what her brother planned to invest in, not only would it help Ben's investigation, but Ben and Adam might be able to offer Byron some protection. It was worth the try.

She sighed, heavily, as if in defeat. "You know best, I suppose," she said.

"I do," he agreed.

"So what does this scheme entail?" She sat in the room's only chair, an armchair beside the fireplace, and hoped she looked a lot more relaxed than she felt.

"Nothing you need worry about," he said. "It's high finance, you see. A bit above you."

Alice tamped down the urge to brain him with the poker. "High finance? What does that involve? I mean, you mentioned raw materials, so…is it to do with one of those?"

He shrugged one shoulder, which confirmed she'd guessed correctly.

"Which one?"

Byron scoffed. "What? So you can run and tell your lover, and he can invest in my stead? Not likely."

She laughed right back at him, and hoped it didn't sound as false to him as it did to her own ears. "Where would Benedict Summersby get the money for that? He's a jobbing actor. Hardly earns enough to feed himself from week to week."

"Ah, but he has rich relatives." Byron looked smug. "Didn't you know?" he taunted. "He has a cousin who is a nabob. He'd only have to tap him for a little and he'd have enough not only to invest in it but to knock all other investors completely out of the game and keep everything for himself."

She hadn't realized he knew about Josh. It made her want to curse. Instead, she smiled sweetly. "His cousin isn't here, is he? There's just me and Ben."

"I'm not taking that chance." Byron shifted slightly on the bed, stretching his back. "Besides, as a condition of being allowed into the deal, we were sworn to secrecy." He grinned. "That's how good it is, Al. These people don't want the world and his wife knowing about it."

I'll bet they don't. "Sworn to secrecy? Even from

me?" She hoped her words carried enough sisterly hurt to make him think that was all there was behind them.

"Especially from you. I know how you women like to gossip."

Hitting him with the poker was becoming a more tempting prospect by the minute.

"I worry for you, By," she said. "It would put my mind considerably more at rest if I knew you weren't in the middle of some havey-cavey scheme. That's why I asked. But you don't have to tell me. I probably wouldn't understand it anyway. I just want to know all is well."

He stood, straightened his coat, crossed the room and patted her shoulder, much as he might pat a dog. Alice tightened her grip on the poker.

"Rest assured, sis. All is well. Or it will be soon." He checked his watch. "I must go. I only came to let you know you're off the hook to Percival." He kissed the top of her head. "I probably won't see you again now. I'll be in the Americas, living like a king." He sauntered to the door. "Take care of yourself, Al."

And then he was gone.

Alice balled her fists in frustration. Not only had she failed to persuade him to avoid angering Milton Percival any more than he already had, but she'd learned nothing that would help Ben in his quest. She didn't know how Byron had found her, nor did she know how the investment tricksters had found him.

All in all, she'd been an abject failure. There was more to carrying out investigations than she'd believed.

In which case, she'd better find Ben, tell him what had happened, and leave the rest to him.

Chapter Eighteen

Ben followed Percival's enforcer from Barrow Street to a tavern on the outskirts of town. Housed in a small, ramshackle building with a misshapen and sagging roof and a wall that looked as if it had bowed outward under the pressure of too many years, the Dirty Dog stood in a side road, on a patch of ground that was little more than mud with a narrow path of sunken flagstones dropped into it. The walls were grey and the windows grimy.

They must serve good ale, Ben surmised, and they must be cheap, for surely nothing else would entice anybody to this place.

The man went inside. Ben did not follow. He would stand out like the proverbial sore thumb in there.

It was a worrying development. If this man had reached Much Wenlock, Byron was probably here as well. But how had he found them? Ben had expected Alice's brother to be in Scotland for some time, leaving no stone unturned in his search for his sister. And even if he'd realized Ben and Alice were not there, he should have been at a loss as to where to look for them.

Clearly, their trail had not been as difficult to follow as Ben had hoped.

Not that the how mattered. The fact was, Byron was here, and he could ruin everything. It had been bad enough when he'd called Ben by name at the Castle

Hotel. If he did the same here, it would be a disaster.

It was also not a situation Ben could deal with alone. Byron had two men with him, including this bruiser. There was no way Ben, on his own, would prevail, if it came to a fight. Not even if the fight was fair, which, he was sure, it wouldn't be. He was going to need help.

He found a young boy nearby and held up a silver threepence. "How would you like to earn yourself a little blunt?"

The boy's eyes rounded. He'd probably never owned a threepenny piece in his life.

"This one is to secure your services," said Ben. "There'll be another when you complete the task."

"Sixpence?" The boy was astounded.

"Go to the Swan and Falcon, ask for Mr. Summersby's coachman, and tell him I need him. When you bring him, I'll give you another threepence." Ben flicked the first coin at the boy, who caught it deftly and pushed it into the pocket of his old, torn breeches before he took off at a run.

Ten minutes later, John arrived. Ben explained the situation and sent him to find Adam. Not only would Adam and his men be able to help should there be trouble, he'd also need to know of this threat to their work, and his local knowledge would be invaluable.

Over the next hour, Ben kept watch as people came in and out of the inn. Most of them were laborers and other low-paid workers. A chimney sweep went inside, leaving his grimy boy to guard the brushes. A couple of lads wearing a thin film of brick dust that marked them as builders sauntered in together. A woman with a lined face, stringy hair, and a too-skinny body came and stood in the doorway, in what she probably thought was a provocative pose. A drunk staggered out, a silly grin on his face, then wove his way, more or less in one continuous direction, toward the town.

John returned with Adam, who slapped Ben's shoulder in greeting.

"Sorry to pull you away from your uncle," said Ben.

"He understood. What do you have?"

Ben explained about Byron and his companions. "The big man went inside, and I've seen none of them since."

Adam nodded. "We should move away from here. You and I could not stand out more obviously if we stripped naked and danced a jig." He gestured to a man who stood nearby. "This is Collins. He's a good man, works for my uncle. He'll keep an eye on the place for us while we go back to the Swan and Falcon to regroup."

"And to see that Alice is safe." To Ben, that was of the utmost importance. For the last hour, while he'd watched this place, his mind had whirled, terrible scenarios filling his imagination. Byron would take her. Byron would lead Percival's men to her. Percival himself would come for her. The possibilities grew ever more dreadful, until his fear for her threatened to overwhelm him. All he knew for certain was that she was alone, unprotected, and unaware of the danger. If anything had happened to her while he was gone, he would never forgive himself.

At the Swan and Falcon, Catherine had commandeered the private parlor. She sat in there alone, reading a book and drinking tea.

"Alice is in her room," she said. "The maid said she's taking a bath. But she knows I am here and she will be down when she is dressed."

Ben nodded. Much as he wanted to see her, to make certain she was all right for himself, he knew it would not endear him to her if he raced upstairs and barged into her room while she was in the bathtub. She was safe enough for now. So he sat down and took the ale Adam had ordered for him.

"So what do you want to do?" asked Adam. "Confront him? Or evade him again?"

Ben grimaced. "I don't know." Both courses of action had their problems.

"We could move to Broseley. Or there are other villages with decent inns."

"What would be the point? They found us here, they'll find us again. At least we know their whereabouts. I'd rather not lose that advantage."

"If he should let on that you're not Josh and Amelia…"

Ben winced. Byron was likely to tell people that, especially if there was profit in doing so.

"Can you not spirit the men away for a few days?" asked Catherine. She looked squarely at her husband. "You're a magistrate, Adam. Is there not a minor statute they've fallen foul of?"

Adam laughed. "I am shocked at you, Catherine Mason! You would have me invent charges and see innocent men locked up?"

"Hardly innocent," she argued. "And for the greater good. We're trying to save lives."

"Moot point, anyway. This isn't my jurisdiction. And, I have to say, I baulk at unjustly convicting a man, even for a good reason. But mayhap there is another way to rid ourselves of them, once and for all." He sipped his drink and thought, then nodded, as if he had agreed with himself in some inner debate. "What say you to Mr. Buck and his fellow travelers taking a trip abroad? Somewhere they could have a new start, perhaps?"

Ben raised his eyebrows. "You want to abduct and impress them?"

"It would be to their benefit, as well as ours. They'll be able to avoid your London gang boss while they're abroad. That may well save their lives, especially Byron's."

Ben couldn't argue with that. Byron was on very shaky ground. Even if he managed to deliver Alice—and Ben was determined to make sure he did not—there was every likelihood Percival would kill him. If not over this debt, over the next.

"And perhaps," Adam went on, "the experience will allow them to turn a leaf. The way they're headed, they'll end on a gibbet. Mayhap we can stop that. As Catherine said, we're trying to save lives." Adam gave his wife a fond smile. She colored prettily and lowered her gaze. Ben studied his own drink, feeling like an intruder in this moment of marital bliss.

After a moment, Adam turned his attention back to Ben. "There's a place, a day's journey from here. Connor's Quay. One can discreetly put somebody aboard a ship there."

"I don't want to know how you know this," said Ben.

"Nor do I," agreed Catherine.

Adam grinned, then sobered. "That sorts the men out. But what of Alice? If this man Percival should come looking for her himself…"

Ben sat straighter. "I'll keep her safe from him."

"How?"

"I'll marry her." It had not been what he was thinking. It wasn't what he'd intended to say. But he said it without hesitation, and he knew, immediately, that he meant it.

Adam was astounded. "Marry her? But she is—"

"A beautiful woman." Ben cut in before Adam could say anything that might require him to call the baron out. He glared a warning. Adam stared steadily back. Catherine looked from one to the other, warily.

"I was going to say, independent," said Adam, at last. "Your Alice is a very independent woman." He glanced at his wife. "That can lead a man into a lot of trouble." Catherine blushed, and Adam continued, "She may not want to marry you. Not every woman is willing to settle."

"I will do what I can to persuade her." Ben realized he meant that, too. And he wasn't thinking in terms of a marriage of convenience, one simply to keep her safe, either. No. Ben wanted a real marriage, a true partnership with her.

This time last month, the thought of marriage would have made him break out in a cold sweat. Now he could honestly say he looked forward to spending a lifetime with her.

"Does she love you?" Adam's question was valid. And awkward.

"I doubt it," Ben answered, honestly. "But I'll do my best to make her happy. To be the husband she deserves." It sounded like a vow. It was one he intended to keep.

Catherine's smile widened, but Adam looked troubled.

"What then?" he asked. "You give her the protection of your name, but will it be enough?"

"Adam…" objected Catherine.

"It's a reasonable question," said Adam. "Percival doesn't strike me as a man to accept defeat easily. Which means you can never take her back to London. Plus, there are other considerations. Can you afford a wife? An actor's income is not great, nor particularly steady."

"I wouldn't be on the stage if I wed. The theater's all well and good for bachelors, but it's an empty world. All greasepaint and glitter, and nothing underneath. It's not for a man with responsibilities."

"What would you do instead?"

Ben shrugged. "I don't know. But I have time to ponder that. For now, we have a more pressing matter."

"There you are," said Alice. She pushed the door open and stepped into the parlor. "Speaking of pressing matters, I have one for you. Byron is in Much Wenlock."

Ben was on his feet in an instant, ready to defend her. "You've seen him?"

"I spoke with him."

"He didn't try to…?" Ben searched for a sign that her brother had hurt her. If he had, he'd be sorry he'd ever been born.

"We spoke," she reassured him. "Nothing more."

He let go of the tense breath he'd been holding, then drew in another when she frowned.

"I think he may have made contact with the people you're looking for," she said.

"What?" Ben and Adam spoke in unison.

"I'll ring for more tea," said Catherine. "I have a feeling we're going to need it."

Ben listened as Alice told them everything Byron had said to her. Afterward, he made her swap chambers with him. It would, he said, give her a little more protection if Byron returned, intent on taking her this time. She argued that he wasn't planning to do any such thing, but Ben wasn't willing to take the chance. Adam agreed with him, and eventually, Alice gave in. She and Catherine went into what had been Ben's chamber and locked the door. John stood guard outside.

Once he knew the ladies were as safe as possible, Ben went with Adam back to the Dirty Dog, hoping to learn something more.

It was dark now. The sky was a deep velvety black, in which were a few stars and a sliver of moon. The town was quiet, all the shops closed, although several inns were open and doing a brisk trade, if the noise of myriad conversations mixed together was any indication.

A cat stalked across the road, its tail held high. In an alley, two more cats screeched insults at each other. A distant dog barked.

Collins was where they'd left him. The tavern had been busy, he said, with lots of comings and goings, but he had seen nobody who matched the descriptions he'd been given. Adam gave him a guinea and told him to buy himself a meal.

"Now what?" asked Ben. "Do you think they'll come out at this time of night?"

"Doubtful, if they haven't been out all day. Although you never know. We'll give them an hour or so, then call it a night."

They stood in the shadows, hardly moving, saying little. Ten minutes crawled by.

"You love Alice, don't you?" asked Adam, out of the blue.

Ben felt his cheeks heat. He didn't see what that had to do with anything. But it soon became obvious that

Adam was waiting for an answer.

"Yes." The word sounded squeezed and out of shape.

"Have you told her?" A brief silence ensued until Adam said, "You have to tell her."

Ben cleared his throat. "I'll think about it."

"Don't think too long. I know it's hard, Ben. Talking of one's feelings, I mean. Not something an Englishman does. But if she's worth loving, you have to let her know."

Ben was saved from answering when the tavern door opened and two men came outside. One was the big man he'd followed earlier. The second man was shorter. He had a broad chest that he thrust out as if he was ready to take on all comers. He walked with a strutting swagger.

"That's them," Ben whispered.

The men moved from the tavern doorway to a copse of trees to one side of the building. There the bruiser pulled a clay pipe and a small sack from his pocket and pushed tobacco from the sack into the bowl of the pipe. As Ben and Adam moved stealthily through the shadows, trying to get closer, the smaller man turned to face the trees. The sound of water hitting the foliage was loud.

"Do you have to do that there?" asked the big man, in a strong South London accent. He struck a light and set it to his pipe.

"What's up wiv ya?" His friend sounded like a St. Giles man born and bred.

"There's a privy over there."

"So?"

The bruiser sighed. "You can take the man out of the

stews, but you can't get the stews out of the man."

"I ain't ashamed of where I come from."

"Never mind." The big man looked toward the road. Ben pressed closer to the trees, whose shadows hid him. "Where's he got to? He should've been back by now."

"He never does anything on time. I've seen quicker snails."

"Long as he does come back."

"He will. He wants what we've got. Long as he thinks we'll turn over Percival's blunt to him, he'll stay around."

The giant puffed on his pipe. The smaller man rebuttoned his falls.

"You don't think he knows?" The giant looked concerned. "About the letter?"

The smaller man laughed. "Not a chance."

"But if he does…"

"He doesn't. I'm telling you, Hawkins, if he even suspected we'd heard from Percival, we'd know. He'd be whining at us, begging us to tell him what was in it."

Ben and Adam exchanged glances. Anxiety shot through Ben. If these men had received a letter from Percival, it meant the gang boss knew where they were. Which meant he knew where Alice was, as well.

Ben's heartbeat raced and his breath caught in his chest. He fought the urge to run back to the Swan and Falcon, to make sure she was safe.

"We don't need to kill him just yet, do we?" asked the big man, Hawkins. He spoke in a matter-of-fact way, as if they were discussing the weather.

"That's what the boss said to do. He's lost all patience with him. And I don't want him losing patience with me."

"But, Dirk…"

"The sooner we do it, the sooner we can go home."

"Yes, but…"

"No!"

"What do you mean, no? You don't even know what I'm going to say."

"Oh, yes, I do." Dirk laughed. It wasn't a pleasant sound. "You want to go in with him on this get-rich-quick scheme."

"Can't see as how it'd hurt. He reckons it won't be long and we'll be rich as the nobs in Mayfair. And he's got a good plan."

"It's a terrible plan. The boss'd have our heads for it."

"He wouldn't know."

"'Course he'd know, you pot o' dripping. You ain't got two ha'pennies for a penny. You turn up in new clothes, with a fortune in the bank, Percival's going to notice."

"I ain't that stupid. I wouldn't spend it at once. I'd hide it. And then, when Buck's all but forgotten, I'll take it and make myself scarce. Percival won't know where I've gone, and if I leave it long enough, he won't work out it came from here."

"Look," said Dirk, on a longsuffering sigh, "I don't care what you do. If you want to be found in the Thames with your toes turned up, that's up to you. But Percival'll put your name with mine, and I do mind that. I like breathing. So I'll do as I'm told and get rid of Buck as soon as I can."

"A once-in-a-lifetime chance, Dirk. You're throwing it away." Hawkins turned his pipe upside down and tapped it against a tree to clear the bowl. "Think on it. We can get the money, then get rid of Buck, go back to London and sit it out for a while. All's well in the end."

Dirk sighed impatiently and Hawkins sped up his speech, as if eager to finish what he was saying before he was cut off. "It'd be better all round that way, Dirk. You're the one what's always saying about misdirecting people. If we misdirect him into thinking we're going with his plan, he'll come along quieter, won't he? Otherwise, who's to say that he won't kick up a stink and draw attention to us?"

"I wasn't planning…"

"I've thought of a misdirection, too. What about this? We get the money, come back here and he's all pleased and happy, like. Then, you and I make a show of leaving without him, and when he turns up dead, nobody'll even think of coming after us."

Dirk gave him a sidelong look. "That's the most cockeyed plan I ever heard. Nobody ever came after us before."

"In London. This ain't London, Dirk. There's less crime to exercise their minds here."

"You're supposed to let me do the thinking," complained Dirk. "It isn't your strong point. What we need to do is…" They continued the argument as they walked back to the tavern door.

Adam tapped Ben's shoulder and gestured that they should leave, too.

Back at the Swan and Falcon, they took the private parlor once more.

"It would seem Percival has grown tired of your friend Byron," said Adam.

"I'm surprised it took him this long, and that man is no friend of mine." Ben sat back in one of the overstuffed armchairs and sipped at the brandy the maid had brought for them. "I'm not so worried about the order to kill him as much as what it means for Alice. Has Percival cut his losses with her too?"

"They said he wanted them to return to London," Adam pointed out. "Which suggests he doesn't want them to continue searching for her." He stood by the fireplace, gazing into the softly glowing coals. "He seems a pragmatic sort. I suspect, if what he wants is within his grasp, he'll take it. But if it requires too much effort or expense, without a worthwhile payoff…"

"I pray you're right." If he was, Alice would be safe, at last.

"I would advise caution, though. A cat may not be willing to chase a rat all over the ship, but if it comes within reach of his claws, he will have it."

Ben vowed to do all he could to protect Alice.

"What of Byron?" he asked, quietly. Byron Buck was a selfish, callous wastrel who didn't have the sense God gave a chicken, but he was Alice's brother and, though he vexed her to no end, she cared for him. She wouldn't want him murdered.

Nor did Ben. It was one thing to learn that someone had died, and that there was nothing he could have done to prevent it. He'd felt the distant sadness such knowledge brought earlier, when Alice told him of Sally's death. But in this case, he knew of the villainous plan beforehand and could do something to stop it happening. That made a world of difference.

"I don't see what we can do for him," said Adam. "If we warned him, I doubt he'd listen. He has his eye on a prize, and he thinks those men will help him to it. Alice said she tried to warn him. Why would we fare any better than her?"

"Because we're men."

Adam raised an eyebrow. "That doesn't make us more logical, or worthy of his attention."

"No, it doesn't." Ben grinned as he thought about Alice's reaction, should she have heard what he'd just said. She would bristle like an outraged hedgehog, ready to impale him on her spines before showing him the error in his words with the irrefutable logic of her own counter-argument.

"A man like Buck doesn't see things as we do," he explained to Adam now. "He sees his sister as a piece of fluff who couldn't think of something clever to save her life. Whereas, when he looks at you or me…"

"I see what you mean." Adam grasped the top of his nose between thumb and index finger of his right hand and massaged it. "Some men are blinded by stupidity. It's a wonder they live as long as they do."

Ben chuckled at that, then became serious again. "We can't let them kill him."

"No. Not if we can prevent it."

"We must prevent it. But how…?" An idea formed. "You wanted to put him on a ship?"

Adam looked askance. "When I had time to plan it. Put men in place to work it. Time's not our friend here, Ben. We cannot just abduct a man with no forethought and expect it to go well."

"He'll go willingly." Ben leaned forward in his chair to emphasize what he said. "Alice says he wants to go to the Americas. What if we give him the seed money and buy his passage? No, don't look at me like that. Hear me out. We won't just give it to him. He'll earn it." Seeing he had Adam's full attention now, Ben went on, "Buck is an opportunist. He takes, if he has the chance. We give him that chance."

"How?"

"He knows the men we seek. We've looked for them for days, with no whiff of success. Byron was approached within hours. He knows who they are, where they are. They're willing to meet with him. All we have to do is follow him and he'll lead us to them. Afterward, we'll…"

Ben stopped when he heard the gasp from the doorway. He turned and saw Alice, standing there, clutching the door jamb. Her face was pale and shocked, and he knew he was in trouble.

Her movements deliberate and precise, Alice closed the door and came into the center of the room. Ben watched her, carefully, waiting for her to strike. At the corner of his eye, he saw Adam stiffen as if he too expected to be caught in the storm.

No storm came. Alice was quiet and calm, and all the more terrifying for that. "You intend to use my brother as bait," she said, in the tone of voice she might use to ask someone to pass the toast. "You mean to dangle him like a worm on a hook and let the fish bite."

Ben could not argue with that. It was, basically, what he'd been proposing. Although… "We would be nearby—"

"Don't try to make it sound more palatable! I'm not stupid. When I add two to two, it makes four."

"Alice, Ben was saying—" Adam tried, but she cut him off with a glare.

"Catherine asked me to say she'd secured rooms for you, as it's too late to return to your uncle tonight."

"Thank you," Adam replied, meekly.

"You disappoint me." She turned back to Ben. "Both of you. I thought you gentlemen of honor, working to rid our country of swindlers and murderers. You're no better than they are."

"Now, steady on—" objected Adam, at the same moment that Ben said, "That's not true."

"I beg to differ." Her tone sharpened. Her eyes sparkled with angry tears, and her chest rose and fell with furious breaths. "The people you seek—because you volunteered to do so—are nasty and vicious. They kill without conscience. And you propose to send an unwary innocent like Byron against them. Because, let me tell you, *gentlemen*," she sneered the word, "Byron *is* an innocent. Not innocent of wrongdoing, perhaps. Not innocent of thoughtlessness and selfish behavior. But he has a childlike way about him, a…naïveté. You would exploit that! You…" She pointed an accusing finger at Ben. "You will follow him? What if you lose him? What if they have assassins waiting in the trees, to shoot him from ambush? How will you save him then? What if…?" She growled her frustration. "He is my brother!"

Ben was on his feet now, as angry as she was. Couldn't she see how unreasonable she was being? "He didn't remember that when he was selling you to Percival!"

As soon as he said it, he knew it was wrong. "I didn't mean…"

Alice cut him off. "Yes, you did." She turned to Adam. "Lord Abberley, I will take the clothes Lord Fremont gave me. Be so kind as to ask him to allow me time to repay him, since I did not complete the task he set me."

Then, head held high, she stalked from the room.

She did not actually slam the door, but it felt as if she had. All the warmth and conviviality within the room left with her.

Ben ran his hand through his hair in frustration. "Hell!" he said. "Hell, hell, *hell*!"

He ran from the parlor and raced up the stairs to her room. She did not answer his knock. He called softly. She ignored him. He tried the latch. The door was locked.

Ben slumped forward, rested his forehead against the wood panel, and wondered how on earth he was going to put this right.

Chapter Nineteen

By morning, Alice was no longer angry with Ben. He was just doing his job, she understood that. Just as she understood he did not feel her compulsion to protect Byron.

It had always been thus. Alice had always been the sensible one, even as a child, and her parents had instilled in her the need to save Byron from himself.

"Look after Byron," Mama would say. "Don't let him get into scrapes."

"Keep your eye on him," Papa had told her. "We don't want him doing anything stupid."

But no matter how she tried, Byron went from scrape to stupid scrape. Nothing had changed, even now he was an adult. The scrapes had just become bigger, the stupidity greater.

In the early hours, she made a momentous decision. She wasn't going to look after him anymore. Byron was a full-grown man and it was high time he took responsibility for himself. Alice would not mend the rips and tears or smooth the creases for him any longer.

Well, after this one last time, that was. She couldn't let him meet with the fraudsters who promised investors so much, took their money, and then murdered them.

Besides, she didn't blame him for falling into this particular trap. He wasn't the first to do so, and some of the victims had far more experience and wisdom than

Byron would ever have. These fraudsters were good at what they did. Gullible, credulous Byron never stood a chance.

She couldn't tell him how she knew it was a fraud, of course. She wouldn't betray the confidence that had been placed in her. Instead, she would say she'd overheard people talking, laughing about gullible investors and parting them from their wealth.

After she'd given her warning, she would sell a dress from her new wardrobe. Hopefully, it would raise enough money to buy a coach ticket to…somewhere she could live cheaply while she prepared for her new life. Then she would send to Catherine for the rest of the clothes and use them as she'd always intended.

By that time, Ben would have returned to London. She'd never have to see him again. Which was a good thing. It truly was. Alice had no desire to see that conniving, heartless man. She didn't want to hear his plans. Didn't care to feel his presence near her.

"The sooner he's gone, the better," she whispered.

It was barely dawn when she left the Swan and Falcon, but the town was already busy. Traders maneuvered handcarts and horse-drawn wagons toward the Buttermarket, laden with the wares they hoped to sell today. There were wheels of cheese and pots of honey, sides of mutton and loaves of bread, chickens and ducks that filled the air with their protests, bolts of cloth and lengths of ribbon, and baskets of mystery. Yesterday, she would have been fascinated to watch and listen to it all. Today, she hurried past.

The Dirty Dog was as tumbledown and dirty as Ben had said. Her spirits sank even lower.

"Oh, Byron. Is this the best you could do?" The

tavern's one advantage was that she might go to her brother's room without too much trouble. A female looking for a male guest at the Swan and Falcon would be ejected without ceremony. Here, they wouldn't care.

It didn't take much effort to discover which room he'd hired, and getting inside was easy, too, since he hadn't locked his door. She shook her head at that. "Good grief, By," she muttered. "I could be anyone. You could be robbed blind and wouldn't know it."

The room was dark, the curtains drawn. Byron lay in bed, snoring softly.

"Byron?" she said in a stage whisper. "Byron!" He didn't stir. "Wake up!"

It took several more attempts, but at last he groaned, sat up, and peered at her through the half-light. "Al?" he asked, perplexed. "What the devil—deuce—are you doing here?"

"I need to talk with you."

"Now? It's the middle of the night."

"It's almost the middle of the morning."

"It's too early. Go away, and come back when it isn't." Byron lay down again.

"Get up!" She pulled at the blankets.

He grabbed them with a squawk of horror. "What are you doing? Stop it!"

"Not until you listen."

"You won't go away until I do, will you?" Byron rubbed his hand across his face. "Oh, very well. Say your piece, then leave me be. You are the world's worst scold. They used to have ducking chairs for women like you."

If he weren't her brother, Alice would walk away, let fate deal him what it would. But then, if he weren't her brother, she wouldn't be trying to warn him in the first place.

Briefly, she told her story of having overheard the villains talking.

"What's that to do with me?" he asked, testily. "Turn your back so I can get out of bed. I need breakfast. Do you have any money?"

"Not a penny." He could buy his own breakfast. Behind her, she heard the rustle of his sheets, the splash of his ablutions, the soft noises of him getting dressed.

"It has a lot to do with you," she said. "Don't you see? Your 'sure thing' is a fraud. They're going to fleece you." She wanted to tell him they would kill him, but she couldn't. That was not something she might have overheard.

Byron laughed. "This is why women shouldn't meddle in business. You don't have the slightest idea."

"I *heard* it," she insisted.

"I daresay you heard something." His tone of voice sounded like a pat on the head. "And, yes, there are fraudsters out there, I make no doubt. But how you can put that together with my deal beggars belief!"

"Byron…"

"Alice," he retorted, childishly. "I'm dealing with respectable businessmen. I've been out to see the mi— the workings. I can't divulge more than that—gave my word, you know. But be assured, everything is aboveboard. And even if it wasn't, I'd be fine. I have my own smarts to keep me safe. And I also have two of Milton Percival's finest protecting me."

Alice rolled her eyes. "They won't protect you. They'll protect Percival's money. All they care about is keeping him happy."

"That's where you're wrong. They don't care about

him at all. They're with me. And we're all going to be rich."

"No, you're not. Listen to me, Byron."

"Well, well, well, what do we have here?"

Alice swung around to see Percival's men in the open doorway. She'd been so intent on warning Byron about the danger he was walking into that she hadn't heard the door open.

"If you don't mind, gentlemen," said Byron, in the voice he used when speaking with those he considered his inferiors, "I'm having a private conversation with my sister."

The smaller man grinned, malevolently. "The elusive Miss Buck." He gave Alice a sardonic bow. "We know a man what's been looking for you, Treacle." He turned back to Byron. "Get packed up. We'll leave as soon as may be, and get her delivered."

"We can't leave now," objected Byron. "I'm meeting with those businessmen today."

"Not anymore you ain't."

The second man, a veritable giant, spoke. "We should let him go to the meeting, Dirk. It's a lot of money to turn our noses up at."

"Sooner turn up your nose than your toes," said Dirk.

The men began to argue. Byron joined in. Alice seized her chance, and made for the door. Dirk grabbed at her, but she shook him off.

"Stop her!" cried Byron.

The giant grabbed her arm and yanked her back, pulling her off her feet, then threw her onto Byron's unmade bed. Dirk closed the door and locked it.

"Byron!" she shouted. "Help me!"

"Be quiet!" Byron answered. He spoke to the men. "We'll have to find somewhere to put her until after we've done the deal, or she'll ruin everything."

Alice gasped in horror. Ben had been right. Byron cared nothing for her. He'd sold her to Percival once, and now he would do so again.

She shouldn't have come. She had to get away before it was too late.

She opened her mouth to scream. Dirk rushed at her. His hand covered her nose and mouth, stopping both the sound of the scream and her breath. He smelled of dirt and sweat, mold and onions. She gagged, even as she hit and kicked out at him.

He cursed and pinned her down while he held her mouth and nose even tighter.

Alice couldn't breathe. The room began to spin. The men's voices floated in the strange, echoey distance.

And then, there was nothing.

****

When Alice came to, she lay on Byron's bed, cocooned tightly inside a sheet, his neckcloth tied around her lower face, presumably to stop her screaming. She struggled but the sheet was well tucked around her, restricting her movements as effectively as ropes would have done.

Two men stood nearby, talking quietly. It took her a moment to recognize them.

"That cove she's been traveling with," said the smaller of Percival's men, "he's smarter than your average toff. He don't just dismiss the lower classes. Look how he sent us on that goose chase to Scotland."

"He's not a toff." Byron sounded affronted that the man would think, even for a moment, that Ben qualified as one.

He's a better man than you are, Byron Buck!

As soon as she thought the words, she knew they were true. Ben *was* the better man. He was honest and honorable, and he would never have stood by and watched while these villains trussed her up like a Christmas goose, then plotted…whatever they were plotting.

"He's an actor." Ben finished his sentence on a sneer.

Better an actor than a blackguard!

To think she'd come here to warn him of the danger. And now she was in danger herself. Far worse danger than Byron had faced, because Ben intended to follow him, watch over him, try to save him from his own actions. But when it came to rescuing her—Ben didn't know she was here. It would probably be hours before he realized she was missing, and when he did, he wouldn't think to look here.

"Don't matter what he is," said Percival's man. "He's protective of that bint."

"Watch what you say! That's my sister."

The other man raised his eyebrow. It was probably the one time in this life that Alice would agree with the villain. It was far too late for Byron to defend Alice now.

"He's protective of her," repeated the man, dismissing Byron's interjection. "And he's not stupid. When she turns up missing, he'll look for her. And wherever you're at, that's the first place he'll go."

Hope fluttered in Alice's stomach, then died when Byron said, "We'll be long gone by the time he comes. We'll be at Edge Farm…"

"You can't take her there!" The man's words were

squeezed through his gritted teeth. He sighed heavily, as if expelling his exasperation. "Her coming here's put the kibosh on our plans, and no mistake."

"Not necessarily." Byron's voice rose, betraying his desperation. "We can still do this."

"Not like you to run from a fight, Dirk," came the deep voice of the bigger of Percival's men. Alice moved her head and saw him push open a connecting door to the room next to this. And, behind him, something that renewed her hope. A young boy was cleaning the fireplace in the second room. If she could get his attention…

"It is when I'm outnumbered," Dirk answered the big man. "They've got friends in this area. Friends what can afford to pay for help." He rubbed his hand across his chin as he thought. Alice heard the tiny scrape of fingers over morning stubble. He looked from the big man to Byron, then back. Alice glanced from them to the boy next door, and willed him to look at her. He didn't.

"All right," said Dirk, at last. "You two go to your blasted meeting if it means so much to you. You'll have to hire a gig, though, because I'll need the coach to take her to London. When you finish, you can catch up. Meet me at Caldmore. It's near Walsall. There's an inn I've heard of there, the White Hart. I'll put up there tonight. You should arrive by morning."

"Walsall?" Byron frowned. "That's not on the way to London."

"I know." Dirk rolled his eyes. The bigger man grinned. The boy quietly laid new logs onto the fire. He still did not look at Alice. She wanted to scream in frustration.

Dirk spoke to Byron as if to a dunce. "The actor'll

expect us to travel down through Kidderminster. But while he rides that way, hell for leather, bent on being a knight in shining armor and rescuing his damsel in distress, we'll be where he isn't. And then... Oy! What are you doing?"

He stalked into the second room, grabbed the boy by the ear, and yanked him to his feet. The boy cried out in pain and fear. Alice's heart jumped to her throat.

"What are you doing here?" demanded Dirk.

"Please, sir, it's my job," squealed the boy.

"Were you listening?"

"No, sir! I promise. I never would. More'n my job's worth!"

"He's just a boy, Dirk," said the big man. "You can't hear nothing from in there anyway."

Dirk looked from the boy to his friend and back. Alice hardly dared to breathe. Tears ran down the boy's cheeks. Byron watched, as if this was a show, meant for his entertainment.

Finally, Dirk let go of the boy's ear, smacked the side of his head and growled, "Gercha!"

The boy did not need the cockney term for "Get out of here!" interpreted. He ran from the room as if the devil was on his tail. And took with him all Alice's hopes of raising the alarm.

****

At first light, Ben and Adam met with the local magistrate and one of Fremont's agents in the parlor. "It's time to end this," said Adam, his face grim. "Before anybody else is killed by these villains." He turned to Ben. "I know you were sent simply to gather information, but if we have the opportunity to arrest these men and stop what they're doing, we must do so."

"I agree," said Ben. "Besides, I can't do what Fremont wanted if I can't attract their attention. The villains don't seem interested in dealing with Josh Summersby, not in the slightest."

"A nabob might be a little too rich for their blood," the magistrate surmised. "He'd have connections powerful enough to make life difficult for them. Still, all is not lost. I'll summon my men and put them at your disposal." He frowned. "What of the gentleman they did approach? You say he's not officially part of the investigation? Do you think he can bluff his way through the meeting until we get there? Wouldn't want him giving the game away, letting on they're about to be caught."

"He won't," Ben promised. *Because he doesn't know.* That sat heavily on Ben's conscience. Byron Buck may have initiated the contact himself, but Ben and Adam had taken advantage of it, and knowingly let him go into danger.

If anything happened to her brother, Alice would be devastated. Whatever his faults, she loved him, which meant Ben must do all he could to make certain Byron survived this.

Then, after the criminals were arrested and their scheme ended, Ben was going to drag the feckless Byron Buck to Connor's Quay and put him on a ship himself, so he could never bother Alice again. He'd lock him in a cabin until they sailed. Hell, he'd lash him to the mast, if he had to. That man was going as far away from his put-upon sister as Ben could manage to send him.

The meeting finished, with the plan agreed. Adam went to his room to bid Catherine goodbye. Ben also went upstairs. He stopped outside Alice's chamber and stood there for several moments. More than once, he raised his hand to knock, but each time, he stopped himself.

She would be asleep, he decided. If he woke her, she'd be concerned. Knowing her as he did, he thought she'd probably insist on coming with them.

If she deigned to speak to him at all, after last night. She'd been furious.

More than furious.

Ben understood her anger, even though he couldn't agree with her. He and Adam had to do this. They couldn't stand back and allow more people to die. Byron's connection to the fraudsters was heaven sent, and they couldn't ignore it.

Besides, it wasn't as if he'd recruited Byron, or coerced him to take part. The man planned to do this, whether Ben and Adam were there or not. At least this way, he stood a chance of surviving it.

'He *will* survive it,' Ben vowed, silently. On that promise, he lowered his hand, walked away, and left her to sleep.

Ten minutes later, he stood with Adam in the shadows outside the Dirty Dog. At this time of day, all was quiet. The only people around were a maid scrubbing the tavern step and the boy cleaning the ground-floor windows.

"I hope the magistrate's men arrive soon," murmured Ben. He had a feeling they'd need strength in numbers to defeat these villains.

"They're already here," Adam answered, equally quiet. Ben looked around but saw no one. Adam grinned. "They're ready to follow us when we leave, but we won't see them. They're good at what they do."

Minutes later, Byron sauntered out of the inn. He made no attempt to step over the newly-washed white step, but scuffed it with his boot blacking. The maid stiffened. Hawkins followed Byron, although he, at least, did make the effort to avoid the step.

The two men walked toward the town center. Adam and Ben followed at a distance.

"Where's the other one?" asked Ben. He looked around. "Why isn't Dirk with them?"

"Good question. Mayhap he's following them, to make sure no one else does?"

"Lord, I hope not."

"If he is, he'll be picked up, should he become a problem."

They trailed Byron and Hawkins along Barrow Street to another inn, where the pair went into the stables on foot, and came out in a gig. They looked squashed on the seat, with Hawkins taking up so much room, and the vehicle dipped noticeably to one side under his weight. Adam watched them leave, then went into the inn's yard while Ben raced back to the Swan and Falcon for two riding horses. By the time Ben returned, Adam was waiting for him on the roadside.

"A place called Edge Farm," said Adam, as he mounted. "It's a modest farm out toward Wenlock Edge, about three miles up the road. According to the ostler, it's out of the way and isolated. To quote him," Adam put on a soft Shropshire burr, "canna see why that last pair of gen'lemen would wanna go there. Leave alone a toff like you." He chuckled. "I'm a toff."

"Congratulations. The pinnacle of your ambition?"

"Indubitably." He became serious again. "I told Fremont's man. He'll make sure everyone else knows."

Adam led the way, Ben followed, and they headed out into the countryside.

Byron and Hawkins drove along a narrow lane that ended abruptly at a square grey stone building. Its slate roof blended with the thunder sky, which seemed to leach the landscape of color. There were several sashed windows on each story, each with wooden shutters which looked as if they'd been recently painted, as did the large front door. There were barns and stables behind the main house. Sheep grazed in fields that sloped up to a rocky escarpment.

Adam and Ben hid their horses inside a copse of trees, then crept cautiously to the building. Hugging the wall and ducking under window ledges, they worked their way around until they reached a room with an open window. A lace curtain moved on the breeze that tried to enter the room, while men's voices carried outside.

"It's really not good form to keep investors waiting," said Byron, in that supercilious tone Ben was coming to hate with a passion. "We do have other demands upon our time, you know."

Glasses chinked and thick liquid chugged. Ben raised his head a little and peeked through the window, using the billowing curtain as a cover. He saw Byron and Hawkins, sitting in chairs near a fireplace. Byron was relaxed, legs crossed, glass of brandy in the hand that rested lightly on the chair arm. Hawkins was less comfortable, on the edge of his seat, legs akimbo and his hands dangling down between his thighs, nursing his own drink. A muscular-looking man in an expensive suit of clothes stood at a side table, pouring brandy into other glasses, which he passed to the two other men in the room. They, too, were expensively dressed. All three looked like successful businessmen. Except now they seemed nervous.

"Where is your other investor?" asked the man who had poured the drinks. His accent sounded educated but not out of the top drawer.

Byron waved the question away. "He had other business."

There was a pause, which reeked of anxious indecision, before the spokesman said, "The meeting is with all three of you. We don't deal by proxy."

If these were the fraudsters Fremont sought, Ben could understand why Dirk's absence had upset them. It meant there was somebody who knew of their scheme, somebody they couldn't immediately silence.

Hawkins looked up, more alert. "He's not here," he said. "What's the problem with that?" He glanced at each of the three men, in turn. Ben could feel the latent menace emanating from him. "Two of us, three of us," the man went on. He put his glass on the occasional table near his chair and studied the men once more. "Doesn't matter, does it? Money's just as good."

"It's not as simple as that," said the spokesman. He sounded as taut as a harp string. "We agreed to three of you investing. We need all three of you here."

The other two businessmen moved slightly. There was nothing threatening in their moves, *per se*, but it changed the atmosphere. Things were becoming more dangerous by the second.

Ben moved back a fraction and gestured to Adam that they should make their move. Adam signaled to the hidden men.

"It's all of you or there's no deal," said the spokesman. He wasn't even trying to hide his animosity anymore.

"Now, see here," argued Byron. His imperious tone said he hadn't picked up any hint of the trouble he was in.

"No, you see here," said the spokesman.

"You can't treat me like this!" argued Byron. "Do you know..."

He never got to finish. From nowhere, a dozen men swarmed the building. There were yells and cries, boots on stone and tile, curses and exclamations, glass shattering, wood cracking, and the snap of flesh against flesh.

"You broke my nose!" cried Byron.

"I'll kill you!" yelled somebody else.

Then, silence.

Which was when Adam, Ben and the magistrate went inside.

The room was a mess. Two chairs were splintered, a third upturned. Broken glass and china glittered on the table and floor. Byron held a bloodstained handkerchief to his nose. Hawkins stood, his hands raised, while one of the magistrate's men pointed a steadily held pistol at him. The three fraudsters stood, each facing more men with guns.

Byron stared at Ben with a look of astonishment that might have been comical at any other time. "Summersby?" he gasped. "What the devil...? What's the meaning of this?"

"The meaning is simple," said the magistrate, importantly. "I am making arrests."

Byron's eyes grew wider. "You can't arrest me!" He sounded more offended than afraid. "I've done nothing wrong!"

"You know these men?" There was a definite accusation in the spokesman's question.

Adam ignored him and asked Byron, "What was your business here?"

"Confidential." Byron bristled with indignation now.

"Not anymore," said the magistrate. "Not if you don't want to swing alongside them."

Hawkins straightened. "I ain't swinging. Not for nothing."

"Then tell us what we want to know," said Adam.

Hawkins looked at Byron, then at the three fraudsters, who all glared at him. He looked to the armed men around the room, then to the magistrate. Ben could see the thoughts parading through the man's eyes as he weighed his chances. The silence was heavy, portentous.

Finally, Hawkins looked at Adam, nodded once, and said, "Silver."

One of the fraudsters yelled. A knife flashed. The man's target was Hawkins, but Byron stepped to the side at the last second, and the knife went through his coat sleeve. Byron cried out and clutched his arm, though it was immediately obvious that he wasn't badly injured. The fraudster pulled the knife back and made to strike again, just as two of the magistrate's men tackled him. There was a scuffle, the man cried out and fell to the ground, the knife embedded in his stomach.

The magistrate's men tended to his wound. Byron howled and stared in horror at his sleeve, wet with his blood. Hawkins stepped back, as if he wanted to meld into the wall. The other two fraudsters stayed still, their hands high.

"We don't know what this is about," said one.

"We're not violent men," insisted the other.

Both protested, loud and long, that they'd acted in good faith, and it was all the fault of their now-dying friend if anything untoward had happened. He'd always been a hothead, they said, and they couldn't be held responsible for anything he might have done.

"*Silence!*" shouted the magistrate.

The men fell silent.

Byron continued to snivel. "This is my favorite coat," he wailed. "Who'll pay for this?"

Ben rolled his eyes. How could someone as wonderful as Alice have a brother like this?

"Better your coat than your life," Adam told Byron unsympathetically before turning back to Hawkins. "Silver?"

Hawkins glanced at the fraudsters again, then at the magistrate, and back to Adam. "Silver," he confirmed. "They found a seam of it near here."

The magistrate laughed.

"You can scoff!" Byron rose to his feet, quivering with anger. "But there's tons of it. He…" He pointed to the spokesman. "He has a nugget in his pocket. Worth a fortune. It was just sitting there, in his field. He didn't even have to dig for it."

"I think I'd know if there was silver around here," said the magistrate.

"They were keeping it quiet," argued Byron. "Don't want the world and his wife coming in trying to grab it, do we?"

Adam held out his hand to the fraudsters' spokesman and waved his fingers as if to say, "Give it to me." The spokesman glared at him, but he reached into his coat, hesitating when two of the magistrate's men cocked their pistols at him. Carefully, he pulled out a piece of what looked like metal and rock fused together. It was about the size of a child's fist.

"See?" said Byron, triumphantly. "Silver ore."

"Hmm." Adam walked to the window and examined the piece in the daylight. He pulled at it, sniffed it, touched the tip of his tongue to it.

The spokesman looked unhappy. His friend was nervous, as was Hawkins, although Byron still seemed eager. The magistrate watched Adam. His men guarded their prisoners, though Ben could see they too were interested in Adam's verdict.

It was a clever scheme. Many men would wish to buy shares in a silver mine. They would understand the need for secrecy to prevent a rush. Secrecy would mean using only cash. A nugget worth more than a house to persuade them…a scheme such as this would make a tidy fortune for the perpetrators. Provided none of their victims lived to complain about it, that was.

Finally, Adam turned back to the room. "It's mundic," he said.

"Mundic?" asked Ben. He'd never heard of that before. Neither had Byron or Hawkins, if their confused faces were any indication.

"Mine waste," explained the magistrate. "It's what's left when they've extracted the ore."

"This looks like molybdenite," Adam said. "Although it could be graphite. Difficult to tell the difference sometimes."

"Graphite?" Hawkins' tone was a mix of incredulity and rage. He glared at Byron, who paled and swallowed. "Graphite?" repeated the big man. "You dragged me out here for graphite? I used Mr. Percival's money for…?

You useless waste of…"

"No!" Byron shouted as Hawkins took a step forward. "It's silver. He said it was silver!"

Time slowed. Movement became deliberate, exaggerated, as if everyone moved through half-set honey, and yet it all happened between one heartbeat and the next.

Hawkins grabbed the magistrate's man nearest to him. In one move, he took his gun, hit him and threw him aside. The man hadn't even landed before Hawkins pulled the trigger, threw the gun away and reached for another.

Several other guns boomed. Blue smoke hazed the air. A strong smell filled the room, a mix of rotten eggs and woodsmoke. Hawkins jerked once, twice, three times, then fell to the floor, lifeless.

Time sped up. The fraudsters stood still, guns still trained on them. The men who had fired reloaded their weapons.

"He shot me!" Byron sounded shocked. "He shot me," he repeated. He swayed, and a red bloom spread over his waistcoat.

No! Byron couldn't die. What would Ben tell Alice? He rushed forward and caught her now-wheezing brother as he fell.

"He shot me," repeated Byron. He took a breath. It bubbled and hissed. "We had…" another breath, more labored. "We had an under…understanding. Why…? He must have…known they'd…shuh…shoot…"

Ben pulled open Byron's waistcoat and tore his shirt. He pressed the tails of the garment into the wound, trying to stanch the flow of blood, though Adam's lack of urgency told him it was futile effort.

"Hanging, face Percival, or die quickly like this." Adam looked sadly at Hawkins' body. "Not much of a choice, really."

"But it was…all right." Byron's lips were bloodied now. "Debt settled. He got…Alice. Duh…Dirk…took her…this…morn…"

Ben froze.

"Tuh…took her…to Perc…Percival. We were… free."

The world stopped. Percival had Alice? How? When? He'd stood outside her door this morning, dithering, too scared to knock. Why hadn't he knocked? He should have knocked! Now he'd lost over two hours. She could be…

"Go," said Adam. "Find her. I'll get this finished, then follow. I should catch up before you get to Kidderminster."

"No!" said Byron. He closed his eyes and struggled for a new breath. "Cold. More…cold…"

Adam shrugged out of his greatcoat and wrapped it around Byron. "Go," he told Ben.

Ben nodded and ran from the house. He had to find her. He had to.

Chapter Twenty

The carriage turned into an innyard. Alice looked out of the window, taking in her surroundings. If she could alert a maid, or a stable boy, to her predicament…

"I know what you're thinking," said Dirk. He moved from the backward-facing seat to sit beside her. She smelled the grease in his hair, the sweat of his body, the stale food on his breath, and she concentrated on not gagging, opening her mouth so she wouldn't have to breathe through her nose. It didn't help.

"You're thinking," he continued, "you'll raise the hue-and-cry. Won't work." He put his arm around her. She shivered, then held herself rigid when he grasped her neck. His voice lowered to just above a whisper. "One peep out of you and I'll snap your neck. You'll be dead before anyone hears your scream."

Alice swallowed. Terror threatened to immobilize her. She couldn't let it. She could not let him know he'd won, even temporarily. If she did, she was lost.

"Mr. Percival won't like that," she said. Her voice was amazingly steady.

The act of bravado, however, did not fool him. "Doubt he'll care." He stroked his fingers up and down the side of her throat. Goosebumps erupted across her scalp and down her spine. "He's already given up on you." He chuckled at her perplexed frown. "He knows when to cut his losses. Wouldn't be where he is today if he didn't."

That made no sense. If Percival didn't want her anymore… "Why are you taking me to him, then?"

"I said he'd given up on you. He hasn't lost interest. If you're offered, he'll take you, thanks very much." He moved closer. She felt his breath on her skin. "Though, who knows? I *might* be persuaded not to tell him I found you."

Her stomach turned over. Hot bile burned her throat, and she shuddered.

Dirk's eyes heated with anger. "What? I'm not good enough for your high-and-mightiness? You give it to that actor but not to me?" He squeezed her neck till she winced with the pain.

That actor. Ben. If he was here…

But he wasn't here. He was in Much Wenlock, following Byron and trying to stop a murderous gang. He probably didn't even know she was gone, yet.

After the way they'd parted last night, the things she'd said, he wouldn't care that she'd gone anyway. Wouldn't spare her a second thought.

No. That wasn't true. Ben wouldn't leave her to face danger alone. It wasn't in him to do so. He would come after her…

If he knew.

But he didn't know. He had no clue where she'd gone. He couldn't help her. Which meant Alice would have to save herself.

Perhaps she could lull Dirk into dropping his guard. If he thought he'd cowed her, terrified her into obedience…

He squeezed her neck harder and Alice realized her fear was not an act.

Lord, she prayed, *give me a chance to escape. One chance. Before it's too late.*

****

Ben had almost reached Bridgnorth, eight miles from Much Wenlock, when he reined in his horse. Something had been troubling him for several miles, niggling away in the back of his mind, and he'd finally realized what it was.

Byron. He'd cried out, *No!*

Why? What had he objected to?

No! He'd shouted it. Then, in typical Byron fashion, he'd complained of being cold. Ben knew he shouldn't be angry at a dying man whose thoughts wandered, but *Lord!*

It took the better part of an hour to realize Byron had shouted *No!* when Adam mentioned Kidderminster.

His first thought was that Byron was still trying to save himself and didn't want Ben to catch up until Dirk had handed Alice over to Percival. But that made no sense. Byron had to know he was dying. Appeasing Percival would avail him nothing now. So why…?

Then Ben remembered the other conversation he'd heard, when Dirk and Hawkins plotted Byron's demise.

"If we misdirect him," Hawkins had said, *"into thinking we're going along with his plans…"*

Ben swore. The horse skittered, and it took a moment to calm it. "We have to go back," he told the animal.

Still, though, he hesitated. If he was wrong, he'd lose two, perhaps three hours. Alice's ordeal would last that much longer. But if he was right, he'd save a day or more of traveling in the wrong direction.

He wheeled around and headed back the way he'd

come, as fast as he could without destroying the horse.

Ben reached the Swan and Falcon just after midday. The town was busy with shoppers now, the hustle and bustle of the place noisy and colorful. He pushed past everybody, thrust the reins into the hands of an ostler, ordered him to make ready a fresh horse, then raced to the Dirty Dog. He could, he'd surmised, spend precious time poring over a map, trying to work out Dirk's likeliest route. Or, he could see if anybody had overheard the villains making their plans.

The landlord at the Dirty Dog was not forthcoming. He stood behind his scarred counter, ineffectively rubbing a filthy cloth back and forth while holding Ben's stare with his own belligerent one.

"I couldn't say," he answered when Ben asked which way Dirk had gone.

Ben pulled out a guinea and held it on the counter. The landlord grabbed Ben's wrist and stopped his offer.

"Your money's no good here," he said in a low voice that hinted at too much Scotch and an overindulgence in tobacco. "How long d'you think I'd stay in business if it got around that I'd peach on my customers every time someone flashed a guinea my way?"

"It's important."

The landlord's move was subtle. Ben almost missed it. The two men at a nearby table did not. They stood, primed and ready.

"I'd leave, if I were you. While you still have legs to walk out on."

Ben raised his hands in a gesture of surrender and stepped back.

"Don't come again," said the landlord.

Outside, Ben ran his hand over his face and tried to

work out his next move. He supposed he could recruit the magistrate's men and send them in every direction. Somebody would be bound to find the trail then. Although whether they'd be in time…

"You looking for the lady, m'lord?" The boy spoke quietly, as if he didn't want anybody else to hear. He carried on sweeping the path, though it was a thankless task, surrounded as it was by mud and waste.

Trying not to look as if he talked to the boy, Ben asked, "Do you know where she's gone?"

"I do. She's…" The boy stopped talking and moved his broom more vigorously. Ben looked back and saw the landlord in the tavern doorway, arms folded across his ample chest as he watched them.

Ben looked around, as if pondering his next move. Barely moving his lips, he asked the boy, "Do you like this job?"

"No, m'lord."

"If you want a better one, meet me at the Swan and Falcon in ten minutes." Then he walked away.

The landlord called to the boy. "What did he want?"

"Asked if I'd seen a lady, but I hadn't. More's the pity. He offered me sixpence."

The landlord grunted and went back inside.

Exactly ten minutes later, the boy ran into the yard behind the Swan and Falcon. Ben's fresh horse was ready. Catherine stood beside it, asking if Ben had all he needed.

"I will have when I've talked to him," he said, nodding to the boy.

"Did you mean it? About a better job?" the child asked.

"He did," said Catherine. "How would you like to

work for Baron Abberley?" The boy's eyes widened. "Please tell this gentleman what he needs to know."

"I was cleaning out the grates," explained the boy. "I saw her, and three men. She was all wrapped up, like me mam wraps me baby brother. She couldn't move."

Ben felt his blood boiling. If they'd hurt her... Two of them might be beyond human justice now, but Dirk wasn't. And, by God, he would pay.

"Two of them said they had business," continued the boy. "They're going to meet him tonight at the White Hart in Caldmore."

"Caldmore?" Then Byron hadn't been complaining of the cold. He'd been telling them where Alice was.

"It's near Walsall," said Catherine. "About thirty miles from here."

Ben swore under his breath. It would take him the rest of the day to get there.

"My sentiments exactly," she said drily.

He closed his eyes, mortified. "I'm sorry."

She shook her head. "Doesn't matter. Go. I'll send John to tell Adam." She turned her attention to the boy. "You come with me. I can hear your bath calling."

The boy looked horrified. "Bath? Nobody said nothing about no bath!"

Ben mounted the horse and set off.

****

The White Hart at Caldmore was an impressive brick building with imposing rounded gables and mullioned windows. The landlord welcomed Ben profusely, called a lad to show him to his room, and promised to send supper up if the gentleman didn't care to eat in the public bar.

Mindful of the way the landlord at Much Wenlock

had guarded his guests' privacy, Ben waited until they were upstairs before he said to the boy, "I'm meeting friends here. Would you know if they've arrived?" He held up sixpence, which completely captured the lad's attention. "He is about so high," he held his hand at the approximate height for Dirk. "The young lady is…" He lowered his hand to Alice's height. "Blonde."

The boy licked his lips at the sixpence. "Came in a private coach?"

"Yes."

The boy nodded. "I'm not supposed to say, sir, but if they're friends of yours…" He took the sixpence and shoved it into his pocket. "You might like to know the lady didn't look none too happy."

"Was she hurt?" Ben's imagination had tortured him every step of the way. What if he didn't get to her in time? What if Dirk took advantage of her for himself?

"Not hurt, sir. Just—unhappy." The boy bit his lip. "Room Six. He said she was his wife."

Over my dead body.

The boy frowned. "Is there going to be trouble? Only, I don't want to be caught up in it."

"There shouldn't be trouble." He hoped there wouldn't be.

The boy scuttled away as fast as he could.

Ben stood in the shadowed corridor outside Room Six and pondered his next move. Part of him wanted to rush in and catch Dirk by surprise. The sooner he freed Alice, the better. But Dirk was a street fighter. What if Ben couldn't best him? He might put Alice in even more danger.

He needed to know what he was up against. So he took a step forward, to listen at the door.

Then jumped as someone clapped a hand on his shoulder.

****

Alice stood in the corner of the bedchamber, pressed into the space between two walls. She had not removed her coat. Her knife was secreted in its deep pocket, and her fingers brushed the handle now. Seated in the coach, she couldn't pull it out easily, but now, she waited for any chance she got.

Dirk rolled his eyes and muttered, "Oh, for God's sake!" He sat on the ladder-backed chair beside the dressing table and rested the foot of his left leg on the knee of his right. He indicated the other chair in the room. "Do sit down."

Alice didn't move.

"I'm not going to hurt you, you silly mare," he said. "Not if I don't have to."

That's not what you said in the coach.

"It's not in my interests, is it? Milton Percival won't want my leavings."

That was true, so mayhap he would leave her alone. Although she wasn't certain enough of that to relax her stance. Mentally, she rehearsed pulling out the knife and stabbing him.

"Get them, and don't be squeamish about it." Sally had given her that advice when Alice started work at the theater. The memory of her friend made her chest ache, and the back of her eyes stung.

"You killed Sally," she whispered, before she could stop herself.

"Who?" Dirk looked perplexed. "You mean the dancer? I didn't kill her." He smiled, ruefully. "Waste of a good woman."

"You sicken me."

He sniffed. "Yes. Well." He stood and moved to the fire, his back to Alice as he stoked the flames.

Slowly, making no sudden movement that might alert him, she drew out the knife.

The door burst open and bounced off the wall in a cacophony of cracking, splintering wood, and thuds and bangs. Two men rushed in. One of them hit the startled Dirk hard, before he could do more than raise the poker in self-defense. Her kidnapper spun under the force of the blow, then fell to the floor.

He scrambled to his feet again, ready to charge his attacker, but stopped dead when he saw the pistol the second man pointed at him. He raised his hands as more men rushed into the room.

"Alice?"

The shock dissipated as the first man looked into her face. "Ben?"

"Are you all right, Miss Buck?" asked Adam, though his eyes never left Dirk, and his pistol didn't waver.

Alice gave a small sob. Ben wrapped his arms around her and held her tight.

****

The landlord of the White Hart was not pleased to learn he'd harbored a kidnapper, and he gave Dirk a kick as he was led away in chains. Then he begged everyone to tell the world he and his establishment were innocent victims. The magistrate nodded a vague agreement, then turned his attentions to Alice. She spent much of the night answering his questions, while he pondered in whose jurisdiction the crimes had been committed.

Adam told her Byron was dead. She wasn't shocked.

She'd almost expected it, if the truth were known.

"If it hadn't happened this time," she said, "it would have happened next." Still, he'd been the last of her family—that she acknowledged—and later, she knew, his loss would hurt very much.

Not that it would make a difference in practical terms. She hadn't planned on seeing Byron ever again, not after he'd so readily handed her to Percival's men. But choosing never to see him while he was living was not the same as being unable to meet him because he was dead.

At dawn, she, Adam and Ben climbed into Dirk's coach and returned to Much Wenlock. Ben held her close all the way home. She savored his warmth, his nearness. Being in his arms didn't feel awkward in the least. Not even with Adam sitting across from them.

They barely spoke for the entire journey. Adam asked her if she wanted a drink, or to stretch her legs when they changed horses. Ben told her to try to sleep. Nothing else.

At the Swan and Falcon, Catherine took her to her chamber and called for a bath. It was then, in the care of the baroness who'd become such a dear friend, that Alice's tears finally came.

****

A week passed. Alice and Catherine returned to Abberley, where she was assured she could stay as long as she wished. She spent her time sleeping, talking with Catherine, or walking through the landscaped gardens, planning her new life as a respected, and respectable, modiste.

Not that the thought of her own shop held the appeal it once had. Then, it had been her heart's desire. Now, it was nothing more than a way to support herself. Her heart desired something else now. Something she could never have.

Adam traveled with Ben to London. They needed to meet with Fremont. After that, Ben would, doubtless, return to the theater. Alice missed him. She would always miss him. Perhaps, given time, the pain of his loss would not be so sharp. Perhaps a day would come when she could think of him with happy fondness and not feel the sting of tears behind her eyes. But not yet.

Today, she sat in the blue salon, sewing lace onto a dress, when the door opened with a soft swish. Expecting to see Catherine, Alice smiled and held up the dress to show her, then dropped it back into her lap when she saw it wasn't the baroness who'd come in.

It was Ben. He stood uncertainly, just inside the door, which he'd carefully left ajar. As if she were a real lady.

Her heart did a funny pit-a-pat at the sight of him. He looked well. His clothes were fresh and clean, which told her he'd taken the time to wash off the journey's dust before coming to see her. His face was tanned, testament to the time he'd spent riding across England.

He bowed to her. She stood and curtsied, rang for tea, then sat so that he could. Her chest was tight, her nerves too close to the surface. She needed to move her hands, to ease the aching urge to reach out and touch him. She picked up her sewing again and clutched it to her lap. She couldn't have set a stitch now if her life depended on it.

"How are you?" he asked after the tea tray was delivered and she'd poured two cups, with hands much steadier than she'd expected.

"I'm fine."

He looked as if he didn't believe her.

She smiled. It felt brittle. "Truly. I am fine."

An awkward silence followed, before he said, "You may not have heard. Dirk was found guilty. He's sentenced to hang. Your name wasn't mentioned. Your reputation remains intact."

"Thank you." What else could she say to that?

Ben stood, paced to the window, and looked out over the garden. "When he took you," he said, "I was terrified. I thought I'd never see you again." He took a deep breath and moved to the unlit fireplace, rested his foot on the surround, and leaned into the mantelshelf.

Alice smiled, sadly. "I didn't expect you to. I'm surprised to see you today, in fact." He frowned. "I thought you'd stay in London. Mr. Tate must be anxious to have you back. Whereas, I'll be..." She gestured, vaguely. As yet, she had no idea where she would be.

He cleared his throat. "I'm not going back."

She blinked, unsure she'd heard him correctly.

"It's not my life anymore. Not what I want." He shrugged, a little too nonchalantly. "The theater's either in your blood or it isn't. It isn't in mine."

He was leaving the theater? What would he do instead? He'd still have to earn a living. She didn't see him in a shop or toiling as a laborer.

"Adam offered me a position," he said. "As his steward."

"His steward?" What did Ben know of being a steward?

"He'll train me, teach me all I need to know."

Oh. "Congratulations."

He would be at Abberley. In which case, Alice

needed to look further afield for her shop. She didn't think she could bear meeting with him, passing the time of day with him, and knowing she could never have him for herself.

"The job comes with a decent salary," he continued, "and a house."

"Good. That's good." Her heart broke. He would have everything she wanted.

"I'd be able to afford..." He huffed in exasperation. "Dash it, Alice! I've never done this before."

Done what? Been a steward? Alice knew that. But he was an actor. Surely he could play the part until he'd learned it?

"I want to say so much," he said. "But one word from you, and I will forever be silent."

What?

"When Dirk took you, I—my heart stopped. All I could think was that if I couldn't find you...my life would end. Because I love you."

He loved her? Since when?

"I understand you don't love me," he continued, "and you have your own plans, and—"

"Who says I don't love you?"

He stared at her, hope and wonderment shining in his eyes. "You do?"

She nodded. Her own eyes probably mirrored his. She felt as if they did.

"Then...you'll marry me?"

Alice stood and moved closer to him. "Yes."

He took her in his arms. "Alice," he breathed. "My Alice." He leaned back and studied her. "But what of your shop? Your dream?"

She smiled. "I have a better dream now. It's you."

He grinned. "All right," he said. "Let's get married."
Then he kissed her.

A word about the author...

Caitlyn Callery lives in Sussex, southern England, near the Regency towns of Brighton and Tunbridge Wells. She is passionate about writing and suffers withdrawal symptoms when she takes a few days away from her work.

Before becoming a full-time writer, she worked in banking, as a waitress, in the motor repair industry, in a call centre, and for a charity. As part of this last job, she helped build a school in Kenya, and drove a vanload of wheelchairs from the UK to Morocco.

She also loves reading, knitting, walking by the sea, the theatre and spending time with her family.

CaitlynCallery.com